Readers adore *The Memory Library*

'An absolute joy to read. Uplifting, beautiful, and
perfect for any book lovers!'
Reader review, ★★★★★

'The Memory Library delivers on its promise of
hope, friendship and second chances. It's a love letter
to the written word.'
Reader review, ★★★★★

'A powerful and poignant story. There were tears
shed.'
Reader review, ★★★★★

'I laughed out loud and had more than one glassy
eye!'
Reader review, ★★★★★

'Beautifully written, with a beautiful message.'
Reader review, ★★★★★

'A real treasure for booklovers everywhere who
completely appreciate the joy, knowledge and healing
that books can bring.'
Reader review, ★★★★★

'There's page after page of wonderful wisdom in this novel.'
Reader review, ★★★★★

'Filled with tender moments of sharing, tears, forgiveness, revelation and healing.'
Reader review, ★★★★★

'What a beautiful, moving story this was! It really had me sobbing my eyes out.' Reader review, ★★★★★

'This gorgeous novel made me cry. It stirred up lots of emotions, released some memories and reminded me of why I love books so much.'
Reader review, ★★★★★

'A fantastic read. You will laugh, cry and laugh some more.'
Reader review, ★★★★★

Kate Storey started her career teaching English and Drama and, when she had her family, combined all three to write novels about family drama. Originally from Yorkshire, she now lives in a London suburb with her husband and two teenage daughters. She has written three novels previously, but this is her debut novel in the book-club space.

The Memory
Library

KATE STOREY

avon.

Published by AVON
A division of HarperCollins*Publishers*
1 London Bridge Street
London SE1 9GF

www.harpercollins.co.uk

HarperCollins*Publishers*
Macken House
39/40 Mayor Street Upper
Dublin 1
D01 C9W8

A Paperback Original 2024

4

First published in Great Britain by HarperCollins*Publishers* 2024

Copyright © Lisa Timoney 2024

Lisa Timoney asserts the moral right to be identified as the author of this work.

A catalogue copy of this book is available from the British Library.

ISBN: 978-0-00-865854-0

Set in Sabon LT Std by HarperCollins*Publishers* India

Printed and bound in the UK using 100% Renewable Electricity by CPI Group (UK) Ltd

For
Zoe and Vicky
X

Prologue

Sally

Thirty-Four Years Ago

Despite her years of experience reading aloud to children, Sally was horrified to find she couldn't stop her voice from wavering. It started when she came to the words 'A woman in a lonely home' in Jo's poem, near the end of *Little Women*. The phrase seemed to describe her so exactly, she lost control of her vocal cords.

She was reading her daughter's bedtime story, so forced a cough to disguise the emotion in her voice. She shuffled closer to Ella on the single bed, giving her thin leg a squeeze through the duvet. Turning the well-thumbed page, she angled the book to catch the light from the bedside lamp and read on, "Be worthy, love, and love will come."

She paused, swallowing hard. Ella looked up, dark eyes reflecting the twinkling fairy lights wound around the bedpost behind them.

Sally gathered a smile. 'You, my darling, are worthy of love.' She tweaked Ella's nose. 'All the love in the world.'

'You are too, Mummy,' said Ella. 'And Daddy.'

1

The last part of her daughter's statement was predictable. There was no Mummy without Daddy in Ella's small world. To be honest, Sally was relieved she featured at all. Ella had been a daddy's girl from the moment she could express a preference and Sally tried not to mind. She was glad, in a way, that Ella's bond with Neil was still as strong as ever. He could do no wrong in the eyes of their daughter, despite being too busy to attend her birthday pool party at the Arches earlier that afternoon. Ella's devotion suggested she was blissfully oblivious to the increasingly frequent arguments and the dismissive way her dad spoke to her mum. Or she didn't care. But that was too unpleasant to think about.

She should be oblivious at her tender age. Being eight was a magical time of life, in Sally's opinion. She adored teaching Year Four children because, at that age, they were smack bang in the middle of living delightfully playful yet serious lives. To Sally, children this age were like butterflies emerging from their chrysalises and she thought it a privilege to be a part of the process.

'I like Jo's poem,' Ella said.

She reached for the copy of *Little Women*, which Sally's own mother had given to her thirty years before, and began to read in a voice a tone infinitesimally lower than her childish voice of last year. She read the poem with a faltering rhythm as she attempted unfamiliar words, pointing to *lament*, then *immortal*, with a bitten fingernail, waiting for Sally to pronounce them and then explain the meaning before reading on.

Sally glanced around the darkening room as Ella read the closing pages of the book, her gaze pausing on the wardrobe and chest of drawers with pink handles, then the duvet cover with its pattern of colourful Russian dolls. How long until Ella wanted a more grown-up bedroom, with posters of pop stars Sally had never heard of?

Ella's voice grew louder as she read, "'Oh, my girls, however long you may live, I never can wish you a greater happiness than this!'"

Sally felt the sentiment of that familiar final line to her core. She pulled Ella towards her and dropped kisses on top of her head. 'Did you like it?' she asked, drawing away and looking into her face.

'I loved it!' Ella squealed. 'I want to be Jo when I grow up!'

Sally's heart swelled. She reached under the bed and pulled out a new copy of *Little Women*. Solemnly, she handed the book with the illustration of Meg, Jo, Beth and Amy on the jacket to Ella. 'This is your special copy to keep forever.'

Ella's eyes grew wide. 'Thank you, Mummy.' She opened the front cover slowly.

Sally held her breath. The tradition of giving her daughter a book inscribed with a message had turned eight years old today, but for the first four years at least, it hadn't held any significance to Ella. To see that she now anticipated the note and opened the book with such reverence made Sally's throat clog with tears. She watched Ella's face as she read what she'd carefully written on the inside page.

A moment later, Ella turned, wrapping her arms around Sally's neck. Despite a bubble bath, her hair still smelled of chlorine from the swimming pool. Sally recalled the joy on her daughter's face when she and her friends had held hands, whooped and leapt into the pool, splashing and giggling with utter glee. She stored it in the album of special memories in her mind, wondering how Neil could choose work, or anything else, above spending today with his only child.

With her arms still around her little girl, Sally heard the bang of the front door closing and her husband's fading footsteps on the pavement of Circus Street below. Her body tensed as she dreaded Ella asking where Daddy was going. Sally didn't know. But she could guess.

Relieved when the question didn't come, she pushed her face further into Ella's hair and whispered, 'Happy birthday, Ella. Happy birthday, my gorgeous girl,' all the time wondering what she needed to do to keep her small family together, and determined not to let Ella see her tears.

Chapter One

Ella

Present Day

The trill of her phone echoed around the open-plan kitchen, making Ella jump. She'd only just poured her first coffee of the day. If she was Queen of the World, no devices would be activated until 100mg of caffeine had been absorbed into her bloodstream. She played the "If she was Queen" of the World game a lot in her head. It didn't get her anywhere. The phone kept ringing.

Glenda's name was on the screen. That made her uneasy. She did the maths; it was seven a.m. here in Sydney, so it was ten p.m. back in London. Why would her mother's next-door neighbour be ringing her at this time?

Ella took the phone off charge and accepted the call. 'Hi, Glenda.'

'Ella,' Glenda's voice sounded tinny and even more cut-glass than she remembered. 'I hope you're well?'

She had a breakfast meeting. No time for small talk. 'Yes, Glenda. Listen,' she said, taking a slurp of coffee and waving good morning to Charlie, who was wandering down their slatted staircase in a T-shirt and boxers. Why couldn't her husband put some trousers on before coming downstairs, like a civilised person? Their open-plan living space was mainly encased in glass, and she was sure random delivery drivers could do without the intimate image of Charlie's anatomy. 'Can I call you back another time? I've got a meeting—'

'It's your mum,' said Glenda. 'She's had a bad fall.'

Ella put the cup down. 'A fall?' Her mother was only seventy-two. She'd seemed fit and healthy the last time Ella had FaceTimed her. When was that – last week? The week before? She certainly didn't seem in any way doddery. She still cycled everywhere. The bike. That must be it. Ella knew cycling in London was a terrible idea. She'd told her mother that plenty of times before. 'Is she all right? Did she fall off that bloody bike?'

Charlie came to her side, eyebrows knitted.

'No, I haven't seen her on the bike for a while. I've just left her at the hospital.'

Charlie was standing too close, his eyes screwed up as if he wanted answers when she didn't know what the hell was going on herself. Ella turned her back on him and marched towards the floor-to-ceiling window. She held the phone to her ear and looked out over the valley. 'What happened? How is she?'

She sensed Charlie hovering behind her and, exasperated, she switched the call to speaker mode and held the handset flat.

'She's gone into surgery,' Glenda's voice boomed into the room.

'Surgery?' Ella's mouth went dry. She felt Charlie's hand on her shoulder and, for the first time in a long time, she didn't want to shrug him off. 'What for?'

'She's broken her right wrist, or maybe it was fractured? Is there a difference? Anyway, they're pinning it . . . or something . . . I can't quite remember what the doctor said. Something about a complicated—'

'Is she all right?'

'Well, no, dear. She's broken her wrist and two of the fingers on her other hand.' Glenda sounded irritated. 'She was very distressed. It was upsetting to see her so vulnerable.'

Ella tasted bitter coffee at the back of her mouth. Vulnerable wasn't a word she would ever choose to describe her mother. But Glenda knew Sally as well as she did, probably better, so what she said must be true. 'Sorry, right. Okay.' The thought of her mother lying on a table in an operating theatre made her light-headed. They might not be close, but she didn't like to think of her mum alone and in pain. 'Is it just her hands? Did she hurt anything else?'

'She's got some bruising on her face. It's a blessed miracle only her hands are broken,' said Glenda. 'And the state of the place! It's going to take some sorting out.'

'What happened?' Ella's mind went back to her childhood home. She saw the handsome Georgian building, which was already in disrepair when she was last there, and that was years ago. Guilt tried to take hold of her, but she fought it. It wasn't her fault that house no longer felt like her home.

'She left the bath running.'

Ella raised her eyes to the ceiling, then glanced at Charlie, whose face was uncharacteristically serious.

'From what I can gather, she rushed in when she realised it was flooding, slipped on the tiles and tried to break her fall with her hands.'

Ella covered her mouth. She could see the scene unfold: the water cascading over the top of the claw-foot bath onto the black and white tiles, her bird-like mother tearing in and skidding on the water, pitching forwards, arms outstretched. The snap of bones.

Charlie took the phone from her, holding the speaker near his mouth. 'Hi, Glenda. Charlie here. Obviously, Ella's a bit upset, so can I get the details?'

'Hello, Charlie.' Glenda's voice seemed to melt. That happened a lot, especially with older women, who found Charlie irresistible. His voice alone seemed to do the trick. He was the type of man who made eye contact and actually listened when women spoke. A rare breed, especially in Sydney. Watching him now, Ella wondered when she'd stopped appreciating that kind of attention. Now his habit of talking about everything just felt inefficient. There wasn't enough time in the day to sit around in your pants, chatting. Not enough time in *her* day, anyway. She felt the minutes ticking away. 'Did she hit her head, or anything?' he asked.

'She must've caught her face on the way down, but the doctors didn't seem unduly concerned about the bruising on her cheek. They checked for concussion. They were very thorough with X-rays and all that business. She's got an infection of some sort, but they're giving her antibiotics for that. She's going to be up the creek without a paddle for a while though, since both hands are scuppered.'

Ella could see where this was leading and took the phone back from Charlie. 'I can't tell you how much I appreciate all you do for her, Glenda. It means the world to know she has you to look out for her.'

'Well, you know I do what I can.' There was a pause. Ella closed her eyes, anticipating what was coming next. 'But it's May in a couple of days.'

Charlie shrugged in incomprehension, but Ella knew exactly what Glenda meant. She'd been her neighbour too when she was a child and Ella remembered waving from the street when Glenda and her husband climbed into a taxi for their annual month away in Antibes.

'When do you fly?'

'In two days. I'm sorry, Ella, but the house in France is ready. I have friends joining me. I can't—'

'Of course,' said Ella. 'Of course.' She scrunched her face, embarrassed. 'I don't suppose there's anyone else . . . ?'

'There are students on the other side now,' said Glenda. 'So, they won't be of much use, though they seem nice enough. One of the girls is American and her family must be incredibly wealthy because they bought the house for her to live in with her friends while she

9

studies at university. Imagine that.'

Ella tried to imagine but failed. The houses on Circus Street would be astronomically expensive to buy these days. She knew it had been a stretch for her parents in the late Seventies, despite them both working and her father making partner at the law firm he worked at.

'And, I don't know . . . your mother seems to have been keeping to herself more recently.'

That didn't sound like her mum at all. Ella's abiding memories were of her mother preparing for a committee meeting at the library, or a jaunt to see her favourite stallholders at the market. It was part of the reason she didn't feel quite so guilty about living on the other side of the world. Her mother was never going to be lonely without her. She was too busy.

'She needs you, Ella.'

She stared through the window at the blue sky. The weather was less predictably warm now May was approaching. Soon, she'd need to remember to take her jacket to work, and before she knew it, she'd be leaving in the dark and getting home after sunset. After Willow was asleep.

She thought of London in the spring, the trees budding in the private garden in the middle of Gloucester Circus. She thought of her mother alone in a hospital bed. 'Is she in Lewisham Hospital? Could you give me the details?'

Charlie opened a drawer, took out paper and a pen and put them on the worktop. Ella set the phone down on the counter and wrote the ward number on the paper with a shaky hand.

'Thank you, Glenda,' she said. 'I'll let you know my plans when we've had chance to discuss it. Take care. Thanks again.'

Ella clicked off the call and blew out her cheeks. She looked up at Charlie and sensed he was going to hug her, so she marched to the cupboard behind the open staircase and unhooked her handbag from inside. He might have time for lingering embraces, but she didn't. If she was Queen of the World, everyone would have a gauge on their foreheads: a traffic-light system, showing green for open to hugs, amber for a quick squeeze and red for leave me the fuck alone. She was already on red and now she had another thing to stress about.

'After my meeting I'll look up care options. We can talk about it tonight.'

'Can't you delay going into work until you've had time to think about what needs to be done?' Charlie said.

'I've got a breakfast meeting.' She didn't know why the urge to get out of the house was so strong. She knew she should cancel the meeting, call the hospital and book a flight to London. That was the right thing to do. The dutiful thing. But people didn't always do the right thing and her mother should understand that better than anyone.

'And what do you mean, *care options?* She's not a decrepit old lady who's too infirm to manage. She's had an accident. It's short-term. She needs you now.'

11

Charlie's voice was soft and that made it worse.

'What am I supposed to do? Drop everything and run off to London?'

Charlie poured himself a coffee. 'Honestly, Ella? Yes.'

Typical of him to think it was so simple. It would be easy for him to run back to England at a moment's notice. His only job now was looking after Willow and the house. The pools he maintained would soon be covered over for the winter. She was the one who had all the pressure and responsibility to keep the roof over their heads. 'It's not that easy.'

He sat on a stool at the kitchen island and looked so relaxed, Ella wanted to push him over. 'Isn't it?'

Squeezing the strap of her handbag until the leather dug into her palm, she took a step towards the door. 'Can you call the hospital to check in? I've got to get on.'

'You need to—'

She turned. 'I've got a meeting, Charlie,' she said. She didn't want to think about London, her mum, or why she had left all those years ago. It was easier to think about work. That was straightforward. If she had a problem at work, she could fix it. The rest of life was so much more complicated . . . and painful.

'Take a month off. Go to London.'

She threw her arms wide. 'Yes, Charlie. Why don't I do that? Why don't I just take a month off work and fly away from all my responsibilities, not forgetting our eight-year-old daughter, for an entire month. What on earth is stopping me?'

12

There was nothing stopping her. She knew that, and so did he. Like everyone at her firm, she was eligible for a month's paid leave after twenty years' service. The problem was, she didn't want to take a month off work. She needed to keep going, fill her life with business and distractions, otherwise she'd have to face all the things that lived in the dark places at the back of her mind.

'What is stopping you?' She was shocked by the chill in his voice. 'You know Willow will be fine. It's not like you see her during the week anyway.'

Both his tone and the truth of what he said stung. 'But people rely on me. I can't let the partners down,' she said, with less conviction.

'What about letting your mum down?'

That felt like a low blow. 'It's her who let me down,' she replied. 'You know that.'

He shook his head. 'I know how hurt you were, but perhaps it's time to put it behind you – or at least to try?'

'Nice to know you'd be happy for me to be on another continent for that long.' She wanted to wound him. He couldn't possibly understand how much her mother's betrayal had affected her. If he did, he wouldn't be making this so hard.

'Happy?' he said. 'It wouldn't make me happy.' He looked defeated. 'But what's the point in you sticking around here when your mum needs you?' He sighed and fixed her with sad eyes. 'Because I think we both know *this* doesn't make you happy anymore.' He gestured out to the room, but Ella knew he meant more than that. He

13

meant their life. He meant himself. 'I know you don't want to talk about it, but it wouldn't do any harm for you to have time to think about what it is you want; what might help you find some joy again. Maybe you could work through what's put this distance between you and your mum. I don't know . . . It feels like so much is unresolved, and it's eaten away at you. This might be the opportunity to—'

'It's not as easy as that.' Did he think she could just go home, have it out with her mum and they could live happily ever after? This was real life, not a fairy tale.

He exhaled loudly. 'Some things aren't easy, Ella. It doesn't mean you don't face up to them. Maybe it's time to stop running away.'

She closed her eyes, visualising her office, with its neat files and ordered desks. She didn't need to have difficult conversations there. At work, there was a system, processes that were followed. It was ordered. It was safe.

Charlie carried on, 'From where I'm standing, it's a no-brainer. You can take a month's paid leave. You can do the right thing by your mum, and . . . well, we can talk about the other stuff when you're ready.'

The other stuff. Ella shuddered. She'd known the other stuff would need addressing one day, but she'd been putting it off, like she put everything off.

'I don't know.' But that was another lie. She did know. Charlie was right about everything. She needed to go back to England for so many reasons, and not one of them was good.

Chapter Two

Ella

Present Day

Ella's stomach lurched when the taxi indicated right into the road where she'd grown up. She'd been feeling increasingly anxious since the car had left the M25, and now she could see the sign for Cheeseboard, the shop on the corner with its bizarre hedgehog logo, above the sign saying Circus Street, SE10, her nausea intensified. The car drove slowly, past Ellis and Jones Fishmongers and the brick meeting hall on the right, eventually coming to a standstill on the left in front of her childhood home.

Beyond the black railings, the white lower half of the building still made the short parade of houses stand out. It shouted *I'm special* to anyone who happened to pass by. The rest of the terraced town house was smart brickwork, starting at the sills of the sash windows of the second floor. Ella had always thought her home looked regal, like the kind of house Sherlock Holmes lived in. She'd been proud to bring her friends here when she was younger, then embarrassed when kids from secondary school would stop on the pavement and look up at the shiny black door, lion-shaped door-knocker and semicircular fanlight window above the doorway and say things like, 'Fucking hell, mate, I didn't know you were a millionaire.'

Later, she'd started to anticipate people's responses, even expecting the taxi driver who was currently hoisting her enormous case out of the boot to expect a bigger tip now he'd seen her destination.

'Nice place,' he said, rolling the case to the bottom of the three steps leading to the front door. 'Want me to take this in?'

'No, I'm fine, thank you.' She handed him a ten-pound note as a tip, the currency feeling foreign despite being what she'd used for the first twenty-one years of her life.

Ella stood, looking up at the house until the car made a three-point turn and disappeared back in the direction of Gloucester Circus. She could see what her friends from school saw. The house was grand, from the ornate railings either side of the steps, to the tall windows, perfectly symmetrical in the brickwork above the white.

But handsome as it was, she didn't want to go inside.

Ella forced her feet to climb the steps. It was only a month; she could survive that. She would do her duty to her mum and then she could get back to work and her family. She reordered that in her head, *her family* and work.

Opening the door onto the hall, Ella let out her breath. It looked the same as ever, just more tired.

The tiled floor had scuff marks, and the curved white archway leading to the staircase needed painting. The walnut banister and beige runner disappearing up to the first floor and down to the kitchen in the basement were still impressive.

She wheeled the case onto the tiles and closed the door behind her. When she breathed in, there was a musty scent in the still air.

Taking a couple of steps in, she noticed a vase of drooping red tulips, heads bowed low, petals scattering the dark wood hall table. There was an inch of foetid water at the bottom of the glass vase. That's where the smell must be coming from. But when she got further into the hall, it got worse, far more pungent than a single vase of expired flowers.

Ella turned left into the sitting room, the familiar sight of a floral three-piece suite stopping her in her tracks. That was the sofa she had sat on to read all through her childhood, her mum with her own book in the matching armchair at the far side of the room, facing the doorway. She could almost feel a paperback in her fingers, see a younger version of herself, legs curled under her as she was lost in another world between the pages. She felt strangely nostalgic for that sensation of being transported. She hadn't read a single novel since she'd been in Australia. She told herself she hadn't had time.

Choosing not to give the thought headspace, Ella stepped into the room. The flowers on the sofa fabric looked the same, but the cushion on the chair where her mother sat had dipped in the middle. The material on the arms was threadbare, like it had been rubbed for decades by restless fingers. The flowers had lost their definition, now just indistinguishable shapes in muted orange, blue and pink. Books were stacked by the side of the chair. Ella picked up the one at the top of the pile, *My Sister, the Serial Killer*. Not her mother's usual choice of reading material. She opened the cover and saw it was a library book. It still had a bookplate with date stamps, but no date had been stamped in for some time. Ella wasn't sure if libraries still used that system in the UK, or anywhere, for that matter.

She put the book back on the stack and scanned the rest of the room. It looked shabby. The magnolia paintwork was marked. She was assessing what needed decorating when her eyes reached the ceiling and widened at the dark, uneven stain blooming from the ornate cornice in the far corner and creeping towards the ceiling rose in the centre. Her heart dropped. Her mum's bathroom was two floors up. It must've been a significant flood to have reached down two floors.

Ella rushed from the room, up the stairs to the first floor, poking her head into the bedrooms. To her relief, they all looked tatty, but undamaged.

Choosing not to linger in the bedroom that had been hers, she crossed the landing to the box room and pushed down the handle. The door didn't budge. 'Oh, for goodness' sake!' she growled at the door. There was no key in the lock. This room was directly above the sitting room and the watermark on the ceiling must've come via there.

The musty smell was worse up here. Ella pressed the handle and pushed against the wood with her shoulder, but it wouldn't budge. Her dad had got locks on the inside doors after a spate of burglaries in the area. 'If someone gets in,' she remembered him saying, 'I'm going to make it as difficult as possible for them. That'll teach the thieving buggers.'

Despite his initial vigilance, they'd soon got out of the habit of locking any of the doors, except when they went on holiday, when he'd go around the house checking each one, then stowing the keys in his case.

She had no idea why her mum would want to lock the room that had been a junk room when Ella last lived there. With a frustrated groan, she let go of the handle and ventured to the top floor. The smell of damp grew with every step. The carpet on the landing was a darker beige and when she stepped towards the bathroom, the fibres squelched under her feet.

The black and white checkerboard tiles on the bathroom floor looked dry at first sight, but when Ella crossed the room, she noticed pools of water under the claw-foot bath, making the black tiles shine like onyx. Someone must've tried to mop up the water using the bath towels from the cupboard because sodden heaps sat behind the door.

Ella remembered the second conversation she'd had with Glenda, where she'd told Ella how her mother had eventually managed to get to the phone in her bedroom and call her neighbour.

'She was cowering at the end of her bed when I got to her,' Glenda had told her, 'shivering with the shock. She hadn't even been able to turn off the water because her hands were broken. Thank God I was in and had the spare key, otherwise the paramedics would have had to smash down the door.'

That was a small mercy, thought Ella, standing in the bathroom and surveying the damage from the flood. Her head was starting to throb with jet lag, but she didn't have time to indulge it. She had to get on with getting her mum out of hospital, then work out what needed to be done in the house to repair the damage.

The cascading water had clearly soaked through the room below and down to the next floor. Ella could only imagine the state of the box room. Whatever was in there would probably be completely ruined. She hoped it was just junk. But if it was, why was the room locked, and where was the key?

Ella dragged her weary limbs back down to get her case. She would unpack, collect her mother and then find out.

Chapter Three

Ella

Present Day

As Ella approached Lewisham Hospital in the taxi, she was surprised at how run-down the area looked. The hospital nearest to her home in Manly was a modern building, reassuringly clean-looking and surrounded by wide roads and greenery. The benefit of Medicare plus good insurance, she mused, then shook her head at herself. If she was Queen of the World, every country would have a fully funded NHS with shiny new hospitals that were fit for purpose. This place was ancient.

Her nerves made her fidget as her taxi joined the queue of cars sitting in bumper-to-bumper traffic trying to enter the car park. As they edged forwards, she remembered her mum bringing her to this hospital when she was a teenager, after she was hit on the forehead by a wayward cricket ball in a games lesson. The teacher had told her to sit down for five minutes and if she didn't feel dizzy, get on with the session. Her mum had looked horrified when she'd walked in that evening with a bruised lump on her head and insisted they went

21

to Accident and Emergency.

Sally had talked at her all the way in the car, telling her the history of the red-brick building. Looking at it now, Ella begrudgingly admitted the facade was beautiful.

'It was built as a workhouse in the early eighteen hundreds,' Sally had told her, in an artificially bright voice. 'I'll never forget reading about it because it said it was built in "the picturesque village of Lewisham".' They'd both laughed at that, looking out of the car window at the heavy traffic and people milling about. It was neither a village nor picturesque. It seemed even less so now.

She'd asked Ella to count how many floors there were, and if she could read what was written on the white triangular plaque under the ornate cupola. With hindsight, Ella could see she'd been trying to work out if she was concussed, but at the time, she didn't even know what a cupola was. It had felt like Sally was trying to trip her up. She'd been irritated. She'd found everything her mum did annoying back then, and after what happened, the feeling had only worsened.

After paying for the taxi, Ella passed through the automatic doors, her shoulder muscles tightening. She rolled them on the way to reception and noticed the woman in the queue in front of her giving her a strange look. She must've looked like she was preparing for a fight. She supposed, in a way, she was.

The smell of cleaning fluid and body odour, as she followed the floor map she'd been given, made her stomach turn. Finally, she arrived at the ward where she would see her mother in the flesh for the first time in years. She took three deep breaths before pressing the buzzer to be admitted.

A minute passed. Nobody came. Tentatively, Ella pressed the buzzer again, practising an apologetic smile to show she was sorry for being so impatient. She knew how ridiculous it was that she was so anxious not to be a bother. So British. It had kicked back in the minute she had landed at Heathrow. Back in Sydney, she had no qualms about complaining about slow service. Everybody did it. But, for some reason, the second she was back in England, she had felt the need to apologise to the taxi driver for the weight of her case. She'd even offered to lift it into the boot herself, despite him being twice her size.

She pushed the button again, setting her face to neutral, but the minute the door opened, an involuntary, 'Sorry,' escaped her mouth, followed by a, 'Wasn't sure the bell was working.'

'Come in, come in,' said a cheerful-looking nurse whose uniform stretched tight across her enormous chest. 'Who are you here for?'

'Sally Harrison,' she said, following her into the ward.

The nurse's flat feet slapped against the linoleum, moving at a surprising pace. 'Sally!' she yelled, making Ella jump. 'You're the most popular girl on this ward.'

Ella looked from left to right, trying to spot her mother, but all she could see were elderly ladies with sunken faces and wild hair, propped against sagging pillows. She swallowed. Surely her mum hadn't deteriorated to this extent in recent years? This looked like God's waiting room. Ella shook the idea from her head and tried to conjure up more cheerful thoughts.

Next to an empty bed, one woman had a visitor who was reading to her from a magazine laid flat on a blue blanket over the wizened woman's legs.

'Sally,' yelled the nurse again, 'you gonna go home and leave me to run this place on my own again?' She laughed.

Ella looked around, but still couldn't see her mother.

The woman reading the magazine turned, and there she was. Not a visitor. Not an old lady, but her mum, slight and upright, her pixie-cut hair almost white, but still looking ten years younger than her age. Thirty years too young to belong on this ward.

She stood when she saw Ella, her eyes glistening above a blueish-purple bruise on her right cheekbone. A blue sling held one arm in a cast across her front and tape was wrapped around the first three fingers on her other hand. Ella's breath caught at the sight of her injured mother.

'Ella,' Sally said, stepping towards her.

Neither of them seemed to know what to do.

Ella felt the nurse's eyes on her back and moved towards her mum, opening her arms, then dropping them again. 'I don't want to hurt you,' she said, making an awkward gesture with her hands.

24

'Come here, love,' Sally said and wrapped her free arm around Ella's back.

Ella closed her eyes. Her mum smelled strange. She was expecting to breathe in Lenor Summer Breeze fabric conditioner, but she smelled of hospital and dusty cotton from the sling strapped around her neck.

'I'm so sorry you've had to—'

'Don't . . . It's not . . . It's fine. Honestly.' The last word stuck in her throat.

Sally let Ella go and grinned. 'Iris, this is my daughter, Ella. All the way from Australia,' she said to the nurse. She turned to the woman in the bed. 'I'm going to have to stop reading now, Judith. I'm going home this afternoon. That all right?'

What was she going to do if it wasn't all right with Judith, thought Ella, stay here, reading back copies of *Woman's Own* until the inevitable happened? Another glance at the woman made the hairs on Ella's arms rise. She looked so weak. The hospital bed she was lying in might be her final destination. It seemed a pitiful end to a life.

The woman nodded.

Iris moved around the side of the bed, took a tissue from the box on the cabinet and dabbed drool from the edge of Judith's mouth. 'We gonna miss our Sally, aren't we, Judith?'

Of course they were going to miss her, Ella thought, with a stab of envy for all these people her mother would have tried her best to take care of. Sally would have done everything she could to make herself part of the community here. She would have been endlessly helpful and chirpy, and they would have all thought she was a saint. Well, she wasn't.

'Let's get you sorted, then.' Ella followed her to a bed with a holdall sitting on top.

'Iris packed for me. I'm afraid I'm pretty helpless at the moment.'

Ella felt guilty about her previous thought. Sally couldn't be too useful with no available hands. She would still have been endlessly cheerful, though. Ella imagined a chirpy patient would be a rare enough treat around here. One who still had the strength to smile would be the exception, by the looks of it.

'Well, I'm here now, so you don't have to worry about that.'

Sally glanced up, her face serious. 'How will Charlie and . . . and your little girl manage without you?'

Ella narrowed her eyes. Had she forgotten her own granddaughter's name? Ella had dropped everything to come here and now it looked like her family was so far down Sally's list of priorities, she didn't know what her daughter was called. If that was the case, Ella was a fool for crossing oceans for her.

'Charlie and Willow will be fine.'

'I feel terrible about you having to leave Willow.'

It seemed like she was repeating the name to imprint it on her memory.

'Charlie's at home. It's really not as disruptive as you

26

think.' Ella said it to punish her. To tell her it was no big deal, her coming to London. It didn't mean that much.

She heard Iris's footsteps slapping towards them. 'Look after this one,' she boomed. 'She's precious.'

Ella smiled. 'I intend to. Does she need to see a doctor, or wait for meds or anything?'

'All done,' said Iris. She turned to Sally. 'You've got your antibiotics?'

'They're in the bag.' Sally glanced at Ella. 'Urine infection. Sent me a bit doolally. My memory isn't what it was at the best of times, and before this infection was detected, I ended up talking all kinds of rubbish. Quite mortifying, really.'

Ella berated herself for condemning Sally for forgetting Willow's name. She must try harder to be kind. Her mother was ill, not uncaring. On this occasion at least.

'Make sure you drink enough water,' said Iris. 'Don't want you forgetting where you are again.' She laughed and shook her head. 'It's not every day a patient thinks they're in a five-star hotel, though. It made a nice change from people complaining about the food and the state of the NHS.'

Ella looked around the stark ward. She'd heard of the delusional effects urine infections could have on older people. It must've been a pretty rough one for her mother to think this place was the lap of luxury.

'I could have gone home the day before yesterday, apparently,' said Sally, fussing over the bag, trying to close the zip with her little finger. 'I've been quite the bed-blocker. They wouldn't let me out until someone was at home.'

'I came as quickly as I could,' Ella said, wearily, feeling the need to defend herself. She eyed the empty bed and felt the urge to curl up on it and close her aching eyes.

Sally's eyes widened. 'No. That's not what I meant. I'm so grateful—'

'Let's get on then.' Ella swooped the zip closed and lifted the bag over her shoulder. 'Thank you for taking care of her,' she said to Iris.

'My pleasure. Watch how you go, Sally. Don't want to see you back in here unless you're a visitor. You hear me?'

'I hear you,' said Sally. 'I'll promise to do my best.'

Ella waited at the door while Sally said her copious goodbyes. Never great at waiting, Ella had to fight her increasing petulance when her mum appeared to know the names of one of the patient's grandchildren. This benevolence was proving hard to keep up. She was relieved when a notification popped up telling them their Uber was one minute away.

'Cab's here,' she called. 'Come on, Mum.'

The silence that fell between them as they walked the corridors towards the exit was excruciating. Ella glanced across at Sally and was surprised to see she looked frail. Against the backdrop of the women with shrunken gums and hands gnarled with arthritis in the geriatric ward, she'd appeared positively youthful; but walking beside her now, she looked like the injured birds Ella had seen on TV programmes, skinny with wet feathers and scrawny limbs. She was surprised by an urge to wrap a protective arm around her.

'You're thin, Mum. Have you been eating properly?'

'Cycling keeps me fit,' she said.

'Glenda said she hasn't seen you out on the bike for a while.'

'Did she?' She looked up at her with a confused expression. She lifted the sling away from her body. 'Don't suppose I'll be able to for a while, will I?'

Ella was tempted to say *good; you'll kill yourself on that thing,* then remembered she'd almost killed herself running a bath. 'Looking forward to sleeping in your own bed?'

'I suppose so,' Sally said, non-committally.

Ella shifted the bag to her other shoulder. 'What? Surely you must be delighted to be going home?' She'd been at the hospital less than an hour and couldn't wait to get away from the smell, the noise, the people in wheelchairs being pushed along with drips hanging from poles like deflated party balloons. The whole place was a screaming reminder of disease, pain and mortality. Three things she'd rather not have to face for a second longer than necessary.

'Yes, it's just . . .'

'What?'

Sally sighed. 'Nothing.'

Ella wasn't going to push her. She didn't have the

energy to pry the meaning of every sigh out of her mother. If she was Queen of the World, people would say what they meant or keep quiet. Winsome sighs and subtexts would be banned.

They reached the entrance. Ella checked the app to find the Uber's registration number, then scanned the cars circling the car park, glad to spot their car heading towards them. She busied herself waving for the driver's attention, then confirming her name and dropping the bag in the boot. She opened the car door for Sally, leaned in to do up the seat belt, all the time dreading being in the house, alone with this woman she felt she hardly knew.

Chapter Four

Ella

Present Day

When the taxi drew up on Circus Street, a boy who looked to be in his late teens was sitting on the steps of the house next door rolling a thin cigarette between his fingers. A black and white cat sat by his side. As Ella struggled to help Sally out of the car to the pavement, the young man put down his tobacco and jumped from the top step down to the bottom. The leap made the grey linen skirt he was wearing flap up, giving Ella a glimpse of black shorts that might have been his underwear.

'Sally!' he said, the 'y' pronounced as a lower case 'e'. 'I've been worried sick about you.' Ella thought he sounded Mancunian, but it was a long time since she'd had to distinguish British accents, so she could be counties out.

Her mother's eyes lit up. 'Sorry, love. I'm an old fool, aren't I? I hope there's no water damage next door?'

'Don't be daft,' said the boy. 'Daddy Warbucks would just throw money at it if there was, don't worry.'

The cat stalked down the steps towards them. Its

head was black apart from a white upside-down heart shape that started between its eyes and spread around its pink nose. One of its ears had a nick out of it and as it started to headbutt Sally's leg, Ella saw its right eye was missing, making the other green eye seem unusually bright.

Sally leaned down to run her thumb over the cat's fur. 'Nice to see you too, Hadron.'

'Hadron?' queried Ella.

'Hadron Collider,' said Sally, straightening up. 'She walks into everything, poor thing. She must've lost her spatial awareness along with that eye.'

'Excellent name.' Ella smiled. 'But aren't cats supposed to use their whiskers for that kind of thing?'

The cat looked up at Ella and made a low guttural noise that sounded like a dog growling.

'Oh dear,' said Sally. 'She's growling at you.'

'Cats don't growl,' said Ella, frowning at the strange creature.

'This one does. We think she must've lived with dogs before. If she doesn't like someone, she growls and . . .' Sally laughed as the cat turned around, stretched out its paws and lifted its tail in the air, displaying its pink bottom, '. . . Does that.'

'Charming,' scoffed Ella, more offended than she should be by this boy's weird pet.

'She'll get used to you,' said Sally.

Ella hoped she wouldn't see it enough for that to be necessary. She had plenty to tolerate on this trip without throwing a cyclops-cat-dog into the mix. 'Let's get in, shall we?'

'You're not in too much pain, are you?' The young man didn't seem to have heard what Ella said and was looking at Sally with concern.

'It's not too bad, thanks, love.' Sally looked down at her sling and bound fingers. 'My career as a world-renowned pianist is over, though.' She shrugged and smiled as the boy guffawed.

'You're a better rapper anyway,' he said. 'Just need to practise your beatbox.' He started to make popping noises with his mouth and, to Ella's astonishment, Sally bobbed her head in time.

She observed the young man. He had an impressively abundant afro, pale brown skin and freckled nose. His frankly bizarre outfit consisted of green tartan jumper, a skirt and the chunkiest trainers Ella had ever seen. She tried to work out who he was and why he was on such familiar terms with her mother.

'I'm Ella,' she said, cutting in over the sound of his lips popping. 'Sally's daughter.'

Sally stilled. 'Sorry, yes.' She gestured towards the boy. 'This is Nathan. He lives next door.'

Ella remembered Glenda saying students now lived in the house next to Sally's. 'Ah, right, yes. Hello,' she said, wondering if she should shake his hand, fist-bump or what. What did the British youth do to greet people these days? She felt suddenly old and oddly Australian. That was a first.

'Right, yeah, Ella.' He nodded. 'From Australia. Always wanted to go there.'

She smiled. Sally's bag was heavy on her shoulder and her head felt soupy with exhaustion. All she wanted to do was get inside and make a nice cup of Yorkshire tea. It tasted better in England, she'd decided when she'd sipped her first cup earlier. Must be something to do with the water. It was the only good thing to have happened since she arrived.

'Me too,' Sally said.

Ella tensed. That was a pointed comment if ever she'd heard one. She shifted the bag on her shoulder. 'We'd better get in. Nice to meet you, Nathan.'

'And you.' He turned to Sally. 'I've hardly seen you since Easter. Might pop round for a catch-up tomorrow. What d'ya think?'

What on earth could her mother and this student possibly have to *catch up* about? Ella eyed him suspiciously, wondering what his deal was.

'How is your mum?' Sally's voice was concerned.

'Yeah, not too bad.' His face scrunched. 'At least we kept the bailiffs away this time. The landlord's all right, really. It's not like he wants to chuck her out, but he's got a mortgage to pay. What can you do?'

'Oh, love,' said Sally. 'If there's anything I can do, you know where I am.' She glanced at Ella, who must've been wearing her impatience on her face because she said, 'Let Ella and I settle in, and then pop around whenever you fancy.'

'Sweet,' he said, skipping up next-door's steps. 'Glad you're home. Be careful with those hands. Don't go overdoing it – I know what you're like.'

How did he know what her mother was like? thought Ella, holding Sally's elbow as they went up the steps. She opened the door wide for her to step through.

The cat started to follow them into the hall. Ella put her foot out to block its way. 'No you don't, pal,' she said. Hadron jumped over her leg. Ella turned to Sally. 'You haven't been feeding Nathan's cat, have you? You'll never get rid of her.'

'She's not Nathan's cat,' said Sally, over the quiet growling emanating from the creature's throat. 'She's mine. At least, she seems to be. I put leaflets up all over Greenwich asking if she belonged to anyone. Nobody claimed her, and that was months ago, so it looks like she's here to stay.'

Hadron turned, dipped her front legs and lifted her tail, showing her bottom again, pink and puckered against her black fur. Ella wished herself on a plane back home. 'Who's been feeding her while you've been in hospital?'

'Nathan. He's very good.'

The cat straightened up and made for the sitting room, knocking into the door frame on her way through with a quiet thud.

'A pet might be a bit much for you, at least until you're back on your feet. Perhaps—'

Sally glared at her. 'I'm sure we'll manage. She takes

a bit of getting used to, but she's been a comfort to me over the last few months. This house felt empty before she came along.'

How typical of Sally to take in a stray. If only she'd shown the same care and attention to her own family as she did for the randoms in her life, then maybe Ella wouldn't be feeling like a stranger in what was once her home.

Hadron had curled up next to her mother's chair, looking like she belonged there. Ella felt a moment's envy for a one-eyed cat. How had it come to that?

Sally's nostrils widened as she breathed in. Ella imagined she could smell the damp too. 'Shall we wait until tomorrow to inspect the damage?'

Sally smiled sadly and nodded.

Dropping the bag onto the hall floor and shutting the door behind them, Ella couldn't keep her curiosity about Nathan to herself. 'What's going on with Nathan's mum?'

Sally moved into the sitting room and fell into her chair. 'The poor woman keeps getting behind on her rent. She's got fibromyalgia, so quite often she's not up to her cleaning job. I suspect Nathan's given her the money from his student loan to stop her being evicted. He works night shifts at the all-night garage, so I hope he's got enough to get by, but I do worry about him.'

Ella had seen endless news articles about elderly people living on their own being taken advantage of. That made her suspicious about why this boy was telling her mother his troubles. Her bottom lip jutted out. She'd had troubles of her own at his age, but she didn't go running to the nearest pensioner to offload. And she couldn't go to her mother. Instead, she flew away to the other side of the world and got on with it.

Ella took a beat to work out whether she should air her concern. She decided if Sally was being taken for a fool, she needed to know. 'You're not giving him money, are you?'

'I'm sorry?'

Ella's cheeks burned. She wished she'd phrased it more subtly, but she still wanted to know the answer to her question. 'It's just . . . it seems a bit unusual that a young man his age wants to pop around for a cuppa with . . .' She paused.

Sally fixed her with a stern look. 'With an old woman like me?'

'That's not what I meant.' It was exactly what she meant.

'Nathan is a long way from home. His mother is unable to support him because she has problems of her own and he doesn't like to burden her. If I can be of any help at all to that lovely young man, I think it's my duty to do so. Don't you?'

Where was your sense of duty twenty-one years ago? screamed the voice in Ella's head. 'I just don't want anyone taking advantage of you. How do you know he's telling you the truth, and not just some sob story?'

Sally closed her eyes and laid her head on the back

of the chair. 'How long have you been in Australia?' she said quietly.

'That's not the—'

'How long?'

Ella walked to the window. She watched Nathan light his cigarette. He breathed in deeply, then out, making little smoke rings that he watched rise, fade, then vanish against the pale blue sky. 'Twenty-one years.'

'And what has happened in that time to make you so cynical? Because the girl I brought up cared about people. She loved Jo in *Little Women* and wanted to be the kind of person who took food to the Hummels.'

Ella's stomach tightened with a mixture of indignation and shame. 'Yes, well, what happened to Beth in *Little Women* when she did what she thought was right? She died. And the real world isn't some kind of fairy tale. People aren't all on some redemption arc. They turn out to be different to who you thought they were, and they let you down. Even the ones you love the most.'

Overwhelmed and exhausted, Ella covered her mouth to stifle her sobs and, without looking at her mother, she marched from the room.

If she had paused for a few seconds and listened beyond the throbbing in her head, she might have heard Sally say, 'I've been trying to redeem myself in your eyes, and my own, for twenty-one years, my lovely girl. You have no idea what I have given up in the hope you might forgive me. It's my only wish in this world.'

Chapter Five

Ella

Present Day

'I might go up to bed,' said Sally at eight-thirty.

'Already?' Ella felt she should protest, but, in truth, she was ready to call time on the quiet, stilted evening. She was glad it was over and unsure how either of them was going to survive four more weeks of tiptoeing around each other. The sooner her mother's hands healed, and she was on a flight back to Australia, the better.

Despite being sure she wanted to get away, the thought still left Ella feeling hollow. There was a part of her that had hoped this trip might be a reunion, a way back to the relationship they used to have.

An image of the two of them holding hands, giggling as they tried to stay upright on the ice rink at Somerset House came into her mind. It was shortly before Christmas when she was twelve, but she could still see the shimmering festive lights and feel the way her thighs ached and her cheeks stung with cold. Afterwards, they'd wrapped their numb fingers around steaming mugs of hot chocolate and watched other skaters glide and stumble. Ella could still feel Sally close by her side. She missed that relationship. She missed feeling mothered.

'I think the general anaesthetic takes a while to wear off,' said Sally. 'And I'm not sure those antibiotics agree with me. I'm not feeling quite myself.' She gave Ella a tight smile. 'Sorry if I'm poor company.'

'No, not at all. I heard it can take a few weeks for the effects of the anaesthetic to wear off.' She wasn't sure where she'd heard it, or even if it was true, but if it gave them both something external to blame for the fact they no longer knew how to be around each other, she was going to take it. 'And an infection can take it out of you. You'll need a lot of rest.'

She followed Sally up to the top floor. Her mother's bedroom looked the same as it had when Ella had left, although the king-sized sleigh bed seemed smaller than in her memory, and the top of the cabinet on the side her father used to sleep on was empty apart from a lamp with a faded pink shade. It had always had a hardback book about some war or other sitting neatly on it with a leather bookmark poking out and his reading glasses folded on top.

Memories of him lecturing her on history and politics came back to her. He had a more didactic approach than her mother, who always encouraged her to question and analyse what she learned, but his absolute certainty and faith in himself was awe-inspiring. He was a man who knew who he was and what he believed in. In Ella's eyes, he was her hero, and now, the day she heard he'd died came flooding back into her mind in a rush that almost made her double over in pain.

Do you miss him too? she wanted to say to Sally. *Did you even love him?* But she knew the answer to that. Her mother could never have betrayed him if she had.

Ella opened the heavy drawer of the old chest Sally directed her to and took out a loose-fitting nightshirt.

Swallowing down the pain of loss that had sat in her abdomen since she'd stepped into the house, she turned on the lamp by her mum's side of the bed and switched off the ceiling light before helping Sally to change. Even in the soft glow, the intimacy felt awkward. She could tell Sally felt it too; her eyes looked anywhere but at her. She manoeuvred the sleeve of Sally's T-shirt carefully over her cast and Sally gave a sharp intake of breath.

'You all right?'

Sally nodded, but her lips were pursed tight. She was in pain and that made Ella's stomach tighten like it did when Willow was unwell.

She tugged at the cotton to widen the armhole, all the time trying not to look at her mother's thin body. She looked fragile in a way Ella hadn't anticipated. Her ribs were visible under pale skin, her breasts almost flat to her chest in a cotton bra top. The strange urge to wrap her up in her arms and protect her returned.

'That's fine,' Sally said, when Ella started to lift the bra top. 'I'll sleep in this.'

'Wouldn't you be more comfortable—?'

'It's fine, thanks, love. Just help me slip on that nightie.'

When she was sure Sally had taken her antibiotics, painkillers and had everything she needed, Ella switched off the bedside lamp and pulled the door almost closed. She left the landing light on and went down the two flights of stairs to the sitting room. She checked the time on her phone and calculated it was still an hour and a half until she could FaceTime Willow. And Charlie, she reminded herself guiltily. Willow and Charlie.

Her mind returned to what he'd said about them needing to talk when she got back and a feeling of dread wound around her. She didn't like *talking*. If she was Queen of the World, all personal problems would be resolved by leaving them alone and getting on with things. All talking did was allow other people to tell you what they thought you were doing wrong. Ella didn't like being wrong any more than her father had when he was alive. Fortunately, both were usually right, in their opinions, at least.

In need of distraction, Ella glanced around the room, looking for the television remote control. It wasn't on the pale green ottoman that sat between the sofa and her mother's chair. She dug down the sides of the sagging cushions, but all she found were crumbs and crumpled tissues.

The cat woke and peered at her with that startling green eye. As if disgusted at being disturbed, she let out the familiar guttural sound, showed her bum and stalked from the room.

'And you, buddy,' said Ella, sticking her tongue out

at Hadron's disappearing rear end. There was a thud, a brief mewl, then the quiet sound of paws on the stairs to the basement kitchen.

Ella searched under the chair and everywhere else she could think of, but couldn't find the controller. Frustrated, she examined the small television in the corner, looking for buttons she could press, but it was sleek and flat and completely devoid of anything that looked like it might allow her to change channels.

With teeth gritted, she scanned the room, finally fixing her gaze on the bookcase filled with exquisite editions of classics and special editions by world-renowned authors. That bookcase had been her happy place as a child. She remembered her heart feeling light when she'd finished one book and was looking for a new story to lose herself in. When she was about fourteen, she remembered Sally telling her she needed to read more than just the classics, much to the disdain of Ella's father.

She hadn't thought about that for decades. How unusual it was, she mused, for a mother of a teenage girl to encourage her daughter to widen their horizons beyond books that were universally admired. Her dad had put forward a case for a classical education without the frivolous distraction of commercial fiction, but secretly Ella and Sally had agreed a rule that Ella would read one book from the bookshelf, then one from the library down the road.

She glanced behind her to the pile of books next to Sally's chair, *My Sister, the Serial Killer* still balanced on top. She would never have imagined her mother choosing that book, but then, what did she really know about her after all this time away? Ella pondered the cover, briefly considering picking the book up, but her gaze was drawn back to the bookshelf.

There was something incredibly comforting about the cracked spines of those novels. She could recall at what point in her life she'd been when she'd read each one.

She lifted out *Pride and Prejudice*, smiling at the familiar Penguin Classics edition with its black rectangle and the portrait of Elizabeth Bennet staring out from the cover. She held the book to her face and breathed in. The smell of paper and dust transported her back to when she was fifteen at school, sitting next to Verity Ibe in English.

Verity was an artist. She loved crafting and painting and hated English literature with a passion. When their formidable teacher, Mrs O'Boyle, finished reading out a passage, Verity would lean close to Ella and whisper, 'Oh my God, why can't they speak bloody English?'

Ella would laugh, but she didn't agree. She adored the formality of Austen's prose and found the satire hilarious. 'It is English,' she'd say to Verity. She'd explain the hidden meaning behind a paragraph to her and Verity would just roll her eyes.

'Does she fancy this Darcy fella or not?' she'd say. 'If she does, then she should just get off with him and save us all the bother of working it out.'

Ella opened the first page now and read, 'It is a truth universally acknowledged, that a single man in possession of a good fortune, must be in want of a wife.'

It felt like being submerged in warm water. The words made the knotted fibres in her muscles untangle. The next paragraph pushed her anxious thoughts from the forefront of her brain. With her eyes still on the page, Ella moved towards the sofa, tucked her legs beneath her, and for the first time since she'd left England, she allowed herself to get lost in a book.

Chapter Six

Ella

Present Day

'Good morning,' Ella said, placing a cup of tea on Sally's bedside table. 'Sleep well?'

'Not bad, thanks,' said Sally. 'I can see why opioids are so popular. The dreams were a bit much, but at least I was out for the count.'

'Yay for morphine, or codeine, or whatever poppy derivative you're high on,' said Ella, wondering whether that was an appropriate thing to say to your mother. Maybe drug-based gags were best kept to peers.

'Yep. When that packet's finished, I'm going to send you down to Deptford to score some heroin.'

Apparently not. 'That escalated quickly.'

'Only kidding,' said Sally. 'I'll ask Nathan.'

'Mother, behave yourself.' She glanced nervously at the packet of pills on the bedside table. 'Does Nathan do drugs . . .'

'Oh, Ella, love. Don't be so gullible. I was joking. Of course he doesn't do drugs . . . Well, he does. He has those things for his ADHD. What does he call them?

Anyway, it's like speed, but instead of speeding him up, they slow him down.'

'So, he does do drugs?'

'Nothing that's not prescribed by a psychiatrist. Anyway, he's far too studious for that kind of thing. Students seem to take their degrees very seriously these days. It's a shame, really. They should be enjoying themselves. When your dad and Andrew and I were at university—'

'How do you want to do this?' Ella cut her off. She didn't want to hear about Sally's university days, and she definitely didn't want to hear about Andrew.

Sally seemed to shrink. She must've realised what she'd said because she avoided Ella's eyes as she lifted herself onto her elbow and swung her legs around, eventually managing to sit up on the edge of the mattress. Ella put out a hand to help, but Sally waved her away. 'How do I want to do what?'

'Get ready for the day.'

'Right, well . . .' Sally frowned. 'I'd like to be as independent as I can be. Can we agree that I'll ask for help if I need it? I'd rather you didn't fuss over me.'

Ella bristled. She wasn't the fussy type and anything Sally could do for herself, she was more than happy to let her get on with. She'd been secretly dreading the moment Sally asked her to help with the toilet, but it hadn't happened so far. 'Will you ask, though?'

'I won't have any choice, will I?' She lifted her arm with the cast to the elbow.

'How will you shower, or do I need to give you a bed bath . . .' She kept her face neutral, as if sponging down her mother's nether regions would all be in a day's work for her. Not a problem. No siree.

Sally shuddered. 'God, no. I don't think either of us want to suffer through that. Before I left hospital, Iris helped me order these plastic cover things with elasticated cuffs from Amazon to put over my arms. They should be arriving today. These fingers' —she held her bound hand up— 'don't hurt too much because they can't really move because of the splint, so I think as long as I keep my hands and the cast dry, I'll be able to shower all right.'

'Phew,' Ella said. 'Not that I'd mind, I mean, obviously . . . whatever you need, fine by me.' She felt Sally's eyes on her and turned away, seemingly unable to stop herself babbling on. 'Yep, no problem at all. Just say the word. Happy to help.'

***

After a breakfast of toast and peanut butter, which Sally ate using her little finger and thumb as pincers, Ella was about to address the matter of the locked junk room, when there was a sharp ring on the doorbell. She hurried up from the basement kitchen, but the bell rang again before she reached the door.

If I was Queen of the World, she told herself, *there'd be a law that you had to wait a full three minutes between goes on someone's doorbell.*

48

When she opened it, an older woman with bobbed, grey hair and a smart trouser suit was standing on the top step, frowning. 'Ella, I presume?' she said in an imperious tone.

'Erm, yes,' said Ella, feeling like she was twelve again and needed to remember how to correctly address her mother's friends. How soon she'd reverted to the child she had been when she'd lived here. 'Hello.'

'Is your mother in?'

'Sorry, can I ask who—'

The woman's chin contracted as though she'd been asked to provide a DNA sample. 'Pru Gardino, from The LCG.'

'The LCG?'

'The Library and Community Group. The LCG for short.'

It was said so haughtily, Ella had the ridiculous urge to curtsy. 'Right, okay, yes. Come in, Pru. Nice to meet you.'

Pru raised an eyebrow and Ella wondered if she expected to be addressed as Mrs Gardino. Or was it Ms? She gave her head a shake. She was forty-two and a successful lawyer. She did not need to be given lessons in etiquette from any of her mother's friends, however intimidating they strove to be.

'Hello, Pru,' said Sally, appearing at the top of the steps from the kitchen. 'What can I do for you?' Her tone was a little more clipped than usual and Ella sensed these two might not be the very best of friends.

Hadron meandered through from the sitting room. When she saw Pru, she growled and showed her bottom, which offended Ella more than it seemed to offend Pru, who glanced at the cat, tutted and looked away. Ella felt strangely like she'd been placed, by Hadron, in the same category as this strident women. Hadron was perfectly cat-like when she was around Sally or Nathan, yet she turned into a judgemental mutt with Ella and now Pru.

'Come through,' said Ella, leading them through to the sitting room.

'I heard about your accident at book group. Apparently, a few of the others from the library popped around to check up on you, but you must've still been in hospital. They left phone messages, but they haven't heard back.' She left a pause, but when Sally didn't reply, she carried on. 'Anyway, someone said your daughter had flown in to look after you, but I thought it was only right to call around myself and see how you are'—she took a box of biscuits from an enormous Mulberry bag and handed them to Ella—'and give you these.' Ella read the Harvey Nichols label on the box and decided they were meant as both a gift and a statement.

'Very kind,' said Ella, clocking that the woman had expressed a duty rather than an inclination to come. Maybe Hadron was right and they had something in common after all. That was a sobering thought. 'And please say thank you to the people who came around. Mum's only just got home.' She felt defensive of Sally, mainly because everything this woman said sounded like an accusation, as if Sally had slighted people by being unavailable. She glanced at the bruise on Sally's cheek, which was fading from purple to yellow, and her chin rose as the protective feeling returned. She turned back to Pru, the politeness taught to her by her mother overriding the urge to show her straight to the door. 'Would you like a drink? Tea, coffee?'

'I can't stop, far too many jobs on the list,' Pru said. Ella heard the words, *unlike you idlers*, in this peculiar women's tone. 'I have to prepare for my Spanish lesson later.'

'I thought the library wanted to offer Spanish conversation,' said Sally. 'Not lessons.'

Ella noted the challenge in her voice and smiled inwardly. Her apparent frailty had made Ella forget how she used to admire Sally's strength of character. She had always stood up for the underdog when Ella was growing up. Ella found herself wondering if she was teaching Willow that trait. The smile wilted at the realisation that, if anyone was, it was probably Charlie.

Pru's chest lifted, reminding Ella of an indignant pigeon. 'Toe-mate-oh, toe-mah-toh. I'm the only fluent Spanish speaker, so it's up to me to lead the less— sessions.' She sniffed. 'Anyway, I just wanted to make sure you're still in one piece and to give you the next book club pick.' She reached back into the bag and pulled out a copy of *The Alchemist*. 'Modern classic this time,' she said. 'Of course, I've read it before, but it has some interesting messages I'd like to revisit.'

'Thank you,' said Sally. 'Very kind of you to bring it round.'

Pru put the book on the ottoman. 'I'll take your copy of *My Sister, the Serial Killer* back for you if you like. Such a shame you missed the discussion, it was very lively. Did you know that Stanley from Chester Road has a second cousin on Death Row in the United States for murdering his wife? Gloria pointed out it wasn't strictly relevant because he only murdered one person, but it was a domestic murder, so I argued it was quite pertinent to the text.'

Sally blinked. 'My Sister what?'

'The Serial Killer,' said Pru flatly, as though that were a phrase she used every day.

Sally looked at Ella, who was still processing the information about Stanley's second cousin. Then Ella remembered looking for the library date stamp when she picked up the book from the pile. 'That's a reading group book, then?'

'That's right,' said Pru. 'The library provides the books for as long as we need them, then they go to another library for their book group.' She turned back to Sally, an irritated V forming between her eyebrows. 'Have you finished it? You can drop it back another time if not, because I really must get on.'

'I don't know what you're talking about,' said Sally.

'The book, Mum.' Ella wanted to get on with assessing the flood damage. The sooner this woman left, the better. '*My Sister, the Serial Killer.* Have you read it yet?'

'I've never heard of it.'

Ella marched to the pile of books by the side of the chair. She held it up for Sally to see. An expression she couldn't read passed across Sally's face. She wondered whether she should tell Pru about Sally's urine infection. It was probably not something she'd want discussed amongst the great and good of Greenwich, but she was clearly not over it yet. Ella tried to remember how many tablets were left in the blister pack of antibiotics. Not many. At this rate, she'd need another course.

'Oh, that,' Sally's voice faltered. 'Right. Yes, no, it wasn't to my taste. I gave up on it and must've forgotten.'

'That's what you said about *The Power*, and I would've thought that was right up your street,' said Pru, with a tone that suggested Sally's street was not one Pru would choose to travel down. She took the book from Ella and dropped it in her bag. 'Well, at least *The Alchemist* is short, so I hope you'll get through that one.' She peered at Sally through narrowed eyes. 'Are you sure you're all right?'

'I'm perfectly all right apart from my blasted hands,' Sally said.

Her terseness seemed to cause Pru's spine to straighten. 'Fine. Good. Well, I'll see you soon, I expect.' She turned to leave the room. 'I'll see myself out.'

Ella followed her to the door, but it closed before she could offer a goodbye. She stood in the semicircle of spring sun shining through the glass above the door, thoughts percolating.

'Mum,' she said, walking back into the sitting room to find Sally sitting in her chair leafing through *The Alchemist* with her thumb. The sight was so familiar, it was like she'd gone back in time. In that second, Ella was eight years old again, and the instinct to sit on the arm of Sally's chair, then slide down by her mother's side was almost irrepressible. She wanted to be tucked in next to her, to hear Sally's voice as she read *Little Women* aloud. She blinked and was back in the present, several strides away from her mother's side. Emotionally, she felt away further still. 'Why didn't you go to the last couple of book groups?'

'Life's too short to read books you don't enjoy,' said Sally, not looking up. Hadron walked over and sat on her feet and Sally stroked her head with her thumb.

'But you used to love the library book group. Surely, it's worth going along for the discussion, even if the book isn't to your taste.'

'Maybe I've decided I only want to read what I choose, not what some library administrator wants me to read. And you can imagine how many opinions Pru has to share with the group. It would be hard to get a word in, even if you'd written the book yourself.'

Ella couldn't argue with that. And she'd read nothing but legal texts for more than two decades, so she was in no position to judge. 'I'm just worried about you, that's all. Glenda and Nathan both seemed to think you haven't been as sociable recently, and your memory—'

'I'm taking the tablets for that,' Sally snapped. 'And

54

I'm getting old. Old people forget things.' She kept her eyes on the page. 'And, forgive me, but I'm not sure how you would be able to tell if my memory, or any other element of my life, has changed recently. Do you?'

Ella closed her mouth. She couldn't argue with that either. The air in the room chilled. She watched Sally run her thumb backwards and forwards along Hadron's spine, feeling like a new chasm had opened up between them.

Chapter Seven

Ella

Present Day

Later that day, it took the two of them the best part of an hour to find the key for the junk room door. Ella craved her tidy house, with its clean cupboards and drawers with dedicated uses and plastic dividers. Not that she'd had anything to do with the kitchen layout. That was all Charlie's doing; but at least she knew where to find everything.

'We'll have to give up. It must be lost for good,' said Sally.

'I'm not the giving-up type.' Ella unhooked the last kitchen drawer from its runners and tipped it onto the table. 'I'm beginning to think you don't want me to see what's in that room.' She visualised the sodden junk and wondered how they'd go about getting a skip parked outside the house, imagining the faces of some of the more snooty neighbours when a big yellow bin was delivered to their precious street.

Sally glanced up, then back at the collection of items. She poked at the pens with missing lids and creased takeaway menus with a confused expression. 'I could have sworn the key was in here,' she said.

'You could have sworn it was on a hook under the stairs, and at the bottom of your second-best handbag, but I'm sure you're right this time.' Ella wasn't about to mention Sally's memory again after being snapped at last time.

'Sarcasm doesn't become you,' said Sally. 'Just wait until you're my age, then see how quickly you can find a key you haven't used since last July.'

Sarcasm does become me, thought Ella. *It's my go-to communication tool.* 'Why last July?'

'Ah, here! Found it.' Sally pinned her thumb on top of a key with a white dot on its side and dragged it to the edge of the table. She tried to pick it up between her thumb and little finger, but it fell and clinked against the tiles. 'Damn and blast.'

'Language, Mother,' Ella mocked, leaning down to pick up the key. 'At last.' She turned the key over in her fingers. 'How do you know this is the right one?'

'I put Tippex on the top,' explained Sally, 'so I'd recognise it.'

'Genius,' said Ella. 'If you hadn't then shoved it in a drawer with four hundred other random bits and bobs.' She gave Sally a quick squeeze and was reassured to feel her mother lean in close.

'All right smarty-pants,' Sally said, smiling up at her. 'We've got it now, so . . .' She paused. 'Anyway, there's no hurry to go up there, is there? Now we know where the key is, we can go any time.'

'No time like the present.' Ella's curiosity had grown in the time it took to find the key. If it hadn't been in the drawer, she might have been tempted to call a locksmith. And now, her mother's reluctance made her even more inquisitive.

Sally hooked her thumb under the strap at the back of her sling and lifted it away from her neck. 'This thing makes my neck ache. Let's go up later, when I feel a bit more—'

Ella pulled out a chair. 'Why don't you sit here and rest your cast on the table – that'll give your neck a break.'

Smiling, Sally lowered herself into the seat. 'Shall we have a nice cup of tea?'

'In a minute. I'm just going to open that room and give it a bit of an airing. Whatever's inside will be soaked through and I hate to think what kind of mould will be growing in there. We should probably have already hired a dehumidifier.' She headed towards the stairs, but turned when she heard the legs of her mother's chair scrape across the tiles. 'You don't have to come.'

'I do,' said Sally quietly, as she followed her up the stairs.

***

The musty smell was strongest outside the junk room door. It had now been five days since the flood and Ella's enthusiasm seeped away when she stood on the landing ready to insert the key into the lock. She hadn't been in this room since she'd left for university. Back then, it was filled with an old filing cabinet, some ancient furniture and suitcases waiting to go into the loft.

She could understand why her mum might be reluctant to go inside. Junk you'd left to fester was depressing enough, so soaked junk that had to be dealt with was even worse. She braced herself, slotted in the key and turned it.

The door opened. Ella stood for a second, squinting, dazzled by shards of light shining through the window at the far wall. They were like beams from torches held in moving hands, shades of yellow and white, narrow near the window, then spreading in glowing triangles, illuminating dancing dust motes. She blinked, waiting for her eyes to adjust and see piles of rubbish, but from what she could now make out, until five days ago, this would have been the loveliest room in the house.

She glanced back at Sally, but her gaze was cast down at the landing carpet. Why hadn't she been desperate to assess the damage to this gorgeous room sooner?

Ella stepped across the threshold, her hand instinctively moving to the light switch, stopping herself just in time. The electrics were likely to be water-damaged, and she didn't want an electric shock, or worse.

Once inside, she saw a dark blue armchair in the right-hand corner next to a wall with pretty floral wallpaper, stained by grey watermarks. Black mould spores speckled the paintwork above the skirting board.

She moved towards the chair and put her hand on the arm. Wet velvet shifted under her fingers. A knitted blanket lay over the other arm, the wool heavy with water. A huge copper reading lamp hung over the chair.

After a quick glance at Sally, who was still standing in the hallway, Hadron now at her side, Ella turned to see a bookcase against the wall to the left of the window. At least, it *was* a bookcase. The cornice had collapsed onto the wood, which was now buckled and twisted. Some of the books had fallen from the shelves and were scattered in a sodden mess on the floor. Books that were still upright were bloated with water, pools of liquid seeping from them and dripping onto the pappy mess below. The light from the window shimmered on the standing water on the dark wood floor.

'What is this room?' said Ella, turning back to the bright hallway, where her mother stood, like a stage-frightened actor caught in a spotlight. 'Mum?'

When her eyes adjusted to the light, Ella saw her mother wasn't frozen, she was moving, her frail body shuddering in great, heaving sobs.

Chapter Eight

Ella

Present Day

'It's my library,' said Sally, when they were settled back in the sitting room with warm mugs of tea. 'Well, not mine really, I think of it more as yours.'

'Mine?' Ella watched a tear roll down the side of her mother's nose. 'I don't understand.'

'You remember how I used to buy you a book on your birthday?'

Ella warmed at the memory. 'Ah, yes. You used to write a note inside the book.' She took a tissue from the box on the side table and tried to hand it to Sally, who smiled sadly when she wasn't able to grasp it and it floated to her knee.

She picked it up and wiped her face. 'I never stopped.'

'What? Buying books?' A rope of guilt knotted in Ella's stomach.

'I bought a book for you every year. Although it wasn't as simple as that. You see – it had to be the right book. I was hoping to give them all to you, one day . . .' Sally scrunched the tissue and attempted to blow her nose.

Ella's fingers itched to hold the tissue for her mum, to help her like she'd help Willow, but she also knew they'd both find that strange. Wiping a grown woman's nose wasn't the same as wiping Willow's when she was a little girl. She experienced a sudden, visceral need to hold her daughter. The feeling shook her more when it occurred to her: that's how her mother must have felt about her. How she had probably felt in the years since she'd left.

'It helped, when I became lonely,' said Sally, 'that search for exactly the right novel. I'd speak to people at the library, pop down to Waterstones and talk to the booksellers there, and every week I'd visit Hannah at the second-hand book stall at the market. You know the one I mean?'

'She's still there?' Ella could almost smell Greenwich market when she thought back. The last time she'd been home, the far end of the market nearest the Admiral Hardy pub had been taken over by stalls selling Thai, Mexican and Indian food. The other half was bustling with arts and crafts, jewellery stalls and rails of brightly coloured clothing.

'Oh yes,' said Sally. 'Every Thursday, Saturday and Sunday, come rain or shine.'

'Is she the one who sent that card?' Ella pointed at one of the many 'get well soon' cards that had been pushed through the letter box and now sat on the windowsill.

Sally turned to the card with a picture of a cat sitting on top of a pile of books on the front. 'Yes, bless her.'

Ella thought of the woman behind the table heaving

with books. She remembered standing, bored and restless, waiting until her mother had finished speaking with Hannah. Then Sally would hand her a bright picture book, and soon she wasn't in the noisy market anymore; she'd be transported to the riverbank in *The Wind in the Willows*, laughing at Mr Toad's antics. The world of the market would suddenly reappear when her mum tugged at her hand and brought her out of the story, her voice echoing that it was time to go. The book invariably went with them. That's when Ella had started to play her 'If I was Queen of the World' game, she remembered. Back then, if she was Queen of the World, she'd let everyone read books all day long if they wanted. What a simple life it had been. 'She must be a hundred by now.'

Sally laughed. 'She's younger than me, although she is a grandma now. You just thought she was old because she was a grown-up when you were a child. She really knows her books, that Hannah. She gave me a lot of ideas and could source a book for me even when it was out of print.'

'How did you choose the books?' Ella asked the question, despite being afraid of the answer. The version of Sally sitting here was nothing like the version that lived inside Ella's head. When Ella was in Sydney, exhausted from a long day at work, she pictured her mother in her beautiful home, carefree and enjoying her unencumbered life. She imagined her cycling everywhere, chairing groups at the library and having lunches with an endless array of friends. She had always told herself her mother was too busy to give her a second thought.

'I asked myself what lesson I wanted to teach you.' Sally glanced across nervously. 'Not in a, you know, preachy way. More a reflection of what I'd learned over the years at certain ages. I thought about mistakes I've made and how I'd do things differently.'

The connection Ella had felt to Sally a second ago disappeared. Her limbs became restless with the familiar urge to flee. She picked up her cup. 'Refill?' She didn't want to talk about Sally's mistakes. Finding out about this flooded 'library' was enough for one day.

'Please, Ella—'

I'm sorry, but I can't do this. Not now.' She gripped the cup tightly, aware of Sally's eyes on her hand as the pads of her fingers turned white with the pressure.

Hadron appeared from behind the chair and growled before circling, then sitting on Sally's feet. She was like a bloody guard cat.

Sally sat back, as if admitting defeat. 'Okay, all right, but can I tell you more about how I built the little library?'

Ella put the mug back on the side table next to the sofa and tried to force her limbs to relax. 'Go on,' she said, hearing the reluctance in her own voice.

'So, I'd find the perfect book, with a little help, then I'd write my message, and at midnight on the eleventh of July every year, I'd add it to the library.'

'On my birthday? Every year?' The words caught in Ella's throat.

'Every year.'

'I don't understand . . . it's such a beautiful room, but you said you hadn't been in there since July last year.'

Sally rubbed the tissue between her fingers. 'I used to go in all the time. It was like a sanctuary for me, because it housed so many books that had touched my heart over the years, and the ones I'd bought for you. That's why it's the only nicely decorated room in the house . . . *was* the only nicely decorated room.' She looked up, smiling sadly. 'I had those two walls wallpapered in that lovely flowery design; did you see? Then the other two walls were painted the same blue as the flowers, and I got the armchair to match. It's so comfortable.'

Her expression changed to one of contentment and Ella imagined her sitting in the velvet armchair with the blanket over her knees, Hadron warming her feet like slippers, the copper lamp glowing yellow over her as she read.

'I've reread your books so many times. Because I'd chosen them for you, they felt like a connection to you. I kept them on the top shelves, in pride of place.' She shook her head. 'I'm a silly old fool, aren't I?'

Ella had to swallow hard before she could reply. 'I think it's lovely.' The knot of guilt was tightening. She used to look forward to the books on her birthday. She could still feel the anticipation of opening the cover and reading the words her mother had inscribed especially for her. But she hadn't even taken the gifts with her to Australia, and she'd allowed the anger and blame to fester since she had left. It had tainted every memory and every thought she had of home. 'Why did you stop going in there then?'

Sally shook her head. 'I don't know.' She sighed. 'I lost the will, somehow. I don't know what changed, exactly, but everything felt a bit hopeless. I haven't had any enthusiasm for anything for . . . well, for a while. Then, any time it occurred to me to go up there, I couldn't remember where I'd put the key, so that scuppered that.'

'Why did you even lock it at all?'

Sally smiled. 'Your dad always said we should lock up precious things. It was the only precious thing here, and now it's gone.' The end of the sentence was said through sudden hiccupping sobs.

Ella moved to the chair and folded her arm around her mother's shoulder. She felt tiny and fragile, not much bigger than Willow. Whatever feelings she'd had towards her mother in the past, it would take a cruel person not to feel pity now.

'I'm sure it's not all ruined,' she said. 'Why don't I go up and pick out a couple of books that aren't too badly damaged. We can read the messages, eh? Shall I do that?'

Sally nodded her bowed head. Ella gave her a gentle squeeze, then jumped up and climbed the stairs. She marched towards the library, deciding to call it that instead of the junk room. She ignored the nagging feeling that it was a fool's errand and strode towards the bookcase, plucking one book from the top shelf. The pages fell out and landed with a wet thud on the floor. She dropped the soggy cover and took one from the bottom shelf. That looked more promising initially, but when she tried to open the pages, they were all stuck together. She tried to part them, but as she did, they disintegrated, turning to lumps of creamy pulp between her fingers.

Her last hope was one of the books on the floor. Maybe they'd survived the torrent of water that had clearly gushed through from above. Ella picked one up, feeling all hope seep away as the cover tore from the binding when she opened it. It was one of the books her mother had bought for her because, on the inside page, there was her mother's inscription. But the ink had run and blurred and, try as she might, Ella couldn't make out a single word.

She dropped it in despair. Pity and guilt were fighting with the decades-old resentment. She was so used to the negative feelings towards her mother, they'd become ingrained, but she was beginning to feel like holding on to the past might have been a mistake. Looking around her now, she couldn't ignore the fact her mother had created this wonderful room in her memory, because memories were all Ella had left her with. And now those memories had been washed clean away.

Chapter Nine

Ella

Present Day

Telling Sally the books were irreparably damaged had been painful. Her face looked older, and a heaviness had settled in Ella's chest. Maybe if they set about repairing the house, they'd both feel more positive.

'I'm going to get some quotes to repair the flood damage,' she told Sally the following morning. 'Can I have the details of your insurance?'

'It's on my laptop,' said Sally, 'in the kitchen. I keep it in a folder in my emails. Better than printing it out.'

'Very green of you.' Ella collected the laptop from downstairs and set it on a cushion on her knee. She opened the lid. 'Are you happy for me to go into your emails?' she asked. White dots circled on the screen as the computer came to life.

Sally looked sheepish. 'Hmm. There might be a few unread ones. I've let things slide a bit recently.' She rubbed the heel of her right hand back and forth along the chair's arm. Ella watched the nervous gesture, understanding how the fabric had become so worn, an indication her mother's life hadn't been as carefree as Ella had presumed.

The screen eventually came to life. Ella clicked on the email icon and gasped. 'Mum, there's hundreds of unread emails here.' Her dad had told her you should only ever touch a piece of paper once, by which he meant deal with everything the moment it arrived. It was a system she'd proudly adopted, only recently realising how much easier it had been for him with a personal assistant at his elbow for his entire working life.

'It all got a bit much.' Sally's voice was quiet and apologetic. 'I used to deal with them every morning, but then, one day I didn't feel like it and the next time I looked, there were so many I couldn't face going through them all and sorting the wheat from the chaff.' Her hand moved over the faded flowers on the chair arm more quickly.

Ella huffed. 'Right, well let's look at the insurance, then do the rest later.' She'd been planning a nice walk along the river in the May sunshine and now it seemed like she'd be spending the whole day sorting out her mother's affairs instead. Managing another adult's life when they operated differently to her was proving harder than she'd anticipated. She felt a hankering to be at home, or, more accurately, at work with a tidy inbox. She knew where she was with that. Everything had a process. It might be tedious, but at least it was organised.

She clicked on the folder titled 'insurance' on the left

sidebar. At least Sally had had the sense to keep that in order. She briefly wondered how Charlie organised their insurance. He was responsible for all the household bills and administration. If she was honest with herself, she'd never given the running of their home much thought.

She opened the document and started to scroll. 'Right, here it is,' she confirmed. 'It's building and contents. Great. All in order as far as I can see.' She scrolled back up to the top of the document. 'Just need to find the phone number to give them a call.' Her finger stilled on the mouse pad. 'Mum,' she said slowly. 'Is this the latest certificate?'

'Yes,' said Sally. 'It must be up for renewal soon, but I haven't heard anything from the broker.'

Ella's mouth went dry. 'You haven't opened any emails in a while though, have you?'

Sally took a sharp breath in. 'Oh God, don't tell me . . . ?'

'It's out of date, Mum. The bloody insurance is out of date.'

***

This already awful day was becoming progressively worse. A trawl through Sally's emails showed the broker had tried contacting her several times by email and telephone.

'Why didn't you answer your mobile?' Ella said, with rising frustration. 'It says here they tried to ring and left messages.'

Sally's face crumpled. 'You see all those adverts about fraud. I thought it was safer not to answer when it was an unknown number.'

'But they left a message.' The irritation was building, and Ella struggled to keep her voice level.

'It's just another red dot on the screen,' said Sally. 'When there are enough, you stop seeing them.' She closed her eyes. 'I got overwhelmed. I'm sorry. I've let everything get on top of me and, to be honest, I don't know where to start putting things back together.'

'That's why you didn't get back to the people who rang to check how you were after the accident,' said Ella. 'You never picked up their messages.' Pity filled her chest as she viewed this woman who had always been so calm and efficient. She wondered how on earth she could have missed this change in her. The version of her mother sitting across from her now in her sagging, worn-out armchair was frail and unbearably sad.

Sally lifted her hand to rub her eyes and winced in obvious pain. 'I never thought I'd miss the dial-up telephone, but at least people didn't leave blasted messages all the time. Bring back the days of the speaking clock, that's what I say.'

'But then we wouldn't be able to FaceTime Willow, would we?' said Ella.

'Ah,' said Sally. 'Then I take it back. Technology is a worthwhile nuisance if I can see that little face every day.' They had both spoken to Willow at eight a.m. that morning and, by the look of joy on Sally's face, seeing her was as sustaining for her as it was for Ella, who was missing her little girl terribly.

'Look,' Ella said, her voice soft. 'It will all be okay. Nothing is unsurmountable. I'm going to pop out and get some nice cheeses for lunch from around the corner, and when I get back, we'll make a plan.' She stood and put her hand on Sally's shoulder. 'We'll sort this out, okay?'

She had no idea how. She didn't have a clue about the state of her mother's finances and was dreading having to ask. It seemed like an intrusion, although she was sure she wasn't low on funds. Dad's estate must've been healthy, and Sally had taught up until she had retired twelve years ago, so there must be a fair amount of money available.

There was no evidence Sally had spent all her savings. The house was in disrepair, and she didn't seem to have made any extravagant purchases. However much pity Ella felt in that moment, she wasn't about to offer her life savings to refurbish this Grade II listed house. She had a home of her own and a family on the other side of the world to prioritise.

Sally nodded. 'Thank you. I'm so sorry, Ella. You don't need—'

'Don't worry,' she said. 'Where's your phone? I'll go through what—'

'No.' Sally's head snapped up. 'I need that.'

'What for?'

Sally swallowed, her eyes on her phone on the ottoman

in front of her. 'It's got my alarms and reminders on it.'

'I'm not going to keep it. I was trying to help.' Ella knew her voice was terse, but did her mum want help or not? It was clear she hadn't checked her messages any more than she'd looked at her emails. She might have missed something important.

'I just . . . For God's sake, will you allow me some privacy?'

'Privacy?' Ella was suddenly standing in front of her mother twenty-one years ago, a letter beside her on the floor, grief and fury coursing through her. 'We've given each other plenty of privacy over the years, haven't we? Neither of us wanted me to be here, trying to sort out this mess, but here we are.'

Sally looked at her with wet eyes. 'You think I wanted you to stay away?'

'It wasn't as if you were begging for a relationship with me, was it?' She shoved back memories of Charlie suggesting she called her mum and her replying that she was waiting to see if her mum called instead. She never did. Ella had set tests and Sally had always failed.

'I was giving you space. I didn't think it was fair to—'

'Space?' Ella laughed in disbelief. 'There's been twenty-one years of that.'

Sally looked confused. 'I thought it was what you wanted. I hoped that one day—'

'What? One day I'd get over what happened, all would be forgiven and we could live happily ever after?'

'No. I knew it wouldn't be as simple as that, but—'

Ella threw her arms up. 'I'm here because you need me. I'm doing my duty.'

'Your duty?' Sally's voice cracked.

The pain in her voice made Ella pause. 'I never got the impression you . . .' *What, wanted me? Loved me anymore?* The thoughts were like shards of glass in her throat. They stuck there, sharp and tormenting. But letting them out might hurt them both more.

'Surely the library tells you how much I wanted you to come home?'

The thought of the ruined books with their illegible inscriptions made Ella stall. She didn't want to think about that room now. If she imagined her mother in that chair, writing an inscription inside a carefully chosen book year after year, she would have to change her view of what had happened over the last two decades, and her part in it. 'I'm hungry,' she said. 'I'm going out to clear my head.'

She checked her face in the mirror above the hall table, wiped away a tear from under her eye, and left.

Chapter Ten

Sally

Nine Years Ago

When Sally saw Ella's number on the small screen of the landline, her heart bounced in her chest. She forced herself to wait for three more rings before she pressed the green button to accept the call. 'Ella, hello, love.'

'Hi.'

She closed her eyes at the sound of her daughter's voice. Ella hadn't rung for thirteen days. Sally had picked up the phone at least once every day, inventing a variety of excuses for calling her, but she always forced herself to lay the phone back in its cradle. There was a tacit agreement between them that Ella would always be the one to ring her. She was a busy woman with an important job. She didn't have time for idle chit-chat, so Sally waited. And waited.

'How's things?' said Sally, wishing she could see Ella's face. God, how she missed that face.

'Good, yeah, I've got some news, actually.'

'Oh, right.' Sally's heart leapt, then danced in her chest. Was Ella coming back to England? Even a visit would be good. It had been years. So many years.

'I'm pregnant.'

Pregnant! Ella was expecting a baby. And she was going to be a grandma. 'Oh, love. Oh, Ella, that's absolutely amazing news. Congratulations!'

'Yeah, we're really chuffed.'

'I bet you are. How far along are you?' Sally tried to keep her voice level. She was desperate to know everything, but she'd come to view conversations with Ella like spotting a deer in the wood – move quickly or try to get too close and she'd disappear.

'Sixteen weeks.'

Four months. She'd been pregnant for four whole months and was only telling Sally now. A heavy weight landed on her heart, slowing it down. 'Wow.' She paused to collect herself and knew immediately that was a mistake. 'And how are you feeling?'

There was a beat before Ella spoke. 'We wanted to be in the safety zone before we told anyone.'

Sally blinked. *Wow* had been the wrong thing to say. Ella had misinterpreted it as a judgement. How could she make it right? 'Very wise,' she said. She needed to recover this. 'I bet Charlie's thrilled.'

'Yeah. You know what he's like – a big softie. He's going to be a great dad.'

Sally didn't really know what Charlie was like. She'd only met him a couple of times, but she'd liked him enormously when she had, thank goodness. She tried so hard to keep the words in, but couldn't stop them from escaping. 'Now I'm retired, I could come over and help, if . . . you know . . . you needed it . . . ?'

'Charlie will be around, don't worry,' said Ella casually. 'Since I earn more than he does and he's not that keen on his job at the planning office, we've decided he'll be a stay-at-home dad.'

'Okay,' said Sally. 'But if you change your mind, I'd love—'

'Thanks, but it's fine. I know how busy you are.' There seemed to be a pointedness in the way Ella said that.

Sally dug her nails into her palm. She was busy, but that was partly to fill the gaping void Ella had left when she had emigrated. Did she really think that anything in Sally's life could possibly be as important as being there for her daughter and her first grandchild? Her throat constricted with the effort not to cry. 'Speaking of busy, that's the doorbell. I'd better get it.'

'Okay. Speak to you soon.'

'Congratulations again, love. I'm so pleased for you. Bye, then,' Sally managed to say, before clicking off the call and setting the tears free.

Chapter Eleven

Ella

Present Day

The midday sun was warm on Ella's face as she walked down Circus Street, trying to calm her roiling emotions. She shouldn't have been short with her mother. She was meant to be looking after her and she was so thin, so much less robust than she used to be. When she'd had time to calm down, she'd go back and try harder.

In an attempt to climb out of her own head, Ella considered the hedgehog painted on the wall above the shop window at the corner of Circus Street and Royal Hill. Not for the first time, she wondered why the spiky cartoon figure was synonymous with cheese. It had been there for as long as she could remember, but when she was younger, it was just part of the landscape of where she lived.

She'd taken so much for granted, she realised, looking across the road at handsome Gloucester Crescent, the trees in its private garden, a glorious springtime array of reds, yellows and greens. Now she could see what a privilege it had been to grow up just a short walk from

Greenwich Park, the river and the bustling market.

As she queued in Cheeseboard, listening to the man behind the counter talk to a customer in a thick French accent, she thought about mentioning the hedgehog, but when her turn came, she didn't have the energy for small talk and ordered a sticky Brie and a pungent blue cheese, along with a bottle of Malbec and some crusty bread. She could still smell the cheese through the brown paper wrapping when she walked a little way down Royal Hill to the florist. It reminded her of coming down to the kitchen at lunchtime on weekends to find her mother licking Brie from her fingers at the kitchen table, a box of crackers and a book open in front of her. She'd always close the book and ask Ella about her plans for the day.

Ella winced at the memory of how short her answers became as her teens progressed. She tried to imagine Willow saying, 'Out,' when she asked where she was going, but it seemed so unlike her chatty, cheerful daughter that the picture wouldn't be conjured. The day would come when it was less hard to envisage; she was sure of that. She wondered if she would bear it with as much grace as Sally had. She doubted it.

She reached the florist and stopped. She'd cleared away the tulips from the table in the hall before bringing her mum home from hospital, and, looking at the colourful displays in the window of Karen Woolven Flowers, she decided a bunch of fragrant hyacinths might look pretty and – more importantly – mask the smell of damp.

She was about to enter the shop when a voice from

inside said, 'Ella Harrison? Bloody hell, it is you, isn't it?'

Ella stepped over the threshold and scanned the room, trying to find the source of the voice when a woman appeared from behind a huge silver tub of sunflowers, wearing an apron over denim dungarees. Ella took in her braided hair, red bandana and tried to place her soft features.

'It's me, Verity. Verity Ibe,' said the woman and Ella felt a rush of nostalgia as the woman's features morphed into the round-faced girl she'd sat next to in English class all those years ago.

'Verity! Oh my God.' She blinked. 'You look . . . amazing.' She really did. The puppy fat Verity used to endlessly moan about was gone, and the teen Ella knew had developed into an extraordinarily attractive woman.

'Really?' said Verity, shyly. 'Thanks. I've been feeling a bit shit recently, so that's dead nice of you.'

Ella didn't know what to say. She was used to people being candid in Australia, where everyone she knew said exactly what was on their mind, but now she was back in England mode, it felt strange.

'How are you?' said Verity. 'You look great.'

Ella was sure she looked anything but. She could feel the puffiness of her eyes when she blinked. Jet lag was not a good look.

'How long are you back in England for?'

Ella was astonished Verity knew she lived abroad. They had been good friends in senior school but hadn't kept in touch when Ella went off to university. 'A month,' she said. 'Mum had an accident . . .'

'I heard, bless her. Sounded awful. How's she doing? She must be glad to have you home.'

Picturing her mother's harrowed face from earlier, Ella wasn't so sure.

Verity carried on, concern in her brown eyes. 'I've been meaning to pop around with some flowers, but I didn't know if she was still in hospital. I've been a bit worried about her, to be honest. We all have.'

'All?'

'Yeah, surely you remember what it's like round here? Everyone knows everyone's business. Loads of people have asked about her when they've come in.'

Ella could recall knowing everyone who lived in the area when she was small, but she'd presumed things had changed. It was London, after all. Cities were fluid places. You couldn't expect to see the same faces you saw twenty years ago. Yet here she was, looking into one now. And it felt good.

She thought back to the suburb in Sydney where she'd lived for a decade. She was on nodding terms with her neighbours but hadn't made any real friends. She was always too busy at work. It crossed her mind that none of those neighbours would worry about her if she had an accident. The thought made her sad.

'She's okay,' Ella said. 'A bit of bruising on her face, one fractured wrist on one side and two broken fingers on the other.'

Verity winced. 'Shit.'

'Yeah, not great, but she's a tough old bird; she'll be all right.' She didn't know why she said that. From what she'd seen since she got back, Sally was nowhere near as tough as Ella had thought.

'She's lucky to have you.'

Ella wasn't so sure about that, either. 'I was going to buy her some hyacinths to cheer her up.' That was a lie. She had been planning to make the house look prettier and smell less. Trying to make herself look better in someone else's eyes was not exactly admirable behaviour. The guilt notched up. Why was being back here stirring up so many complex emotions inside her?

She looked around at the blooms, breathing in the mingling scents of roses and lilies.

Verity strode to where purple, pink and white hyacinths sat in individual buckets. 'Some of each colour?'

'Yes please.'

Verity bundled them together with sprays of something white and various green fronds. Ella watched in admiration as she wrapped them in paper and tied a rustic-looking string in a bow at the bottom.

'They're gorgeous. You were always the arty one, weren't you? Glad to see some things don't change,' Ella said, taking the flowers and admiring the bouquet.

'Thanks.' Verity's eyes shone.

'How much?'

'They're on me,' said Verity. 'On one condition.'

'What's that?'

'You let me take you for a drink while you're here.'

Ella grinned. 'You're on. But I'll buy the first round.' Her mood lifted at the thought of a night out. She couldn't remember when she'd last gone out for a simple catch-up with a friend. These days, all her evening events revolved around work. Come to think of it, she couldn't remember the last time she and Charlie had a date night.

'Great,' said Verity, 'I want to hear all about your fabulous life in far-off lands.'

'Not much to tell there,' she said. 'All very standard. Husband, child, job – you know, just life.'

'Ha! I don't believe your life is standard for a second. You loved your stories too much for that. I bet you've got a million adventures to tell me about – all I've got is one miserable marriage and a job as a florist.' She grimaced.

'Oh,' said Ella, slightly taken aback by the oversharing. 'I, erm, look forward to hearing more when we go out.' Her marriage wasn't in the best condition ever, but she wasn't about to disclose that over a bunch of daffodils. 'How about tomorrow night?'

'Cool. I'll call for you at about seven. It will be like the old days, me knocking for you on our way to the pub. Fancy going to The Gypsy Moth?'

'I do!' Ella's heart swooped. She could almost taste the sweet cider she used to buy using her fake ID back when they were in sixth form. They'd sit in the beer garden on warm spring evenings like this and talk about their futures. Momentarily, she wondered what her seventeen-year-old self would think of the life she'd built. Disappointed, she imagined.

'We can go anywhere we like,' said Verity. 'We could go to Paris on the Eurostar and stay for a fortnight, and I don't think my other half would notice.' She laughed, as if trying to make a joke, but it didn't have any humour in it.

'I'm looking forward to it already,' said Ella. She thought of the Post-it notes Charlie stuck on top of the dinner he left in the fridge whenever she was late back. He noticed when she wasn't home. He always drew a smiley face and a kiss. It was a long time since she'd written a thank you note for him to find in the morning. Perhaps she should do that more when she went back.

'Can't bloody wait. It's so good to see you,' beamed Verity with a grin as Ella made her way to the door. 'Give your mum a big kiss from me, and I'll see you tomorrow.'

'Thank you,' said Ella. 'See you.'

'And Ella,' said Verity, when Ella reached the doorway. 'Yes?'

'That cheese fucking stinks.' She laughed and disappeared to the back of the shop.

**

On her walk back past Cheeseboard and into Circus Street, Ella decided to try harder with Sally. She was only here for a short time so she should make it as painless as possible. When her mum could fend for herself, she could go back home and pick up her life where she'd left off. The thought of that didn't bring Ella as much joy as it should. She'd thought her job was the one part of her life she had got right, but she wasn't missing it at all. Whenever she thought of home, it was Willow she craved, even though she spent most of her waking hours at the office.

'Mum,' Ella shouted from the hallway when she closed the door behind her 'You'll never guess who I bumped into.' She kicked off her trainers and stuck her head around the sitting room door. Sally wasn't in her chair. Hadron was curled on the floor. 'Where is she?' Ella said quietly. Hadron lifted her paw and batted at her tatty ear, then closed her eye again. 'You're no help,' Ella muttered, wondering when she'd started talking to the cat. She carried on down to the kitchen. 'Mum?'

She wasn't in the kitchen either. Ella presumed she was upstairs having a nap. She put the cheese in the fridge, then had a second thought. She dug around in the cupboards until she found a Tupperware box with a lid that actually fit and put the blue cheese in, then slid it back into the fridge.

After arranging the hyacinths in a vase, she took them up to the hall and placed them on the table. She breathed in the heady scent and was pleased with herself, until the smell of damp added its dank undertones to the mix. After grabbing some bin bags from under the kitchen sink, she went up to the library room and pushed open the door. The wallpaper was peeling away from the bottom of the wall and the dark spores of mould seemed to have spread further since she had last assessed the damage.

The sodden books made wet thuds as she dropped them into the bag. After the first few, Ella stopped opening the covers to see if she could find an inscription. The disappointment of seeing nothing more than blurred pen marks when she had, dragged on her heart, making it as heavy as the bloated books. Soon, the smell overpowered her and she went back downstairs to research local builders to get quotes for repairs.

Half an hour later, she'd arranged for a dehumidifier to be delivered and made appointments for two sets of builders to visit. Satisfied she'd made a start, at least, Ella closed her browser and sensed the quietness of the house. She wondered whether it was a good idea for Sally to sleep this long during the day. She stepped quietly up the two flights of stairs to her mother's bedroom, tiptoeing up the last steps in case Sally was asleep. She wasn't there. She wasn't in the bathroom or any of the other rooms Ella looked into on her way downstairs.

Back in the sitting room, she started to panic. Sally had been upset when she'd left. She was still disorientated after the anaesthetic and infection. She couldn't use either of her hands properly, so how would she manage outside on her own? Ella scanned the room for any clues as to where Sally could have gone, but the only thing she could say for certain was Sally's phone was missing as well. She pulled out her own phone and dialled her mother's number, listening helplessly as the ringtone went on and on unanswered.

Chapter Twelve

Ella

Present Day

Ella scoured the sitting room for anything that looked like an address book, or list of phone numbers. She wished she'd asked Pru for her contact details. She might at least have some idea where Sally might have disappeared off to. Ten minutes later, Ella was considering going out to wander the streets in search of her mother, when she heard voices outside. She rushed to the window. A mixture of relief and annoyance jostled inside her when she saw Sally chatting to Nathan.

Nathan was in his usual spot, smoking a roll-up, brushing falling tobacco from wet-look leggings he'd teamed with a frilly white shirt. Her mother was in jeans, a vest top and a cardigan Ella had helped her into that morning. They looked like the most unlikely friends.

Ella breathed in and out slowly to try to quash her frustration. She opened the front door and stood on the top step, forcing herself to smile when they both turned to look at her. 'There you are,' she said. 'You didn't say you were going out. I've been trying to call you.'

Keeping her voice steady was a monumental effort. She gave herself an internal round of applause.

'Have you?' said Sally. 'Sorry. I always have my phone on silent.'

Ella wanted to scream. And she did . . . inside her head. External Ella was fighting to stay calm. 'What's the point in having a phone if it's always on silent?'

'I set myself alarms,' said Sally. 'Alarms still work when it's on silent. I would never have remembered the doctor's appointment without it.'

'What doctor's—'

'I do that too,' Nathan cut in. 'I wouldn't remember a thing if I didn't set a reminder.'

'Nathan has ADHD,' Sally said to Ella, as if she hadn't already explained the boy's medical history to her previously. 'The inattentive subtype. His working memory is affected.' She turned back to Nathan. 'That's right, isn't it?'

'You're learning.' He grinned. He looked up at Ella, squinting. 'I got diagnosed when I was twelve, thank God. It's all been good since then, with the meds and that.'

'Erm, right, good. Well done.' Ella hadn't a clue what she was meant to say. Had she been in Australia so long she'd absorbed the myth about English people being buttoned up? Everyone she'd met since she came back seemed to want to tell her their life stories. She wouldn't be surprised if the woman across the road walking her terrier approached them to ask their opinion about a boil on her backside.

Hadron followed her outside and weaved her way clumsily between Sally's legs, bumping into her shins. That's all Sally needed, to be tripped up by the spatially challenged cat and end up breaking more bones. As if reading her mind, Hadron stopped, dropped onto her front paws and pointed her bum at Ella.

'I didn't know you had an appointment, Mum,' she said, doing her best to ignore the cat. 'I would have come with you.'

Sally flapped her hand. 'No need. I can walk to the surgery and back, no bother.'

'But what if I'd been out when you got back? How would you have got in? You can't use the key with broken fingers.'

'I know that,' said Sally. 'That's why I gave Nathan a key. Glenda has one, but since she's away this month, I gave one to Nathan when I went out.'

Nathan dug a hand into the pocket of his impossibly tight trousers and drew out a key ring with a book on the end. The silver door key glinted in the sunshine. 'Ta-da.' Hadron saw the shiny object and tried to bat at it with her paw, missing by a mile.

Ella watched the key dangle from Nathan's fingers and wondered if her mother had gone mad. Giving a key to Glenda, who'd lived next door for half a century, was one thing. Giving one to a student she hardly knew who had self-confessed money problems was quite another. 'Well, you're back now, so shall I take that?' She walked down the steps with her hand outstretched.

'Nathan can keep it,' said Sally, just as Nathan was about to hand it over. 'It's always useful to leave a key with a neighbour.'

'But . . .' But what? She could hardly argue her case with the boy sitting in front of them. It had barely been five minutes since their last row. And it was her mother's house, not hers. 'All right.' She gave Nathan a tight smile.

'If you're not comfortable with me having it, that's okay,' he said, and Ella was surprised to hear no resentment in his voice. He looked down at the pavement, an expression of sad resignation on his face, as though he expected to be mistrusted and had come to accept it. 'You don't know me from Adam, so I get that I might look a bit, well . . . strange.'

'Not at all,' said Ella. She was surprised to realise she meant it. When she'd looked from the window, she had to admit, she was taken aback by his outfit in the same way she had been when she first saw him in the skirt, but viewing him now, she thought the clothes suited him. 'You look like Adam Ant.'

'Ace,' Nathan crossed his arms in front of him. 'Stand and deliver!' He laughed. 'My nan loved him.'

'Me too,' said Sally. 'I liked his punk era best, although his early Eighties pop was good too.'

Ella had forgotten her mum loved music and dancing. Her abiding memory of her late teenage years had been of a quiet, withdrawn woman. If she thought back further, she could remember kitchen discos, them both dancing to the radio as they made cakes together. What had changed? Where did that version of her mother go, and why had Ella forgotten she had ever existed?

'Keep the key,' said Sally. 'Come on,' she said to Ella. 'Did you get that cheese? I could eat a horse.' She turned back to Nathan. 'Fancy joining us for a bit of bread and cheese for lunch?'

'Thanks, but I'm not hungry,' he said.

Something in his eyes told Ella that wasn't true. As she walked back up the steps, she suspected it was her presence that was putting him off. She suddenly felt like a terrible person. He seemed like a perfectly nice young man and his skinny frame suggested he could do with a few hearty meals. It was then that she decided to try harder not to judge.

'Why *does* he smoke on the front step instead of the garden?' she whispered to Sally when the door was closed behind them – her decision not to judge proving short-lived.

'He likes to people-watch,' said Sally, scratching Hadron under the chin with her thumb. 'I think he gets lonely.' She allowed Ella to take her handbag from the crook of her elbow and set it on the floor next to the hall table. Sally noticed the hyacinths and took a deep breath in and smiled, patting Ella on the arm. It felt like a full stop to what had happened earlier. 'The two girls who live with him are nice enough, but they seem a bit aloof. They're like a couple of socialites, constantly drifting from one party to another, enveloped in expensive perfume and fruity vapes. Nathan gets on with them, but they're not his people, if you know what I mean. He likes to chat about everyday things like the news and books.'

A motherly pang squeezed Ella's heart. She imagined Willow at university in a town far from home. She couldn't bear the thought of her being lonely.

They went down to the kitchen. Sally sat at the table while Ella got the cheese from the fridge and sawed the crusty bread into thick slices.

'So, this doctor's appointment,' she said, pouring red wine into a glass and putting it next to her mother's plate. It felt decadent to have wine with lunch, but she was on a holiday of sorts. It was a poor justification, and she knew it. What she really wanted was to blur the edges of her day. 'Was it about your fingers, or the urine infection, or . . . ?'

Sally tried and failed to grasp the cheese knife between her little finger and thumb. 'Nothing important,' she said. 'Just a check-up.' She smiled her thanks as Ella cut the bread into chunks and smeared a portion of cheese onto each.

'You should have let me take you. Did they give you another course of antibiotics? I've got the feeling the infection is hanging around. I'll pick it up for you this afternoon if you like.' She remembered that you're not meant to drink while taking certain antibiotics and immediately felt guilty about opening the wine.

'You've got enough to do,' said Sally, balancing the glass well enough to take a sip. 'I'll probably need you to come with me to the hospital to get the cast off and all that palaver, so I thought, since I can walk to the doctor's myself, it was better not to bother you.'

'But you didn't even mention you were going.'

Sally's glass slipped when she tried to put it down and Ella's hand shot out to just about stop the red liquid spilling. She definitely regretted opening the wine now. What was she thinking? There was little she could do about it without treating Sally like a child. It would seem patronising to suggest her mother didn't drink in the daytime, especially when it had been Ella's idea.

There was a knock on the door, followed by the ring of the doorbell. Ella rushed upstairs from the basement kitchen, then came down with a cardboard package in her hands. 'Amazon delivery,' she said. 'All right if I open it?'

'Yes. I hope it's my arm condoms.'

'What?' Ella spluttered, ripping the tag to open the package.

'That's what Iris at the hospital called them,' said Sally. 'The plastic things that go over your arms, so you don't get your dressings wet. Arm condoms.'

Ella pulled out the contents and read the label, 'Small Adult Half Arm.' She opened the wrapper. 'Imagine if you had to order that over the phone. You'd sound like a cannibal. Hello, I'd like to order a small adult, half arm, please. No, not a full arm, I'm still full from lunch.' She shook out the sleeve with a black elastic cuff, the strong smell of plastic battling with the cheese.

'Oh, that's great,' said Sally, standing and undoing

the Velcro of her sling with her thumb and dropping it on the table. 'Let's try it on.'

Ella helped her off with her cardigan, then opened the elasticated end and gently tugged the sleeve up over Sally's cast. The end closed above the elbow. Sally's thin arm looked fragile, the skin wrinkled and puckered where the elastic ringed it. 'Is it too tight?'

'It's probably supposed to be,' said Sally. 'To be honest, I don't care. As long as I can stand in the shower and feel the water flow over me, I'll put up with restricted blood supply for twenty minutes. I can't wait.'

'Maybe you shouldn't drink wine before going in the shower,' said Ella, glad to find a plausible reason to put right her mistake.

'Fine by me.'

They ate in silence for a few minutes, then Ella's curiosity got the better of her. 'What did the doctor say?'

'Sorry?'

Ella knew a distraction technique when she saw one. 'At your check-up?'

'Nothing much. The appointments are so short, these days, you hardly have time to pass pleasantries.' She popped the last piece of bread and cheese in her mouth. 'Right, time for that shower.'

'But, what—'

Sally stood. 'I haven't had a proper wash since I left the hospital. I don't think I've ever been this excited about getting clean.'

'I was just—'

Sally was walking away. 'Could you bring those arm condoms up and help me down to my undies. I think I can take it from there.'

Sally clearly wasn't going to say any more about her appointment. Following her mother upstairs, Ella couldn't help wondering why.

Chapter Thirteen

Ella

Present Day

On the way back downstairs, Ella saw Sally's handbag where she'd left it on the floor near the hall table. She stepped closer, the smell of the hyacinths strong as she bent to take hold of the brown leather straps. The nagging sense that her mother was hiding something made her pause before putting the bag where it usually sat by Sally's chair in the sitting room.

She instinctively listened for footsteps at the bottom of the stairs, even though she knew her mother was in the shower and had specifically asked to be left alone for twenty minutes. Still, Ella crept back into the sitting room and sat down quietly, placing the bag on her lap.

Justifications jostled with judgements in her mind. Right now, she was essentially her mother's carer, so she needed to know what was going on medically. That was all she was looking for. Nothing else. That thought fought with the knowledge that even opening the bag was an invasion of privacy.

Hadron lifted her head and shame coloured Ella's

96

cheeks at being watched. It didn't help when Hadron jumped onto the ottoman and sat, her one bright eye staring directly at Ella. Bloody cat.

With a deep breath, she looked away from that judgemental green eye, unclipped the top of the bag and put her hand inside. The first thing Ella found was the TV remote control. No wonder she couldn't find it before. She lifted it out, huffing in disbelief. What on earth was her mum doing carrying the TV remote around in her handbag? She definitely needed more antibiotics if this was the kind of thing she was doing. She glanced over at the chair and imagined it falling off the arm and into the open bag below. It was unlikely. She put it on the ottoman next to Hadron, who was still staring at her.

Delving back in, Ella pushed aside packets of tissues, receipts, a biro and a roll of extra-strong mints, half of which had spilled out and were dotted around the lining at the base. She unzipped the inside pocket and then her fingers found what she was looking for: her mother's phone. She put the bag at her feet and held the handset in her palm. She felt terrible, but after the insurance debacle, it was only right she made sure Sally wasn't getting herself into any more trouble.

The phone must have been at least five years old. It still had the button at the bottom for fingerprint recognition. When she tapped on the home button, it asked for a passcode. Ella puffed out her cheeks. This probably wasn't going to work. She was going to give herself away by locking them both out of the device by inputting too many guesses. She tried to remember how many attempts you were allowed before the security system locked you out.

With a touch of irony, she put in her own date of birth, not imagining for a second her mother would have chosen that as her most important numbers. To her astonishment, the lock screen opened.

Ella glanced towards the door, then opened the calendar app. Today's appointment was there with an alert set for half an hour beforehand. It must've gone off after Ella had left to get the food. She scrolled back, looking for other appointments, to see if she could find a clue as to why Sally was being secretive. Two weeks ago, there was an entry that just said *clinic*. What clinic? There was no address. No other information at all.

She clicked on the NHS app, her stomach churning with shame, but when the site came up, it asked for the password, and after a couple of feeble attempts, Ella gave up trying to guess. She examined the various screens but couldn't find any other apps that might give her the information she needed, so she decided to put the phone back in Sally's bag.

Just as she was about to send the phone to sleep, she noticed the photo app, her curiosity making her finger hover over the icon. What did her mother take photos of? What did she find interesting enough to capture and store?

She tapped on the icon. Willow's face appeared on the screen, filling Ella's heart with adoration for her gorgeous little girl. The memory of taking that picture at the park came rushing back. It had been a glorious day and Willow was sticky from working her way across the monkey bars. She'd got all the way to the other side for the first time and in the photo she was pumping her fist in triumph. Ella had carelessly WhatsApped it to her mum, thinking she was keeping her up to date and fulfilling her duty.

Her mum must've saved it to her camera roll. It must've meant something to her. Perhaps what she'd said earlier was true. The thought sparked a warm feeling inside Ella, which was a welcome change from the guilt and exasperation she'd become accustomed to. Maybe their relationship going forward could be more than the dutiful, perfunctory habit it had become. Now she wished she'd known Sally had kept the picture. She might have written a longer message, maybe sent a selfie with them both in it.

She scrolled to the next picture. That was Willow too, and the next. Ella changed the screen to thumbnails and scrolled upwards. Every single picture was one that Ella had sent.

Tears clouded her vision, blurring the screen. She'd had no idea. She'd persuaded herself their distance was mutually agreed, that Sally was, if not content, at least as resigned to their fractured relationship as she was. But the pictures told the same story Sally had been trying to tell her earlier.

Continuing to scroll, Ella stopped at the sight of a

room. She tapped on the image, examining the pretty floral wallpaper, the velvet chair and the copper lamp. The little library. It was beautiful. The next picture was of the bookcase. Her heart swelled at the sight of those undamaged books, neat on their shelves. And now she knew that the ones on the top shelves had a hidden, handwritten message inside: a representation of her mother's desire to connect with her. Curiosity niggled at her. If only she could know the words concealed within the pages.

Chapter Fourteen

Ella

Present Day

Ella followed the two men carrying the bulky dehumidifier up the stairs and directed them to the library. She was glad Sally stayed downstairs. The room looked even worse than the last time she'd been in, with black mould creeping further up the walls.

'Keep all the windows and doors closed,' said the man who seemed to be in charge, after showing her how to empty the water tank. 'It'll take a few days, with this level of water damage.' He rubbed the back of his neck and blew out his cheeks and Ella saw the mess afresh through his gaze and tears pricked the corners of her eyes.

'Fancy a trip to the library?' Ella said to Sally after seeing the men out. She needed some fresh air. Her nostrils were still clogged with the smell of damp, and the house, which had always felt enormous with its high ceilings and well-proportioned rooms, was starting to feel strangely stultifying. She needed a change of scenery.

'You go,' said Sally. 'I'm all right here.' She appeared

to be reading *The Alchemist*, but Ella had been watching her and she hadn't turned the page for the last five minutes.

She crossed the sitting room to the window. Outside, the sun was shining. May was one of the more clement months in the UK, but it was no more predictable than any other in Britain. Ella knew from experience that, despite the bright blue sky she was now looking at, it could hail or even snow the following day. 'Come on, Mum. I'd really like to see the town again. Let's get out for a bit. It might tip it down tomorrow, then we'll be sorry we didn't make the effort. Anyway, I need your library card to get a copy of *The Alchemist* for myself. Charlie's already read it and you know how competitive I am.'

When she'd told Charlie about rediscovering her love of reading, his reaction had surprised her. She'd been moved by his suggestion that he read the books she and Sally were reading too. It would give them something new to talk about. A chance to reconnect. Lying in her childhood bed at night, she was surprised at how much she missed his solid form and the sound of his soft breathing next to her. When she'd stepped on the plane in Sydney, she'd been concerned that she'd enjoy a break from her marriage. Now, she was beginning to think it wasn't her marriage that was the problem.

'You get that competitiveness from your father,' said Sally.

Good, thought Ella. It was an admirable quality

she'd inherited from an admirable man. She thought back to games of Scrabble and Monopoly she'd played with him when she was a child. He'd never let her win, telling her that she had to learn to defeat people on her own merit. The first time she had beaten him at Scrabble she'd expected him to be proud of her, but instead, he'd sulked for days. She'd inherited that trait too, and even she had to admit that was less commendable.

'You can borrow this one.' Sally lifted her hand from where it rested on the open book and the pages fluttered.

'Thanks, but it would be nice if we read it at the same time, don't you think? Like our own little book club.'

Sally nodded and slipped a bookmark between the pages before closing the book. 'All right then.' She pushed her elbows onto the chair arms to help herself stand up. 'I can't remember when I last went to the library.'

Ten minutes later, they were at the wooden gates blocking cars from entering Circus Street from the busy main road. On Greenwich South Street, Ella stopped to look in the window of The Junk Shop. A pair of enormous knickers hung on a rickety bookshelf under a paper sign saying *Big Knicks*. She remembered them being there when she was a teenager and felt oddly sentimental about a pair of saggy, pink pants. Two walking sticks were hooked over the case, which heaved with a haphazard collection of books, vinyl records and, inexplicably, a bowl overflowing with colourful neck ties.

'I can't believe this old place is still here. Still as bonkers as ever. Has it still got the tearoom at the back?'

'Tearoom?' said Sally, with a confused expression.

'Yes, at the back of the shop?'

'I don't . . .' Sally looked up at the sign written in black Art Deco font above the green paintwork. 'The Junk Shop,' she read, as if for the first time.

'What are you looking so confused about? This was here before you and Dad moved here.'

Sally scrunched her eyes closed and shook her head.

'Are you okay?' Ella took her elbow. Maybe coming out wasn't such a good idea after all. Sally was clearly still suffering from the effects of the infection.

'Are we going to the library?' Sally said.

'Only if you're up to it?'

'Okay.' Sally started walking away from Greenwich High Road, back towards home.

'Mum, for goodness' sake, where are you going?'

Sally stopped, turned back and followed her in the right direction. Ella hooked her arm through Sally's as they walked and wondered whether she was pushing her to do too much, too soon.

Ella was surprised by a burst of nostalgia at the sight of the red-brick library. Even as a teen, she'd been able to see it was a stunning building, but in comparison to the blocky constructions that had sprung up along the high road, the library – with its pale stone architraves, cupola and lead dome – stood out in a way that took her breath away.

She stopped in front of the huge central window and read the black plaque on the balcony above, 'The gift of

Andrew Carnegie Esq. He was all right, that Carnegie fella, wasn't he?'

Sally followed her gaze. 'Do you know what that black plaque's called?' she said. Ella shook her head. 'A cartouche. It's a pleasing word, isn't it?'

Ella inwardly groaned at the fact her mother could remember an obscure word, but not where they were going. The woman was an anomaly. She hoped she'd get back to normal soon.

She watched her closely as they walked up the steps and under the ornate lintel with 'Public Library' carved in relief. As ever, as soon as she crossed the threshold, her eyes were drawn up to the ceiling of the first of the three rooms. Held up by four columns topped by embellished mouldings was a beautiful dome. She gazed up, marvelling at the eight ornately divided sections, each one painted duck egg blue. Light flooded through the octagonal cupola at the dome's peak and the semicircular windows at the lower section.

'It's even more stunning than I remembered.'

'It's breathtaking, isn't it?' Sally stopped by her side. 'Thank goodness it wasn't closed down.'

Ella had been ten when her mother and a passionate group of local residents had formed The Friends of West Greenwich Library to campaign against its threatened closure. She remembered the celebrations when they'd won the fight to keep the library.

The sound of footsteps behind them broke their reverie. They shifted out of the way of a woman in a pink hijab, carrying a large bag. She turned back when she passed them, breaking into a broad smile. 'Sally,' she said. 'I thought it was you when I saw you from behind.' The woman dropped the bag and started to make gestures with her hands, touching her fingers to her head in a salute, then moving them in a pattern on her palm.

Sally tapped the swollen fingers of her right hand to her forehead. 'That's all I've got for you today, Mina,' she said. She lifted the sling away from her body to show the woman, whose smile dropped.

'What happened?'

They moved onto the carpeted area as a noisy group of young women arrived with babies and toddlers in tow, all making the same saluting sign to Mina and Sally as they traipsed past to the far end of the library.

'Bit of a fall,' Sally shrugged off. 'Good job I'm not reliant on signing. I hadn't thought of that. Imagine if you hurt your hands and you were hearing impaired.' She looked terribly sad for a second, then seemed to snap back into the room. 'This is my daughter, Ella. She's come over from Australia to keep me out of any more trouble. Ella, this is Mina. She runs the baby signing sessions.'

'Ah,' said Ella. Now the salutes made sense. 'Nice to meet you.' She turned to Sally. 'I didn't know you could sign.'

'She's amazing,' said Mina. 'I'm pretty sure she could take the class on her own.'

'I don't know about that.' Sally looked abashed.

106

'Seriously. I'm not sure I would have coped when I started if your mum hadn't offered to help. She showed me how to manage a group, you know, teaching tips? She's a lifesaver.'

'Wow. I had no idea. What else are you keeping to yourself, Mum?' Ella said, only half joking, but Sally's head turned away as a voice Ella recognised boomed across the room. So much for libraries being quiet spaces.

'Ah, Sally. Glad to see you out and about.' Pru Gardino gave Ella a curt nod before turning back to Sally. 'How are you getting on with *The Alchemist*?'

'Hi, Pru.' Mina gave a nervous wave, mouthed goodbye and scurried in the same direction the mothers and babies had gone. Pru clearly terrified everyone she met. Ella imagined coming up against her in a boardroom. She seemed like the kind of woman who broke the glass ceiling without offering her hand down to help other women up. Ella looked at her mum with fresh eyes. After seeing her interact with Mina, she knew Sally would always throw down the rope, even if it meant cutting herself on the glass. It was the very first time in her adult life that she wished to be more like her mother. The realisation made her scalp tingle.

'Almost finished,' said Sally.

'How are you finding it?'

'Best save that for book group, don't you think?'

Ella wondered why Sally was lying, but her train of thought was interrupted by a loud squeal from the far end of the library, followed by crying.

107

Pru's head snapped around. 'They really should control their offspring,' she said. 'This is a library.'

Ella would have loved to point out the hypocrisy, but the set line of Pru's mouth stopped her from uttering a word.

A slight man with thinning blond hair wandered over. He had a green lanyard around his neck and carried a bundle of books under his arm. 'Well, well, well, if it isn't the elusive Mrs Harrison. How the devil are you?' he said, coming over and kissing Sally on both cheeks.

'Hello, Jakub. Sorry I haven't been in for a while.' She looked down at her cast. 'I've been somewhat indisposed.'

'So, I've heard. Hope that's not as painful as it looks.'

Ella followed his eyes to where the ends of Sally's fingers emerged from the cast. They looked pale and bloodless. The bruises on the parts on the other hand she could see were a sickening mixture of yellow and black.

'It's not too bad. Just annoying not being able to do everything for myself.'

He grimaced. 'Poor you. How's that fabulous house of yours? Not too much damage, I hope?' His free hand danced as he spoke.

Pru sniffed, but when nobody turned their attention back to her, she mumbled something about having to get on and marched to a table in the middle of the second room, bending her head over a book.

Sally glanced across at Ella. 'The house isn't great, is

it, Ella?' She waved her hand between the two of them. 'Jakub, this is my daughter, Ella.'

Ella shook Jakub's hand, wondering how many other people they would meet on this trip. It felt like being out with an A-list celebrity.

'Please tell me that lovely little library of yours wasn't spoiled.'

'Oh, Jakub, it's ruined,' sobbed Sally.

Jakub's hand flew to his mouth. 'All that hard work!' He dropped the books on the nearest table and took Sally in his arms. 'Darling woman, I'm so sorry.'

Ella was ashamed of herself for envying this man's easy way with her mother. She wished she felt comfortable enough to hold her like that. 'It's such a shame,' she said. 'The books are pretty much pulp.'

'No, no, no!' exclaimed Jakub. He held Sally in front of him and looked into her face. 'That's awful. It was your life's work.' Ella thought that a little dramatic, but dramatic seemed to be this man's MO. A guilty voice in her head asked: *Was the library really her life's work?*

'All gone,' said Sally, her voice wavering. 'I've racked my brain, but I can't even picture what was there.'

'You're probably still in shock. You've been through quite the ordeal.' He rubbed his hands up and down Sally's upper arms as if trying to save her from hypothermia.

Sally nodded. 'It hasn't been my favourite week ever.'

'I can imagine. But you've still got the photos?' said Jakub.

'What do you mean?'

'On your phone?'

Ella had been visualising the photographs of the library on Sally's camera roll, but she couldn't say anything without giving herself away.

'Remember, you were asking me about *One Hundred Years of Solitude* for your collection, and when you told me about what you were doing, I asked you to take a picture of your little library for me? You took the photo on your phone and showed me the next day.' He led them over to a circular table directly under the blue dome. They all sat. 'Did you delete the pictures?'

Sally shook her head. 'I don't think I did. They should still be there.' Her voice sounded hopeful. She put her bag on the table. 'Could you get my phone out, please?' she said, gesturing to Ella.

Ella did as she was asked, making a show of looking in the centre of the bag before unzipping the side pocket.

'The passcode is your birthday,' Sally said. 'Can you find the photos on there?'

They sat in silence as Ella tapped the phone open, smiling at Sally when the screen lit up, hoping she looked pleased and surprised at the same time. She scrolled through the pictures she'd seen before, grinning at her mum as she pretended to see Willow's face on the device for the first time. 'Here we go.' She laid the phone on the table so they could all see the screen, then enlarged the picture of the bookcase with her thumb and forefinger, until the spines of the books came into view, blurred, but just about distinguishable. 'Is there a way to print this out here?' Ella said to Jakub.

'Email it to me, and I'll print it off now,' he suggested.

'That's a good idea. We could stick it up at home,' remarked Sally, sadly. 'It would be nice to have a reminder of how lovely it was.'

Chapter Fifteen

Sally

Twenty Years Ago

The hour hand on her wristwatch clicked to midnight. It was the eleventh of July, Ella's birthday. Sally lifted the book from the ottoman and made her way up the stairs to the first floor. She ignored the scuff marks on the wall and the increasingly threadbare stair carpet, pushing down the feeling that having the old junk room decorated had been an indulgence she couldn't really afford. She should probably have spent the money she'd saved on freshening up the hallway or fixing the broken drawers in the kitchen. Maybe she'd do that next year, or the year after that when Ella came home.

Until then, this room, her book haven, was her solace. It felt like a way of connecting herself with her daughter, and she needed that like she needed air. She pushed open the door and used the dim light from the window to find the floor switch for the lamp. She put her slipper on the button and felt it click as the bulb sprang to life, lighting the room in a soft orange glow.

Sally moved towards the bookcase that housed the

twenty-one books she'd bought for Ella, one every year since her birth. Ella had left them behind when she had moved away. That hurt, but nowhere near as much her absence did. Sally prayed that one day – soon hopefully – Ella would come back and see this little library, made entirely out of love for her, and understand how much Sally wanted to make amends.

She opened the front cover of *The Catcher in the Rye* to see the inscription she'd written there. The words made her eyes sting with tears. If only Ella would come home and read it, then she would know how sorry Sally was. Nothing was exactly as it seemed, but she could see why Ella, in her grief, had jumped to conclusions. She'd tried to tell her the truth, but it was hard to make someone listen from the other side of the world and she'd given up, hoping time would build a bridge between them.

Even now, a year later, she understood why Ella felt betrayed. She'd been complicit in allowing Ella to see her father as a man he was not. She had made so many mistakes. Regret was her most familiar emotion, these days. That and a bone-deep loneliness that only Ella could resolve.

The last part of her handwritten inscription shimmered and moved as she read it through her tears. Her mother had written a quote from the book about some things being only partly true, not all true:

I've learned the hard way that Holden's right in this. If only I could tell you the parts you don't know, then perhaps we could sit in this little library I've made for you and read together again. It is all I want in the world, Ella. That and to be able to wish you a happy birthday in person, my darling, darling girl.

Chapter Sixteen

Ella

Present Day

Verity knocked on the door at exactly seven p.m. She held out a glass vase filled with purple tulips. 'For your mum.'

'Aw, that's so kind. Come in,' said Ella. 'Mum's through here. She wants to say hello.'

Verity followed her to the sitting room, where Sally was in her usual chair. She started to rise.

'Don't get up, Mrs Harrison. I brought you some tulips. Where should I put them?'

Ella took the vase from her and put it on a coaster on top of the bookcase, trying not to feel left out when Hadron came over and bumped her head against Verity's legs. No backside for their guest, it seemed.

'They're beautiful, thank you,' said Sally. 'You're still calling me Mrs Harrison?' She laughed. 'Surely you can call me Sally after all this time?'

'I even call you Mrs Harrison in my head,' said Verity. 'Can't help it. It would seem disrespectful to call you . . . Nope, can't do it.' Hadron lay on her back so Verity could tickle her tummy. Ella didn't know why she was so bothered, but she felt like growling at the cat, see how she liked it.

'Do you know, in my head you're still ten years old,' remarked Sally. 'Little Verity Ibe, drawing pictures in all her books, always reluctant to read in quiet time.' Her voice was warm, as though the memory was special.

'You did your best,' said Verity, grinning. 'I read more during the year I was in your class than at any other time in my life, if that's any consolation.'

Ella watched the exchange, wondering how she'd feel if she was in the home of one of her primary school teachers three decades later. She was glad her parents hadn't sent her to the school her mother taught at, and enormously relieved that when she met lots of her mother's ex-students at secondary school, none of them had a bad word to say about her.

'So, how are you, Verity? Still enjoying floristry?'

Verity appeared to grow taller. 'I am, thanks. I love everything about it, from designing the bouquets, to spending all day smelling the flowers.'

'Glad to hear it.'

'How are your hands? I was so sorry to hear about your fall.'

Sally looked down at her dressings and sighed. 'These things are sent to try us. I'm not too bad. At least it means I'm getting to spend some time with Ella.'

Verity grimaced. 'Sorry, I probably shouldn't be dragging her out tonight.'

'Not at all,' said Sally. 'You can have enough of a good thing.' She winked at Ella. 'I'm glad you two have the opportunity to catch up. I have everything I need here, and Hadron will keep me company.' She gestured to the mug of tea and plate of biscuits next to her and the book on her lap.

'Hadron?'

'Hadron Collider,' chuckled Ella, as the cat made its way over to Sally, bumping into the corner of the ottoman on her way.

'Right,' said Verity, drawing the word out as Hadron pointed her bottom at Ella before settling on Sally's feet.

'You two have a lovely time, you deserve it.'

***

'I can't believe I used to take all this for granted,' said Ella as they crossed the road and the enormous clipper ship, the *Cutty Sark*, came into view. 'Who stops seeing a ship with huge rigging like that parked down the road?'

'I know, right?' exclaimed Verity. 'I went on a tour of the naval college a couple of years ago, and it was the first time I'd really looked at it – you know what I mean? We had this amazing guide called Nina. She was funny and knowledgeable, and she made it all so interesting. It was like being back in your mum's lessons.'

'I'd forgotten you were in Mum's class before you mentioned it earlier,' said Ella. 'It must be a bit weird, still seeing her around.' She pushed open the door of the ancient pub, the sight of its dark wood interior taking her back over two decades in an instant.

'It's not weird at all. It's nice.' They approached the bar. 'You got your ID?' Verity raised an eyebrow and they both giggled.

'Should we have pints of cider to toast the old days?'

'Why not?'

They took their drinks out into the beer garden and Ella tasted the fruity liquid and sighed. A warm breeze ruffled her hair and, as she stretched her arms back, she noticed the muscles at the base of her neck had relaxed for the first time since she'd arrived in England. 'This is the life,' she said, looking out in the direction of the Thames, the rigging of the *Cutty Sark* reaching towards the blue sky. 'Do you come here a lot?'

Verity shook her head. 'I don't go out much, to be honest.'

'What about date night?' said Ella, curious about Verity's relationship. Since she'd been back, she'd had time to think and, if she was honest with herself, she couldn't pinpoint exactly what it was about her own relationship she found so dissatisfying. Maybe talking with Verity would help her to quantify it.

'Ha. As if.'

Ella turned away from the ship and assessed her old friend, taking in her youthful appearance that easily defied her age. Her hair was intricately woven into zigzagged cornrows, she wore huge sunglasses, cherry red lipstick and a chic monochrome maxi dress. Ella then saw her own reflection in Verity's glasses and was surprised to see how well she looked too. The perpetual dark circles under her eyes from endless early mornings seemed to have gone and her square jaw, her favourite feature, was still firm. They were a good-looking pair, she thought to herself.

'Charlie and I never go out together either,' she said. 'Not ideal, is it?'

'Yeah, Luke's too busy on his bloody PlayStation, or he's out with his mates. Doesn't give me a second look these days.'

Ella thought of Charlie's warm hand on her shoulder when she got the call about her mum. The last thing Charlie was, was inattentive. Perhaps it was his attentiveness that bothered her. She was always too busy to reciprocate. It felt like pressure, another thing she had to fit in to her already unmanageable life. 'But you're gorgeous. What's wrong with the man?'

'Yeah, what's wrong with him?' Verity laughed unconvincingly.

'Seriously, though.' Ella put her drink on the table. 'Are you happy?' Ella loved the fact that, even though she hadn't seen Verity for so long, it felt like they'd fallen back into their old relationship, exactly like when they were teenagers and would lie on top of Ella's bed, surrounded by Westlife posters, sharing their secrets.

'Ooh, deep,' said Verity. She rolled her lips over her teeth. 'Well, since you ask, I'm not, not really. I mean, I'm not really unhappy, but I'm not living the life I thought I would. I love work, and, well, that's it really. I like my house, but I feel like I'm alone there, you know? I'm not alone, a lot of the time. But I still feel like I am.'

'What do you want to do about that?'

Verity took a gulp. 'What can I do? I've made my bed and now I'm lying in it. I'm forty-two, we'd decided not to have children, and I'm still okay with that, but we'd planned to have . . . I don't know, a bigger life. I feel like he's settled down like his dad did. He's happy to go to work, see the lads and play that bloody machine.'

A shiver ran through Ella. Did Charlie think their life was small? Did he feel alone in their house? Because if she was honest, Ella knew she wasn't really present when she was there. She was always thinking about work. 'Do you miss him? The man you married?'

Verity scrunched her nose. After a few seconds, she said, 'I don't think I do. If I'm completely honest with myself, we've drifted apart because we're just not into each other anymore. Annoying as it is that he's always off doing something, if he suggested a date night, I'd probably try to wriggle out of it.'

Would Charlie be pleased or run in the opposite direction if she suggested a romantic dinner? Ella knew the answer. He'd dress in a shirt he knew she liked, shave carefully, book the table and order the taxi. He'd listen and try to make her laugh and when they got home . . .

For a moment, she craved him next to her, which was pretty inconvenient when she was in a beer garden, over sixteen thousand kilometres away from her husband.

'Sounds like you might be better off on your own.

That way, you'd have the chance to meet someone else.'

'Nah,' said Verity. 'What's the point? I never meet anyone. I'd be living on my own, with no one to share the bills with, forever.'

'Defeatist, much?' Ella picked away hair the breeze had stuck to her lipstick. 'What about going to an art class or something like that? I remember the paintings you did at school. You were by far the most talented in our year. You could reignite that artistic flair and, you never know, you might meet someone more like-minded while you're at it.'

'Don't be daft,' said Verity. 'It's kind of you to say all that, but I can't go back to school now.'

'I'll tell Mum you said that,' warned Ella, 'and she'll tell you off. She's a huge advocate of lifelong learning, my mother.' She paused, took a sip, then added, 'I was at the library today, and they've got a gallery along the wall. Have you seen it?'

'I haven't been to the library for years,' admitted Verity. 'Isn't it just for books?'

Ella shook her head. 'I bet they have art classes. Let me check. Is that all right with you?'

There was a new, excited glint in Verity's eye. 'Ah, why not? Anyway, that's enough about me, let's talk about you. What's it like being back here after all this time?'

Ella pulled her denim jacket around her. The breeze had turned chilly now the sun was going down. 'Shall we go inside?'

Once at a table in the glass conservatory overlooking the garden, Ella hoped Verity had forgotten her question. She changed the subject, 'So, are you in touch with anyone from school?'

'Nice try, but we haven't talked about you yet. Must be weird living with your mum for the first time since you left home. I think I'd throttle mine.'

'Yeah, it's strange. Mum and I grew apart after Dad died, and maybe even before that, if I'm honest. When I was little, we were so close, but when I got a bit older, I suppose I drew away.'

Ella thought back to when she was preparing to sit her A levels. Her dad had been so exacting, insisting she wasn't working hard enough, while Sally had encouraged her to take breaks, read something for pleasure rather than revision. She could hear Sally's voice now, saying, 'All work and no play is no way to live a life. Remember, nobody will be interested in what grades you got when you're at university. These exams are just a means to get to the next stage.'

Ella already had an unconditional offer from her first choice of university, so, Sally was right, and even at the time, Ella knew her friends would appreciate the kind of advice her mother was offering. But she'd seen it through her father's eyes, believing not striving for top grades demonstrated a lack of ambition. Her mother and father were so different, she felt like she had to pick a side, and she'd chosen his.

'That's a shame.' Verity traced a finger around the

top of her pint. 'Can I tell you something embarrassing?'

'Go on.' Ella leaned in.

'When I was younger, I used to wish your mum was my mum.'

Ella didn't know what she expected, but it wasn't that. 'Really?'

'Don't sound so surprised. She's ace, your mum. She was so lovely at school – dead calm. And she'd give you a cuddle if she thought you needed one. I still remember what it felt like, to get a cuddle off Mrs Harrison.' She stared off into the distance with a wistful look on her face. 'I'd go home, and my mum and dad would be shouting at each other and slamming doors, and I'd imagine Mrs Harrison being there instead, baking cakes and reading bedtime stories.'

A lump formed in Ella's throat. Her childhood had been almost exactly as Verity described. She remembered arguments between her parents, but they were rare and always in hushed tones. 'She's not a Disney character,' she said. 'We all have our faults.'

'I know that.' Verity drained her glass. 'But it was my little escapist fantasy. And, anyway, even if she was as perfect as I thought, you wouldn't be able to see it, would you?'

'What do you mean?'

Verity stood and rummaged in her bag, bringing out her purse. 'That's how it works, isn't it? You were a teenager when you left home and you never lived there again, or even in the same country, did you?'

'No.' Ella couldn't grasp what Verity was getting at.

'So, you're probably stuck in that awkward phase where you automatically find faults with your parents. Everything they do sets your teeth on edge like when you're a teen. Am I right?'

Ella blinked away images of her clenching her teeth at something her mother had said or done over the last few days. 'Erm . . .'

'Ha, your face says it all,' said Verity. 'You're a forty-two-year-old teenager – admit it. Another pint, or do you want something more grown-up?'

'More grown-up, please.' She didn't want to drink fizzy apple juice anymore. She wanted a glass of crisp white wine. Because she was an adult.

And when it came to her mother, perhaps she should start acting like one.

* * *

When Ella got in, the house appeared to be in soft focus. She walked woozily into the sitting room, flopped onto the sofa and took out her phone. She opened a message from Charlie and saw he'd sent selfies of him and Willow grinning from their garden at home.

She called him. 'Hello. Thanks for those pictures.'

'No problem. How's things?'

'All right.' She was slurring slightly. She wondered if he could hear it. 'Is Willow okay? When I FaceTimed her yesterday, she seemed a bit flat. I asked about Harper and I'm sure I saw her well up. Is everything all right there?'

'She says Harper isn't her friend anymore, but she won't say any more than that. I'll keep trying. Other than that, she's fine. Don't worry.'

'If I was Queen of the World, nobody would be allowed to be mean to my Willow.'

She heard a snort of laughter. 'I haven't heard an *If I was Queen of the World* for a while. Have you had a glass of wine . . . or two? You sound . . . more cheerful.'

'Do you mean drunk? The cheek. Actually, yes, I went out with an old school friend, Verity, tonight. It was so nice to be in an old English pub and just chat. I'd forgotten what it was like, not to always have a million things I need to do. I've got so used to seeing leisure time as wasted time, but it's not, is it?' She didn't know where that came from. She hadn't thought about it before she said it, but it suddenly felt piercingly true.

'Who are you and what have you done with my wife?'

'Very funny. Seriously, though, when did I stop feeling the breeze on my face, or looking up to admire the rigging?'

'You've lost me now. Is that a euphemism? That kind of sentiment suggests to me that you've finished *The Alchemist*. Do you think you're starting to value the simple things in life again?'

'Ha! It's so sweet of you to read all the books Mum and I are reading.'

'It's the least I can do. She made a library dedicated to you. I'm not sure you appreciate how incredible that is.'

'I do,' said Ella, feeling chastised. The library was

on her mind a lot and she was beginning to appreciate how much thought and love had gone into it. It was humbling, and humbled wasn't an emotion she was used to feeling. 'And I have finished the book. Bloody loved it. I'd forgotten how mesmerising reading is, and how it makes you think about your own life, that book especially. It's so wise! I've been thinking about how we all got to where we are; how me and Mum ended up sort of estranged.' She cradled the phone between her neck and shoulder and ran cold water into a glass.

'Verity had an interesting – if not a bit insulting – insight on the situation. She said I was stuck in a teenage relationship with Mum, because I left for uni when I was eighteen, then moved away straight after. She reckons I'm still in the automatically hating your parents phase, where they're permanently annoying and embarrassing.'

'And what do you think?' He sounded hesitant.

'Very tactful. Don't think I didn't notice you not giving your opinion. I suppose she could be right. I haven't forgiven Mum for what she did and I've seen everything since then through that distorted lens.' Wow, she was wise this evening. 'Since I've been back, I've had an insight into how everyone else sees her, and she seems to be universally adored. Either I'm wrong or everyone else is.'

'Is that you admitting you might be wrong . . . ?'

'Ha bloody ha. Actually, I'm blaming it on the drink. I'd never admit to something so ludicrous if I was sober. I'll have a hangover tomorrow. I'd probably better get to bed. Night-night, love you.' Where had that come from? She hadn't said *love you* at the end of a phone call to Charlie for a long time. The only person she ever said it to was Willow.

'Drunk Ella is my favourite kind of Ella. It's good to hear you relaxed for a change. Night-night. I love you too.'

Her mood dipped. Did he really have to add *for a change*?

Chapter Seventeen

Ella

Present Day

As Ella indulged in the breakfast her hangover desperately craved, her thoughts wandered again to her mother's library, pondering which book within it best captured the essence of her teenage years. She peered at the photo Jakub had printed off, which was stuck to the fridge door with Sellotape. She tried to focus on the beautiful room as it was, and not overlay the mouldy mess she'd seen that morning, when emptying the dehumidifier tank of foetid water had made her fragile stomach churn.

Sally followed her gaze, lifting her cereal spoon to her mouth with the fingers of her left hand. She was becoming more agile by the day. 'It was lovely, wasn't it?'

'It really was.' Ella walked closer to the picture, squinting at the spines of the books on the top shelf. *The Catcher in the Rye* immediately caught her attention. She'd never read it, but she'd heard that it was the quintessential teenage novel. She wondered what words her mother had chosen to inscribe in that one. 'I'm planning a trip to the market this morning. Fancy coming along?'

Sally looked at the rain dashing against the window. 'Not in this,' she said. 'I can't put my hood up and down or hold an umbrella with these blasted hands.'

'I'll hold the umbrella.'

'If it clears up, I'll go for a walk this afternoon.'

Her mother sounded decisive, so after she'd cleared up the breakfast things, Ella borrowed Sally's raincoat and ventured out alone. The recent sunshine had lulled her into thinking the British weather was better than she'd remembered. She tugged the raincoat around her, but it was too small and she couldn't make it meet over her T-shirt. By the time she reached Greenwich Picturehouse, she had a wet stripe down her front. She firmly believed the weather was worse than what she had imagined while sipping rosé wine on her sun terrace at home, where she often thought about England's grey skies and rain-soaked pavements. When she was over sixteen thousand kilometres away, it had made her feel smug; like she had made a better decision than everyone who chose to stay on this dreary island.

But now, walking the zebra crossing and turning left under the curved sign, down the alleyway into the market, the cobblestones under her feet reminded her of the long history of her hometown. It was called *Historic Royal Greenwich* for a reason. It held stories in every building, every pathway, from the majestic naval college to the Royal Observatory, which watched over the resplendent park from the Prime Meridian Line. It made her feel like a part of something important in a way she had never experienced in Australia. She supposed it was called *the New World* for a reason. At that moment, the old world sang out to her like a Siren.

Passing the ancient shops on the narrow market approach, Ella forgot about her damp T-shirt sticking to her stomach and appreciated their pretty bay windows and colourful displays like a tourist might. When she reached the end of the alley and the busy market opened up before her, she experienced a sense of homecoming. She wasn't a tourist. She belonged here. This wasn't a dreary island with terrible weather. Well, it was; but it was also deep in her DNA.

Once under the glazed roof, she tugged down her hood and breathed in the smells of the market. Spices and barbecue mingled with the aroma of burning incense. She meandered along the first row of stalls, picking up a silver bangle from a table sparkling with shiny jewellery and wondering if Willow would like it. Suddenly, she was desperate for her daughter to be by her side, squealing about how much she *needed* to get her ears pierced so she could wear the gorgeous earrings hanging from thin wires along the top of the stall. She bought the bangle and slipped it in her pocket, then moved further into the market.

Soon, there it was: the stall where she and her mum had spent so much time when she was small. Even the green tablecloth with geometric print was the same, not that much of it could be seen under the neatly stacked rows of books. Stepping closer, Ella could see it was set out exactly as it always had been: children's books to the right, under which magazines were displayed in upturned crates. In the middle of the huge table, adult fiction books sat in rows, the odd one flat so its cover was in full view. To the left, classic copies of old books were stacked, their dark blue and claret spines distinguishing them from the colourful modern novels.

Behind the table, a woman was sitting, reading a book. Her long dark hair was streaked with grey, and she wore glasses now, but she was still as familiar as the stall itself.

Ella approached, curiously nervous. 'Hannah,' she said. 'You probably won't remember me, but—'

The woman looked up. 'Ella?' Her mouth opened and she put the book face down on a pile. She stood and shook her head. 'You're a sight for sore eyes.'

'I didn't know if you'd remember me,' Ella said, blushing.

'Remember you? You and your mum were my best customers,' she said. 'Your mum still is, bless her. And you haven't changed a bit!'

Ella knew that wasn't true, but there was something about being back here that made her feel more youthful somehow, like her cares were less heavy despite the circumstances she'd arrived to. It was probably being away from work and all the adulting of having a house and husband and child. It crossed her mind for a second, she wasn't really responsible for any of that stuff in Sydney, so what did that leave? Work? Herself? 'You haven't changed either.'

'Ah, get away with you.' Hannah grinned. 'And how's your poor mum?'

Everyone in Greenwich seemed to know about Sally's fall. 'Not too bad. A bit sore and obviously quite upset about the damage to the house. She would have come with me today, but . . .' She gestured to the rain spattering on the market's glass roof.

'I don't blame her for staying in on a day like this. I'm glad she's well enough to be out and about, though. I did call, but I imagine her phone has that many messages she didn't know what to do with them. Tell her I miss her, won't you?'

'I will.'

'And tell her I won't expect her back at work until she's ready.' She chuckled.

Ella was confused. 'Work?'

'Only kidding. She used to sit with me back here sometimes to keep me company, and if I needed the loo or a cuppa, she'd take over.'

'Ah, right.' Ella was learning so much about her mum's life from other people. It didn't sit right. She should have known more about Sally's day-to-day through speaking with her over the years. She thought back to their phone conversations and realised she was the one who always cut the call short, saying she had some work to get on with, or Willow needed something.

'I was so grateful to her when she ran the stall for me when my Caroline was having Darcie. You don't want to miss the birth of your first grandchild, do you?' Hannah looked out at the other stalls. 'I mean, I doubt they would have taken my pitch off me if I'd missed a few days, but your mum offered to help out, so I didn't have to worry about it.' She hugged herself and grinned. 'Ooo, Darcie was a lovely baby. I can't believe she's already at school. Time flies, but you know that. Those first weeks are so precious, aren't they? Sally made it possible for me to be there for all of it. Caroline reckons she's a saint, says she wouldn't have coped without me there.' Her face looked suddenly serious. 'Must've been hard for you and Sally when you had your Willow, with you being all the way over there and your mum stuck here. She's a gorgeous little thing,' Hannah continued. 'Sally shows me all those pictures you send. We both think she looks just like you did at that age.'

'Thank you,' Ella said, her mind racing as Hannah's words flew at her. Her mum had made it possible for Hannah to spend time with her first grandchild. She showed her pictures of Willow and allowed her to think it hadn't been possible for her to be there when Willow was born. In truth, Sally had offered to travel to Australia to help, but Ella had put her off, saying it was too far and she would be fine. Now she could see how that rejection might have felt. She'd told her mother she didn't need her, but hadn't considered how that might feel to her.

Admittedly, she had been fine, but that was because Charlie had taken care of them both. And had been doing so ever since, she realised, with not much in the way of gratitude if she was completely honest. Still, she worked hard. That was her part of the bargain, but was that enough? Perhaps her kind, reliable husband deserved more from the deal than she offered.

'Can I get you a drink?' she said to Hannah, needing to be on her own for a moment to swallow the guilt that threatened to overwhelm her. 'I fancy a coffee.'

'I'd love an oat milk cappuccino, if it's not too much bother. I've gone all modern in my tastes, haven't I? Oat milk – what am I like?'

Ella gave her a thumbs up and rushed away towards a converted van at the far end of the market advertising hot drinks on a chalkboard strapped to the windscreen, wondering how she had become someone who was too bitter and resentful to allow her mother to spend time with the only grandchild she had?

Chapter Eighteen

Ella

Present Day

Hannah found a copy of *The Catcher in the Rye* after a couple of minutes of looking in crates of books she couldn't fit on the table. It was an old edition in good condition, with a yellow title over an orange illustration of a galloping stallion.

'How much?' said Ella.

'The price of a posh coffee.' Hannah winked and sipped from the cardboard cup.

Ella started to argue, but Hannah shook her head, so she thanked her and made her way out of the market, after promising to return with Sally soon.

The rain had stopped, and slivers of blue sky marbled the clouds. Ella avoided puddles as she marched towards West Greenwich, past conversations with her mother replaying in her head. Each one was brief, mainly consisting of Sally asking her questions. She realised she'd asked little in return, just getting the bare bones of her mother's life. From that, she'd invented a narrative where Sally went about doing good deeds as penance.

She'd imagined her mother trying to make up for her wrongs by being on committees and chairing book groups. But she was quickly learning the truth held little resemblance to the life she thought her mum lived.

Sally was a kind neighbour who a struggling teenager could turn to when he was in need. She was a much-admired ex-teacher who helped a woman run her baby signing lessons. She was a booklover who made it possible for her friend to spend precious time with her family. She was not the woman Ella had told herself she was. She wasn't doing penance; she wasn't a do-gooder. She was exactly who she'd been all the time Ella was growing up: a teacher, a good neighbour, a friend. More than any of that, she was a mother. A kind, caring, funny, loyal, loving mother. And that's why she had stayed away when Ella had asked her to.

She wasn't sure she could look Sally in the eye in that moment, so decided to go into the library on her way home. The quiet atmosphere in the first room had a soothing effect on her spiralling brain. A few people tapped on computer keyboards in the allocated space under the enormous window. An old man sat at the central table under the blue dome, a book that must've been a thousand pages long open in front of him.

She walked to the wall to the right of the entrance and stood in front of the display of watercolour paintings. The first was a beach scene, the soft sand merging with the aquamarine, which blended into a cloudless sky. The next was a row of white cottages. Pink roses climbed the wall of the last house; at least, Ella thought they were roses. The pink shapes were blurred, giving the impression of flowers, and Ella could feel her tight muscles unfurling as she took in the peaceful scenes on the canvas.

'Glorious, aren't they?'

The voice behind her made her jump. Ella turned to see Jakub examining the painting of the cottages over her shoulder.

'The artist lives around the corner. It's his first exhibition, which is astonishing, isn't it? The brushwork is so accomplished. I love the way he blends the scene' – he pointed at the beach painting – 'making the sand, sea and sky all one amalgamation. It says a lot, to me at least.'

Ella nodded. 'They're beautiful.'

Jakub took a breath before speaking again. 'I'm glad I caught you on your own. I hope I'm not speaking out of turn, but it appeared to me your mum wasn't quite herself when you both came in the other day.' He tapped his fingertips together in front of his lanyard.

'In what way?'

He scratched his cheek, stubble making a crackling sound under his nails. 'Hard to say, exactly, but she seemed . . . It's probably nothing. She's had an accident, so she's probably still in shock.'

While Ella agreed with that, Jakub had latched on to something that had been bothering her too. 'She seems different to me too. I can't put my finger on it either.' She

137

couldn't admit that she was comparing her to the Sally she knew twenty-one years ago.

'If she were a dimmer switch . . .' Jakub held up his finger. 'Stay with me on this; it's a bit like she's been turned down a notch. She's still shiny, but not quite so bright.' He closed his eyes. 'That came out completely wrong. There's a reason I'm a librarian, not a writer. Imagine Evelyn Waugh using a dimmer switch as a metaphor. I'll be comparing these paintings to lawnmowers next.' He pursed his lips. 'I didn't mean she's not bright—'

'I know.' Ella smiled. 'And that's a good analogy. The light. Not the lawnmower.'

'Definitely no lawnmowers here.' He wafted his arm in front of the paintings. 'Do you think she might be depressed?'

The thought had crossed Ella's mind when she'd heard her mother hadn't been out and about much lately. It was so unlike her. There was also that elusive doctor's appointment. 'I don't know.'

'It wouldn't be a surprise. I'd be low mood personified if I lost the use of both hands.'

His hands moved so frequently when he talked that Ella imagined he'd have to stop conversing altogether if he couldn't accompany his speech with gesticulation. 'It's possible, isn't it? If she is . . . I'm not sure what to do.'

'I think just having you here is the tonic she needs.'

Ella smiled, trying to disguise how difficult it was to hear that. 'Maybe. I hope so. We used to be very close, when I was growing up, but, well, it's hard to keep up when you're on the other side of the world. I feel like I'm getting to know her again.' She wasn't usually so candid with relative strangers, but there was something so warm about this man, she felt like she could trust him with the truth. Or some of it.

His eyes misted over. 'Have you got a minute?' he said. 'I'd like to tell you something about Sally that you probably don't know.' He led her to a small table in the second room under the next blue dome. When they were seated, Jakub took a breath and said, 'She made up the name of my drag act.'

Ella sat back in the chair. 'She did what?'

'I'm serious.' Jakub sniggered. 'By day, I'm Jakub, a handsome librarian of Polish decent.' He covered his face with his hands, then pulled them apart like curtains, revealing a seductive pout. 'But, by night, I'm Bridget Bard-Oh.' He made the Oh at the end sound like a delighted gasp.

'Bridget Bard-Oh?' Ella blinked, wondering if she was actually dreaming this exchange.

'Like the Bard, you know, Shakespeare, but with a bit of Brigitte thrown in, with a big Oh.'

'That's genius!'

'I know! It was your mum's idea.'

Ella was definitely dreaming. Although they were talking about a woman who'd named a stray cat Hadron Collider, so, maybe not.

'We were chatting about the act, and I gave her a

139

bit of a preview.' His hands had taken on a life of their own, flying in front of them. 'I perform comedy poetry and I'd tried out loads of names but none of them fit, or they'd already been taken, and she came out with it, just like that. She was so sweet. Even came to my first open mic night. She brought her neighbour – what's her name?'

'Glenda?' Ella tried to visualise her mother and Glenda, whose comedy tastes struck Ella as more *The Good Life* than experimental drag, sitting in a comedy club, while Jakub performed poetry in a wig and lipstick. Nope. She couldn't conjure it.

'I'm learning more about my mother every day, but this one is the most unexpected, I can guarantee you that.' She took in Jakub's corduroy trousers and sensible shoes. 'And you're a dark horse.'

Jakub grinned. 'Expect the unexpected.' He waved his fingers in front of his face. 'And that's the point of parents, isn't it?'

'Eh?'

'They're not really people, are they?'

'I don't follow.'

Jakub put his hands to the side as if he were about to explain something obvious. 'If we accepted our parents were individuals in their own right, like we are, then we would have to accept we are not the centre of their world. They are. And we'd know they're fallible, and that wouldn't work for us, when we're kids at least, would it? Parents have got to be right all the time. They have to be in charge and make all the right decisions. That keeps us safe.

'When we realise they're actually human, it's a bit of a blow, because then we know they can't always protect us. We have to reframe our world view. I don't think many of us choose to do that. We prefer to keep them as saviour figures. It's why we cry for our mothers when we are in the worst situations, because they can protect us from anything. Heartbreaking, really, when you think about it.' He gave a bouncy shrug. 'That's my theory, anyway.'

As Ella absorbed what he was saying, she realised that was exactly what had happened to her. In fact, she'd learned of her mother's fallibility on the day of her father's funeral, and her world was rocked like a dinghy in a storm. Up until that point, her mother would have been a port, but all of a sudden, she couldn't be trusted, so Ella ran. Ever since then, she'd relied on herself. She didn't even allow Charlie in. Not completely. She didn't ever want to be let down like that again.

But her mother hadn't directly let her down. She'd made a terrible mistake, and she had lost her entire family because of it. Sally wasn't a monster. She never had been. She was human, so wasn't it time Ella accepted that?

Chapter Nineteen

Ella

Present Day

'I can't believe you didn't tell me about Jakub's drag act,' Ella shouted from the hallway when she got home. She kicked off her wet trainers and hung the raincoat on the banister before going through to the sitting room.

'Bridget Bard-Oh?' Sally grinned. 'She's really very good.'

'You call Bridget "she"?'

'I asked what pronouns Jakub would prefer. I thought he might prefer she, or they/them, when he's in character. He prefers he/him in his everyday life and she/her when in character.'

When had her mother become so right-on? 'How did you get Glenda to go and see him – I mean her?'

'I told her it was a lot like Morecambe and Wise.' The lines from the edge of Sally's eyes crinkled down her cheeks as she grinned, 'Which wasn't a complete lie, because those two were always in bed together.'

'Mother!'

'What? It's a simple fact. If I'd told her it was drag,

she'd have assumed it wasn't her thing. You should have seen her face when the first act came on. I thought she was going to choke on her sherry. I needn't have worried; by the time Bridget came on, she was laughing harder than anyone. She's always asking when the next open mic night is. She's watched every episode of *RuPaul's Drag Race* since then.' She winked. 'Fancy making me a cuppa?'

Ella shook her head in disbelief, grabbing her bag from the hall before following her mum down the stairs to the kitchen. Near the top of the stairs, she noticed steam on the window overlooking the garden at the back of the house. That was odd. As she reached the lower ground floor, the room felt strangely humid and when she turned on the light, a mist hung in the air. 'Why is it foggy down here?' she said, unease spreading out from her stomach. She breathed in a sulphurous odour. 'What's that smell?'

'I don't know.' Sally looked around, as though seeing the room for the first time.

The was a rattling sound and Ella saw a pan on the hob. She rushed towards it, and found an egg, its shell burst open, juddering in a centimetre of bubbling water. 'Mum! You left this to nearly boil dry!' She turned off the hob and stood over the pan, the steam hot on her cheeks. 'What were you thinking?' She sensed Sally behind her. 'You could have burned the house down.'

'Sorry,' said Sally. 'I forgot I'd put that on. I fancied a boiled egg . . .'

Her voice wavered, turning Ella's exasperation down a notch. Of course she hadn't meant to forget, but that didn't alter the fact that this was a dangerous mistake. 'What if I hadn't come home when I did?'

'I said I'm sorry,' said Sally. 'Haven't you ever left a pan on?'

'No,' said Ella, although she knew she could only be sure of that because she rarely cooked at home. That was Charlie's domain.

'Wait 'til you're my age,' said Sally, as Ella moved the pan into the sink. She ran the cold tap and water sizzled as it met hot metal. 'You'll see how easy it is to let a pan boil dry.' She hovered, watching Ella turn off the tap. 'There. No harm done.'

Ella wasn't so sure. She wanted to ask if this had happened before. In truth, she wanted Sally to promise her that she wouldn't try to boil anything except the kettle in future. But how realistic was that? She'd be back on the other side of the world before long and Sally couldn't eat raw food for the rest of her life.

'Maybe stay in the kitchen when you're cooking?' Ella suggested.

'Will do,' replied Sally. 'Now, tell me what else you got up to this morning.'

Ella knew she was trying to change the subject, but went along with it anyway. 'I went to see Hannah.'

'Oh, lovely Hannah. How is she?'

'Good. She wants to see you though, so we'll have to pop down next market day. I bought this.' She took the book from her bag. 'Do you remember this was in your library?' Thinking of the library was calming. She wished the room was in its original state and that she could curl up in the armchair now, surrounded by the books her mother had chosen for her.

Sally narrowed her eyes and read the title, 'The Catcher in the Rye. Ah, yes. Poor little Holden Caulfield, always in trouble. Always blaming someone else, bless him. He didn't want to grow up.'

'I'd like to read as many books from the top shelves of your library as I can before I go home.' The word 'home' felt strange in Ella's mouth. Greenwich had started to feel like home again. Even the sofa where she was spending more and more time reading seemed to have moulded back into her shape. Could you call two places home?

Sally's eyes filled with tears. 'That's lovely.'

There was a clattering sound and Ella turned to see Hadron eating cat biscuits from her bowl under the window. Her bottom was in the air, but at least this time it didn't seem like an insult directed at Ella.

She wasn't sure she wanted to hear the answer to the question she was about to ask, but Ella asked it anyway, 'Do you remember what you wrote in the inscription?'

Sally sat at the table and picked at her thumbnail. 'I bought that one the year you left for Australia.'

Ella's mouth went dry. She'd thought as much and now it was confirmed, she wasn't sure she wanted to hear any more. But her mother had accused her of not wanting to understand her, so, if she wanted them to have a relationship, it was time to listen. 'Go on.'

'I don't remember exactly what I wrote, but from what I remember, the themes in the book are the protection of childhood innocence; Holden is so scared to grow up, and tied in with that is the fear of dying.' She glanced at Ella, then back at her fingers. 'You'd been forced to face up to all of those things, and I wanted you to know I understood how hard it was for you.'

The memory of getting the phone call telling her her father was dead hit her like a blow to the chest.

Sally continued, 'In the book, Holden's enemy is the adult world. At that time, I knew you saw me as the enemy, and I wanted to explain to you what really happened.'

'Your affair?' Ella didn't want to hear it, but she knew she had to.

'There was no affair.'

Her vision pixelated with the effort not to scream. She ran the cold water, then filled the kettle, glad not to have to look her mother in the eye. 'I saw the letter.' What she wanted to say was: *How can you lie to me now? I'm trying to forgive you, to understand you.*

'I need you to listen and understand what I am saying,' Sally said, her voice seeming loud when Ella turned off the tap and put the kettle on to boil.

Ella froze, holding on to the edge of the work surface, watching her knuckles turn white. She waited, a hollow feeling in the pit of her stomach.

146

'It was not an affair,' Sally said.

'He said he loved you.' Ella turned, spitting the words out. 'I read the letter, so don't try to deny it.'

'Yes,' said Sally. 'We loved each other. I admit that, but not in the way you think. I was never unfaithful to your father . . .' Sally's voice shook. 'But my friendship with Andrew meant a great deal to me.'

'Friendship?'

'Yes, friendship. Please hear me out. Sit down. Please, Ella.'

'I'm happy standing.' Ella's head pounded. Could she have been wrong for all those years? She leaned against the granite, the hard edge cold against her back.

'Andrew and I had been friends since university. The three of us were a gang, once, before . . .' She paused. 'Back then, me, your dad and Andrew, we were all close. I suppose I always knew Andrew had a soft spot for me, but I couldn't see beyond your father. He shone so brightly, both Andrew and I were in his shadow.'

Ella remembered her father's charisma, making his already impressive frame appear even bigger. He could fill a room by force of personality alone. God, she missed him. 'Your feelings of inferiority are no excuse to go behind his back,' Ella said.

'I know, but Andrew was kind to me. He listened, and he cared. He supported me when I needed it most.'

'Why didn't you turn to Dad? He was your husband.'

Sally shook her head. 'There's a lot you don't know. It wasn't always easy, living with your father.'

147

'You're going to blame him for your deceit?'

'I didn't plan to deceive anyone. Your dad held a grudge against Andrew ever since—'

'You can't really blame him for not being too keen on the man who was infatuated with his wife.'

It was as though Sally hadn't heard her. 'So, Andrew and I wrote to each other in secret.' She looked up, her eyes imploring. 'That's all it was: letters, friendship, nothing more.'

Ella tried to take it in. She searched beyond her simmering fury to find some rationale. If this was true, her mum had deceived her dad, but only through continuing a friendship without his knowledge. There was no affair.

'What would you say if Charlie was having an online friendship with another woman behind my back? A woman who said she loved him? Would you think that was all right?' As soon as the words came out of her mouth, her brain conjured up an email exchange where another woman professed undying love for her husband. She wanted to retch. She was surprised at the vehemence of her response.

'No,' said Sally. She bowed her head. 'I've always understood why you were as hurt as you were.'

Ella baulked at the hypocrisy. 'I know I'd be devastated. Destroyed even. Poor Dad.'

Sally started. 'Your dad didn't know.' She looked horrified. 'Is that what you've thought all these years. That Neil discovered something going on between

Andrew and I?'

Ella couldn't stop her sobs. 'Isn't that what happened?'

Sally stood and wound her free arm around Ella, dragging her close. 'No, absolutely not. Oh, darling girl, it must've tortured you to think that. Oh, sweetheart, I'm so sorry I didn't try harder to tell you. I knew you were angry with me, but I had no idea you imagined your dad died thinking I'd betrayed him. That's not what happened at all.'

Sally's collarbone was hard against Ella's cheek, but she didn't draw away. 'Are you sure?'

Sally released her and stroked tears from her face. 'He never knew Andrew and I wrote to each other. After they fell out, he had no idea we were even in contact. I swear on my life, on Willow's life, that it was never more than letters, and your father never knew. After you found that one on the day of your father's funeral, I never sent a letter to Andrew again. Your reaction made it clear that you saw it as disloyalty, a breach of trust, and I didn't ever want to make you feel that way again.'

Ella gulped down tears. She looked into her mother's eyes, and she believed her. 'You stopped because of me?'

'I would never knowingly hurt you, Ella. I never sent a letter to him again,' she repeated.

And that was enough to lift the weight Ella had been carrying since the moment she had found the letter. The thought of her mother's betrayal and her father's despair had dogged her for twenty-one years. Now her mother

149

had sworn it wasn't the case and she had stopped writing that day to prove that her daughter was her priority, she felt that a boulder, which had stood between them for all these years, had been rolled away. Now, at last, they could move on.

Chapter Twenty

Ella

Present Day

The following day, Ella and Sally got up early to let two of the builders in to quote for repairs. Ella had made a list of all the things she could see that needed attention, but suspected there was a lot more work required. Her mother had let the house slide since her father's death, as if she wasn't aware ongoing maintenance was the only way to keep on top of an old house like this.

They sat in the kitchen, listening to the footsteps and rumbling conversations above. Sally was on the last few pages of *The Alchemist* and Ella was distracting herself by scouring the details of the library picture.

'Right,' said the builder, his clumpy boots appearing on their stairs, followed by blue overalls and then his egg-shaped bald head. 'I've given it a good coat of looking at.' He sucked air in through his teeth. 'A lot needs doing. Not going to be a cheap job.'

'Yes,' said Ella, annoyed by the performative teeth sucking. 'I thought as much.'

'I'll need my electrician to come around before I can

give you a full quote.'

'All right. Get them to give me a call. I've got a couple more builders coming over the next few days, so we'll be around.'

'Oh.' His mouth drooped with pantomime sadness.

Ella wasn't taken in by this artificial display. She'd disliked the man on sight. He was full of bluster and had gone around the house shaking his head and sighing at every minor crack in the plaster. She imagined he'd assessed the street and the house, found two women inside, and thought his luck was in: an inflated quote for as little work as possible, and a nice holiday off the back of it. If she was Queen of the World, everyone would have a nose like Pinocchio that grew whenever they told a lie. On second thoughts . . .

The builder's partner appeared behind him. 'When do you want us to start?'

'They're getting more quotes,' the first man said.

'Oh.' The second man's chin puckered. 'You want to be careful, two women on your own. You don't want to let just anyone in. There's a lot of cowboys out there.'

Ella knew this was designed to make them uneasy. She laughed and enjoyed the surprise on their faces. 'Don't you worry about us,' she said, walking towards them with confident strides. 'I can spot bullshit from' – she looked pointedly at the distance between them and her – 'about a metre and a half.' She crossed her arms, standing with legs wide, and gave them a plastic smile. Hadron walked in front of her and growled at the men, who looked from her to the cat, as though either one might attack at any moment. It felt nice to have Hadron on her side for a change.

'Right, well, we'll leave you to it,' said the first man, looking a foot smaller than before. 'I'll get the electrician to give you a bell, then we'll get on that quote.'

Ella followed them to the door. 'Thanks for coming,' she said. 'We'll let you know if you win the job.' She closed the door, then glanced around the hall. It really was jaded. Near the bottom of the stairs, she recognised the deep scuff mark on the paintwork from where she'd dragged her rucksack against the wall, almost falling under the weight of it, when she, walked out after finding the letter.

Both she and Sally had turned to look at the gouge in the lining paper the bag had made. She remembered silently daring her mother to comment on it. She hadn't. She'd just watched Ella leave while tears streamed down both their faces.

Ella shoved the memory back. She was looking forward to seeing this place done up. But it wasn't going to be by the two jokers who'd just left.

'What did they take us for?' said Sally, when Ella came back downstairs. 'I'll ask Glenda for the number of the nice chaps she got in to do her new kitchen.' She stood.

'Where are you off to?'

'Next door, I told you.'

'Glenda's in Antibes,' Ella said.

Sally looked at her, brows furrowed as though calculating something in her mind. 'Antibes?'

'Yes. It's May.'

'Is it?'

'You're worrying me now. It's ages since your operation and you can't possibly still have a urine infection. Your brain fog should be getting better now, not worse. I think I need to take you to one of those memory clinics and get you checked out. Maybe the painkillers are too strong. Do you think you still need them?'

'I don't know.' Sally looked down at her sling as though it was the first time she'd seen it. 'Maybe not.'

'Try without, and if it's too sore, you can always take them again.' Ella put their breakfast things in the dishwasher, then looked out of the window, up towards street level, straining to see the sky over the houses opposite. The day was overcast, but the clouds were white, and the weather forecast didn't predict rain. 'It's better weather today,' she said to Sally, turning back to where her mother sat at the table. She looked terribly sad. 'What's up?'

Sally turned towards her. 'I'm, erm . . . Nothing.'

'I was thinking of getting *The Great Gatsby* today,' said Ella. 'That should put a smile on your face.'

Sally blinked. 'I'm sorry, what?'

'Let's go and see Hannah, get a copy of the book, if she's got one, then go to the library and get another copy so we can both read it – or, in your case, reread it – at the same time.'

154

Sally smiled. 'I'd like that.'

'Come on then. Let's do this.'

***

Hannah grinned as soon as she saw Ella and Sally approach. 'I've missed you,' she said, shuffling out from behind her stall and hugging Sally gently. 'How are you?'

'All right,' said Sally. 'I wouldn't be able to manage without this one, though.' She smiled at Ella, and Ella felt able to accept the compliment without wondering if there was a hidden meaning, or some kind of manipulation, for the first time since she'd arrived.

Hannah offered Sally her chair behind the stall and the two women chatted while Ella got coffees for them all. When she returned, Sally's head was thrown back in a fit of laughter and Ella was hit by a dart of uncomplicated love. This was the mum she'd grown up with. It was wonderful to have those feelings back.

'Your mum said you're looking for a book,' said Hannah. 'But couldn't remember which one.'

'Honestly,' sighed Ella. 'She wasn't always so forgetful, was she? I'm getting worried, quite frankly. It's *The Great Gatsby*.'

'That's it,' said Sally. 'I knew it began with a G. Please don't worry about me.' Her voice was pleading. 'I'll be back to my old self soon. It's just been a lot. That's all.' She picked up a book and clumsily turned to the first page. 'The doctor said I was right as rain.'

Ella searched her face. 'When?'

'Last time I went.'

'Did you talk about the memory stuff?' If she had, why didn't she mention it before when Ella had quizzed her? Why wait until now to say there was nothing to worry about?

'Yes.' Sally turned the page with her thumb. 'So there's no need to keep talking about it.'

'Doctor or no doctor, you said the book began with an S, not a G,' said Hannah. Her fingers hovered over the books on the table, then expertly flicked through the paperbacks, plucking one out and dropping it on top of the rows. 'Here it is.'

It was a Penguin Modern Classics edition with a black and white photo of a woman pictured from above on the cover. She wore a 1920s-style dress and beads and was reclining next to a seated man, a table with drinks and cigarettes beside them.

'Bloody love that book,' Hannah said, slapping her hand on the cover. 'I reckon I would have thrived in the 1920s. I would've made a brilliant flapper.' She started to dance, palms circling in front of her. Passers-by grinned and watched, before wandering off to other stalls. 'I'm putting off the customers.' She grimaced and picked up her coffee from where she'd balanced it on a copy of *The Time Traveller's Wife*.

Ella picked up the book, still turning over what Sally had said in her mind. If there really was nothing to worry about, that would be a huge relief. But something didn't feel quite right. 'Brilliant. How much?'

Hannah lifted her coffee and nodded. 'You know the rate of exchange.'

Ella started to argue, but Hannah cut her off.

'You can pick up a second-hand book for a quid in most places. You can get them for free from the library. Even a newly released eBook might only set you back 99p. How much was this coffee? Two quid, three?'

It had been three pounds fifty, but Ella wasn't about to disclose that. She mimed zipping her lips.

'Take the book. I insist.'

'Thank you.' Ella dropped it into her bag. She pointed at her mum. 'Think about the message you wrote inside. See if you can remember any of it.'

Sally smiled. 'Yes, miss.'

'I love that you built a library especially for Ella.' Hannah smiled at Sally. 'I might start doing it for my Caroline.' She grinned. 'I might make her do it for me, too. Then I'd see what she really thinks of me.' She laughed. 'I think everyone should have a library that's been made for them specially, with lovely words about why a particular book was chosen – it would be a hell of a lot more meaningful than a card. Anyone who's survived another year on this earth deserves a few hundred pages and a dedication. That's my opinion and I'm sticking to it.' She crossed her arms and stamped her foot, pouting like a toddler.

Ella agreed. It would.

On the way back to the library, she thought about what Hannah had said. Her mother had created a library especially for her. As they passed through the doorway of the beautiful building, she decided to spend the rest of her time in Greenwich rebuilding it. Better still, wouldn't it be wonderful to make a special library for Sally too?

Chapter Twenty-One

Ella

Present Day

Jakub greeted Sally and Ella like old friends when they arrived at the library. He sat with Sally at the central table under the dome, while Ella perused the fiction looking for F. Scott Fitzgerald so she could borrow a copy to read alongside her mum. Charlie had picked his copy up from their local library in Sydney and had told her how much he was enjoying Jay Gatsby's world.

It took Ella far longer than it should to find the Fitzgerald book because she kept coming across books she was compelled to take off the shelf. Titles called to her, then cover designs. She got lost in blurbs and found herself drawn in, opening books she couldn't resist and reading the first page. It seemed like every book she opened was enticing her to read on, exactly as they had when she was younger.

How had she resisted all these magical stories for so long? And why? She had to admit, it was a rejection of all that Sally loved. Under some delusional sense of not being like her mother, Ella had denied herself one of life's most simple pleasures: living multiple lives through someone else's words. Well, no more. It was time to make reading a priority again and she would encourage Willow to do the same.

She forced herself to leave the books, telling herself she could come back any time and retrieve them, but for now she just needed *The Great Gatsby*. She found a copy with an illustration of Gatsby on the cover, leaning on a balcony, smoking and looking wistfully off into the distance, and joined Jakub and her mother at the table. 'Got it.'

'Excellent,' said Jakub. 'You should get a membership of your own.'

Ella flushed, feeling like a child caught stealing from the corner shop. 'Is it against the rules, me using Mum's card?'

'Well,' he said, looking awkward, 'technically, yes, they are non-transferable, but Sally is with you, so I won't get out the handcuffs. But what I meant was, you're here for a while, aren't you?'

A shadow descended on Ella's mood, taking her by surprise. She'd been missing Willow terribly, and was experiencing an unexpected ache to see Charlie, but even so, the thought her visit was already halfway through made her toes curl up in her trainers. 'Only another two weeks.'

'Is that all?' said Jakub. 'Aw.' His head fell to the side and Ella couldn't look at her mum. She didn't want to see the sorrow she knew would be written all over her face.

'I've been meaning to ask, do you have art classes here?' The change of subject was clunky, but she needed to shift the focus away from her going back to Australia.

'We do.' Jakub's hands danced as he told her the times and dates.

Sally seemed distracted, her eyes on an unkempt man who had shuffled in pulling a battered shopping trolley behind him. The man was muttering something about Jesus. He wandered aimlessly, his lips moving constantly.

'Malcolm,' said Sally, standing and crossing the room to greet the man. 'I haven't seen you in ages. How are you?'

They started a conversation and Ella watched, mesmerised by her mother's gentle way with the man.

Jakub watched them too. 'Bless our Malcolm,' he said. 'He's been telling us Jesus is coming to save us for at least a decade by my reckoning. Ha! Reckoning. Look at me being all punny.' He grinned, still watching Sally. She and Malcolm were seated now, chatting earnestly. 'She's a superstar, your mum. Everyone loves her.'

'Even Pru?' Ella said. 'She doesn't seem too keen.'

'She struggles, our Pru. She seems to think an admission of humanity would be considered weakness. She's an anomaly, that one. She does so much good for the library, and the whole community, but smiling seems to be against her odd set of personal rules. I wish she'd lighten up. I'm sure there's a lovely woman in there somewhere, but she's determined to hide it.'

'She terrifies me.'

He leaned forwards. 'Me too. Sally's the only person who doesn't bow and scrape to her. That's probably why she gets the extra frosty Pru. I admire your mum for it, but I'm not brave enough to try it myself. Pru asks for a photocopy, I say *how many*?'

Malcolm was stroking Sally's cast, a concerned look on his face.

'She's probably the only person who's spoken to him all day,' said Jakub. 'We always have a few words, but there's usually someone who needs our attention before he's got through whichever Bible passage he wants to recite.' Jakub glanced up at the desk behind a Perspex screen, where a young woman was waiting. 'Speak of the devil. Oops, there I go again.'

He hurried behind the desk and apologised for keeping the young woman waiting. While he was occupied, Ella sent a text message to Verity with the details of the art classes before the information slipped from her mind. She grinned at the list of excited faces, paintbrushes and thumbs-up emojis that Verity sent in reply.

'She's still there,' Jakub said, when he returned a couple of minutes later. He nodded to Sally and Malcolm. 'She'll know the whole of the First Testament if you don't extract her soon.'

'Before I do,' said Ella, 'I wanted to ask you something.'

'Ask away.' Jakub fluttered his fingers, then knitted them together in front of himself.

'Would you consider helping me with a little project?'

'Go on.'

'Hannah, who has the book stall at the market, gave me the idea,' said Ella. 'You know how Mum built that library in our house over the years? With inscriptions in the books she chose for my birthday?'

'Yes. Such a gorgeous thing to do. I wish someone had built something like that for me. It must feel so special.'

'It does. I'm very fortunate.' She was beginning to understand what the accumulation of the library over all those years meant. The thought and love that had gone into it was more than some people experienced in a lifetime. 'And I'm going to rebuild it. I've already got a few of the ones I saw on the photo, and I'm planning to get the rest before I leave.'

'How lovely.' Jakub beamed, then frowned. 'How can I help?'

'I was thinking of doing the same for her: creating a library of books that mean something special.' The idea had taken shape in Ella's mind and now she couldn't keep the excitement from her voice. 'I've seen how much she means to everyone around here. I've met so many people since I've been back whose lives she's had a positive impact on. I was hoping you and some of the others might help me build a library of books from all of us to replace the special ones she lost. Would you choose a book that says something about what she means to you, and write an inscription inside? It doesn't have to be long—'

'Oh my God, yes!' Jakub interrupted. 'Absolutely! You know this is a librarian's dream? What a glorious idea.' His fists were bunched, and Ella could feel the enthusiasm coming off him. 'I want to start now. I'm going to make a list. It will be hard to find exactly the right one.' He glanced back at the desk and saw a man standing next to the screen. 'It's a yes from me. I won't be able to think of anything else until I've found the perfect book,' he stage-whispered over his shoulder as he went back to the counter.

Ella stood, about to reclaim her mother from Malcolm when, in her peripheral vision, she saw a figure hovering on the walkway near the library's entrance. Something about the furtive movements made her look more closely. It was a young man wearing black jogging bottoms and a grey hoodie, standing next to a metal cage-like box with no lid. Above was a sign that read: *Food bank contributions.*

She watched as the boy looked from left to right, then dipped his knees, reached into the cage and grabbed a tin from the inside. He shoved it into the pocket of the hoodie and walked nonchalantly towards the door. As he reached the exit, he glanced back over his shoulder. He caught her eye, then dipped his head and quickened his pace, rushing towards the street.

The clothes were different, but there was no mistaking the round face and the smattering of freckles on his nose. It was Nathan.

Chapter Twenty-Two

Ella

Present Day

Sally was quiet that evening.

'You all right?' said Ella, after dinner.

'Just tired, love,' said Sally. 'Okay with you if we sit and read tonight?'

'Perfect for me,' Ella replied. She couldn't wait to get back to Jay Gatsby and Long Island. She soon lost herself in the story, only stopping when, about seventy pages from the end, she read the words, '"What'll we do with ourselves this afternoon?" cried Daisy, "and the day after that, and the next thirty years?"'

She was reminded of the last conversation she'd had with Charlie. He'd read those words too and said to Ella, 'What do you really want from your life?'

They were getting on better than they had for a long time and now she thought about it, it was because they were talking more. Not the kind of talking they did at home, which was mostly about Willow, or who took the bins out last. They were talking about how they felt.

Now, in *The Great Gatsby*, she could feel the heat

and tension rising to a crescendo. Something terrible was about to happen. She thought about her relationship with Charlie. It didn't have the passion she felt coming from these pages, but it was deeper, grounded in trust and respect. She'd taken that for granted. She'd seen his steadiness as dull and his cheeriness as irritating and it had taken her to travel to the other side of the world to value him again, to hear what he had to say.

What would they do with themselves for the next thirty years? This novel was about how important having a purpose is. Charlie had said, 'Now Willow's older, I'd like to find a new purpose.'

Ella had been surprised, but it made complete sense. She was ashamed that she hadn't considered his needs. She'd been too busy feeling pious about how hard she worked. Now she could see this could be an exciting opportunity for real change in their lives. And what about her? Her purpose had been work, but was it truly fulfilling? She would give it serious thought.

'Mum.' She looked across at Sally, who was nearing the end of the short book. 'Why did you choose *The Great Gatsby* for the library? Do you remember?'

Sally slipped in her bookmark and turned towards her, her face serious. 'I hope you won't see it as a criticism.'

Ella inwardly winced, expecting a few home truths. This trip was a humbling experience, and humbled still wasn't her first choice of emotion. 'I'm braced.' She plumped a cushion and straightened to face the blow.

'I bought this one when you got that big promotion

at work.'

Ella cast her mind back to when she had been promoted two pay grades in a company restructure. It had felt dizzying and thrilling. She remembered emailing her mother the news.

'I was worried about you,' said Sally.

'Worried?' That didn't make any sense. She'd been excited. Proud even. Surely a mother could be expected to feel the same when their child achieved something. 'Why?'

Sally sighed. 'Don't take this the wrong way.'

Nothing good ever followed that phrase.

'But the email you sent felt like a corporate announcement. It was all about how senior your role was and how wonderful it was you'd been recognised in that way.'

'What's wrong with that?'

'I read about the restructure online. A lot of people lost their jobs.'

Ella blinked. 'Well, yes, but . . . That wasn't my fault.' Her jaw tightened.

'No, but you didn't mention it. There wasn't a hint that, although your luck was in, other people had suffered.'

'Jesus, I can't win with you, can I?'

'Let me finish,' Sally said, firmly. Ella had almost forgotten that part of Sally's success as a teacher was her ability to discipline calmly and effectively. If someone was generally warm and humorous, then people listened when they were sharp. 'It's not that I wasn't pleased for you. It was more that I was worried I hadn't done a good enough job as a mother.'

'What?' How could that possibly have anything to do with her getting a massive promotion?

Sally held the book up between her thumb and little finger. 'This is all about elitism and how privilege can ruin lives. The message is that what you have is nothing in comparison to who you are. I believe that to my core, but I was concerned that bringing you up here, in this house, in this affluent neighbourhood, had skewed your value system. Your father had a materialistic side. He wanted this house so badly, we almost went broke trying to pay for it. He wanted to be seen to be the best at everything, and money became more important to him than . . . I just didn't want to see you going down the same road and that email . . . it made me wonder.'

'I'm not obsessed with money,' said Ella. 'I was proud of what I'd achieved. I thought you would be too.' She was pouting and she couldn't shake the sense of injustice.

'I'm sorry if I misinterpreted you,' said Sally. 'Maybe if we'd spoken more . . .'

Ella huffed. She turned the book over in her hands, thinking about the reprehensible behaviour of Tom and Daisy. The comparison stung. 'Do you really think I'm spoiled and heartless?'

Sally laughed. 'Don't be such a drama queen. That's not what I said. If you listened, you'd know I said I was concerned we'd spoilt you.'

'That's not exactly what you said.'

Sally leaned forwards, a glint in her eye. 'Well, it's exactly what I meant.'

'So, you basically think I'm entitled and lacking in empathy.'

The book dropped from Sally's fingers, making a dull thud on the floor. Neither of them moved to pick it up. Hadron left her place by the chair and nudged the book with her paw. After a moment, Sally said, 'Let me give you an example of what I mean. You know when you met Nathan?'

'Yeah.' Ella's voice was sulky.

'You were ready to believe he used drugs and you also thought he was asking me for money.'

'I didn't—'

'I saw your face when I let him have the key to this house.'

Righteous indignation swelled in her chest. 'I was right. He's a thief.'

Sally shifted in her chair to stare at her daughter. 'What do you mean?'

'I saw him steal from the library earlier today.'

'A book? That doesn't make any sense. It's a library. It's free.'

'No, no. He took a can of something from that metal cage thing. The one for the food bank.'

Sally gasped. 'That poor young man.'

Ella paused, surprised by her mother's reaction. All of the indignation left her when she saw what her mother saw. Not a thief, or at least, not only a thief, but someone they both knew was struggling going to extreme measures because they were hungry. 'God, you're right,' she said.

Tears pooled in Sally's eyes. 'I told him to come to me if he was finding things hard.'

Ella remembered the way Nathan had looked at her in the library. He'd looked frightened. She wasn't surprised he hadn't visited Sally while she'd been there. She hadn't exactly been warm towards the poor boy. 'I bet it was me who put him off,' she said.

Sally stood. 'I'm going to put a few things from the cupboard in a bag,' she said, 'and drop them around now.'

'Let me.' Ella got to her feet. She put her hand on Sally's arm, then drew her into a hug. 'I'm sorry I haven't been empathetic, Mum. I do see what you mean, and I'm not proud of it. I'll pop to the shop and get a few essentials and drop them round to him.'

'Get him some treats, too,' said Sally. 'He's a good lad, you know. He's doing his best.'

***

Out in the cool evening air, Ella let the shame soak in. She had never been hungry in her life. When she was a student, her parents gave her an allowance that meant she only had to work during the long summer breaks, and she only used that money to pay for her holidays. She'd been so proud she'd paid for her own backpacking, but now she looked back, her summer holidays were spent working at the law firm where her father was partner. Pure nepotism. She did filing and covered the phones when the receptionist was on vacation, but it was hardly a stretch, since her dad drove her there and back, and, being the daughter of one of the bosses, she was always treated well.

Her mother was right; she'd lived a life of privilege and had told herself, because she worked hard, she deserved all she had. But hadn't her mum said that Nathan's mum had a cleaning job she couldn't always get to because of her illness? And she knew Nathan worked night shifts at the garage. Those were hard jobs. Probably harder than hers, especially at the level she was at. While Nathan's mum cleaned other people's toilets, Ella cleaned up corporate mess, which, more often than not, included mopping up after companies who were greedy, or mistreated their employees.

The mini-market's door swooped open; the air-conditioner cold on her face. Ella took a basket and filled it with staples, adding in crisps and packets of biscuits. After she paid, she walked from the shop, her steps made a little lighter with the hope of making amends.

Chapter Twenty-Three

Ella

Present Day

Nathan opened the door. His face fell when he saw Ella on the top step. He leaned on the door frame, gaze dropping to his trainers. 'All right?'

Ella lifted the carrier bag. The straps dug into her fingers. 'Can I come in?'

'It's not a good time.' He didn't look at the bag.

She shook it. 'I've brought some groceries.'

He raised his eyes to hers and she was surprised to see challenge there. 'Thanks, but I think you're better off donating that to the food bank.'

She let the bag fall back to her side. 'The food bank?'

'Yeah, I know you're trying to be . . . but I don't need saving.' He started to close the door.

Ella was so cross, she pushed the door with her foot. 'I'm trying to do the right thing here.'

'What?' said Nathan. 'Give to charity? I think we both agree there are probably more worthy causes.'

'I don't understand.' Ella was truly baffled. The boy was clearly in need of help. Why wouldn't he accept it?

172

'My mum was going to come but—'

'I'd have let Sally in.' He emphasised her mother's name in a way she found infuriating.

'Why?'

'Because she's my friend. Because she doesn't look at me like some kind of scrounger.'

Ella thought back to their earlier interactions and she couldn't say for certain she'd managed to keep her first impressions to herself. 'I'm sorry. I've been a judgemental idiot and I'm sorry.'

Nathan looked at her, clearly confused himself. 'Okay. No worries.' He nodded his head towards the hall, 'I've got to get ready for work, so . . .'

'Actually, I've come to ask you a favour,' Ella said. 'If you've got a minute, I'd really appreciate it.'

His eyes widened. He shrugged his shoulders briefly, then opened the door, stepping back to allow her in.

At first glance, the hallway appeared to be in a worse state than Sally's, but when Ella looked more closely, the decor was fine: it was the mess that gave the impression of disrepair. A shoe-shop's worth of trainers and sparkly high heels seemed to have been kicked off on one side of the hall and handbags and totes lay where they'd been dropped on the other, creating a peculiar runway down the middle. Coats of various styles and colours draped the banister and the light from a standard lamp that stood on the floor was muted by a pile of baseball caps sitting on top.

'That might be a fire hazard,' Ella said, pointing at the hats.

Nathan lifted them off and the room brightened, which did nothing to improve the look of the place. 'Ignore the mess,' he said. 'I've tried telling them, but they both have cleaners at home, so they seem to be waiting for the fairies to clear up after them as usual.'

There was a weariness in his voice. Ella wondered what it was like for him, living in luxurious surroundings that were treated so casually by those who were used to the privilege. 'How did you end up living with your housemates?'

'Cheapest option,' he said. 'Bonkers, right? Carla's dad doesn't need the rent, so he told her whatever she could get from letting the rooms, she could have as spending money. She sees herself as a bit of a saviour too.' He raised an eyebrow at her. 'So she lets me have it for under what they charge in halls as long as I don't complain about the mess and the parade of morons they bring around. It's a win-win.'

It didn't sound like much of a win to Ella. She'd lived with close friends at university. She remembered those years with enormous fondness, despite having lost touch with most of them when she moved away. Regret spasmed in her chest. It was like she'd shed the skin of her past when she went to Australia, but she was starting to realise she'd peeled off the good with the bad. And even the bad wasn't so bad after all.

She followed Nathan into the sitting room, which

was exactly the same dimensions as Sally's, but this one was filled with giant beanbags with random items of clothing scattered over them.

Nathan lifted a pink hoodie from the plumpest beanbag and gestured for Ella to sit. 'What can I do for you?'

She dropped the shopping on the floor and sat, feeling the air escape as she sank down. She was tempted to struggle into a more upright position, but didn't want to make a fool of herself, so stayed where she was, lying back with her arms squeezed to her sides. 'It's two things, really. The first is about a project I'm doing for Mum. You know she lost her library in the flood?'

'Yeah. That must've hurt. She loves her books, doesn't she?' His face brightened when he talked about Sally.

'I'm trying to rebuild it before I go home, and I want to add a few more books, and that's where I need your help. I was wondering if you could think of a book you love, that could relate to Mum in some way, and write her a short inscription in it.'

He looked confused. 'Can you give me an example?'

Ella thought for a second, then decided to lay herself bare. 'Okay. The one Mum and I were discussing before I went to the shops was *The Great Gatsby*.'

'What was the message: *be careful who you party with*?'

He'd clearly read the book. Ella was impressed. Then felt patronising for being impressed. 'I wish. It was actually: *don't be such a capitalist bastard*.'

Nathan barked out a laugh. 'Sally wrote that to you in a book?'

'Not exactly. I'll never know what the original inscription was, but it was along the lines of: *check your privilege and remember that who you are is more important than what you have.*'

'Nice message.'

'Unless it's from your own mother.' Ella bit her bottom lip and smiled. 'I probably needed to hear it, though. Just a shame it took decades longer than it should have for me to learn it.' His eyes had more warmth in them, and she was glad she'd come clean. 'But your message can be anything, maybe what you admire about her, or what she's taught you.'

'I like it.' He nodded. 'I can definitely do that. When do you want it by?'

She'd been ignoring the fact she only had a short time left in Greenwich, and now the reminder struck her like a blow. 'Next week? Is that okay?' She reached into her pocket and pulled out a ten-pound note. 'I know books are expensive . . .'

'No,' said Nathan. 'Thanks, but if I'm buying a present for Sally, it's coming out of my wages.' He checked his watch. 'And I need to get to work in a minute. You said there was something else?'

Ella struggled to her feet, the beanbag scrunching with her movements. 'I was wondering if you'd be able to meet me at the library tomorrow at four-ish.'

A shadow passed over his face. 'Are you going to

tell—'

She held her hand up. 'God, no, nothing like that. There's somebody I'd like you to meet.'

'All right,' he said, standing with considerably more agility than she'd managed. 'Mysterious. You've piqued my interest.'

'Good. This your uniform?' She pointed to his grey slacks and green fleece. 'Not half as interesting as your usual get-up.'

'Stops me being punched in the face by the locals for wearing a frilly blouse though, so every cloud . . .' He shrugged.

'Every cloud.' Ella wanted to hug him. Instead, she smiled and walked towards the door.

'You've forgotten your shopping.'

She turned. 'It's really heavy,' she said, pretending to droop. 'I can't carry it. Can I leave it here? Please?'

Nathan shook his head, a shy smile creeping onto his face. 'Just this once,' he said, wagging his finger.

'Just this once,' she agreed, and grinned all the way to her own front door.

Chapter Twenty-Four

Ella

Present Day

The builder who came around the following day was a different breed. He introduced himself as Bill the Builder and input all the information on an iPad, spending much of the time admiring the original features and talking about ways he could try to keep costs down. Ella watched Hadron sidle up to him coquettishly, definitely purring, not growling. Why didn't she do that with Ella? She'd started to think of the cat as a good judge of character, which wasn't ideal since, if this morning's bottom showing was anything to go by, she still found Ella decidedly lacking.

'I'll have a quote with you by the end of the week,' Bill said on his way out. 'I'll try to make it as painless as possible. They're money pits, these old houses, aren't they? I don't want you to worry. We'll sort it however it works for you.'

Ella joined her mother in the sitting room. She'd finished *The Great Gatsby* and was ready for another book from the list. 'Fancy coming down to Hannah's stall with me?' she said. 'I want to get a copy of *A Room of One's Own*.'

'What day is it?' Sally squinted at the small wristwatch she'd worn for as long as Ella could remember.

'That doesn't have the days of the week on, does it?' Ella asked.

'What doesn't?'

'Your watch. You asked what day it was, then looked at your watch.'

'Did I? Well, I didn't mean to look at my watch.' Sally viewed her through narrowed eyes, as though she didn't know what she was talking about.

'For goodness' sake, if the doctor hadn't said otherwise, I'd think you were definitely losing your marbles.' Ella watched Sally's reaction.

She bent and hooked the handles of her handbag over her cast, lifting it onto her knee.

'What are you looking for?' said Ella.

'Sorry?' Sally snapped, looking across at her, her face blank.

'You asked what day it was, then started rummaging in your handbag. Are you looking for your diary?' Ella pressed. 'Oh, it's not market day, is it? That's what you meant.'

Sally nodded, although her face didn't seem to register what Ella had said. She put the bag back down without taking anything out.

'I might pop to Waterstones, then. Won't hurt to buy one or two new, will it? I've got that book in my head now and it's a short one, so I could have it finished by the end of the day.'

'My little bookworm is back.' Sally was smiling at her in the way an adult smiles at a child. It was unnerving, especially after the previous confusing exchange.

'When's your next appointment at the doctor's?'

Sally frowned. 'What for?'

'Your hands.'

Sally lifted her hands and looked at them as though seeing the cast and bandages for the first time. 'Oh.'

Fingers of unease crept up Ella's spine. 'Mum,' she said carefully. 'I'm really worried about you. You seem a bit confused, like you're forgetting and misremembering things.'

'I've told you, I'm fine,' said Sally. Somehow, it seemed like she was back in the room with Ella. 'Brain like a sieve these days, that's all. The downside of getting old,' she added, now sounding completely normal.

'I think we should talk to the doctor at your next appointment.'

'Please, Ella, don't treat me like a child.'

There was nothing she could say to that.

***

They chatted normally for the next half an hour and Ella began to think she was imagining the apparent lapse in Sally's memory. After lunch, Sally decided to have a nap while Ella took a walk along the river.

She'd popped into the library on the way down

to Greenwich to talk to Jakub about Nathan, and her mood was high when she passed the clusters of excited schoolchildren queuing near the visitor centre surrounding the *Cutty Sark*. She turned right at the jetty where the boats set off to cruise up the river to Westminster and on to the Thames Path.

As Ella followed the path, the elegant pale stone of the naval college on her right seemed to glow in the sunshine as the wide river ran dark on the other side. She stood back against the railings as a small girl careered towards her on a scooter, sparkling tinsel flying from the handles as her mother, with a baby strapped to her chest, rushed after her. Much as this place had wound its way back into Ella's heart, the craving she felt for her own little girl at that moment was like a gnawing inside.

When she reached the Trafalgar Tavern, memories crowded her mind. Her parents had taken her to the naval-themed pub for birthday meals out in the fancy dining room upstairs, but her most vivid memory was of one winter night when she and her friends from sixth form had met up when a storm was brewing. They'd sat at a table near the enormous window that looked directly out over the river.

When they had first arrived, it was growing dark. Rain lashed at the window. She remembered being mesmerised by the patterns it made on the glass, tracing the rivulets with her finger. As darkness fell, the storm blew in and the water grew choppier, swells rising and falling, and that's when they saw a small boat being thrown about like a toy in the centre of the river.

Soon, everyone in the pub was watching as the boat was lifted and tossed. Ella's heart raced with every undulation, until, at last, the orange hull of a lifeboat came into view. They watched breathlessly as it sliced through the waves and came alongside the small vessel. There'd been a spontaneous round of applause when the RNLI boat appeared, and she could still feel the camaraderie and the sense of relief when the two boats travelled together along the black river and out of view.

Verity had been sitting next to her during all of it. Riding the wave of nostalgia, Ella took out her phone and invited her for dinner that evening, before popping into Waterstones and picking up a Penguin Pocket Hardback of *A Room of One's Own*. It was a beautiful edition with a sage green cover adorned with a pattern of diamonds and stripes.

Next on the list was the library. Nathan was already there when she arrived. He sauntered towards her, wearing a fabulous combination of red silk shirt, black waistcoat and harem pants that floated with every step.

'You look amazing,' she said. 'Thanks for coming.'

'What's with all the mystery?' he said.

'No mystery. Follow me.' She led him to where Jakub was standing behind the Perspex screen, checking out a pile of picture books for a toddler with her mother.

As they waited in line, he kept looking up and

grinning at them and when it was their turn, he clapped his hands together. 'Is this the young man you told me about?' he said.

Nathan looked at her, eyes full of concern. 'What did you say?'

'Only that I think you're entitled to more help than you're currently getting,' she stated. 'Last time I was here, I noticed that sign for free SIM cards.' She pointed at a green sign with a purple banner running across the top which said: *Speak to a team member today.* 'Jakub is a team member, and he's an expert on benefits and entitlements, so I thought it would be good to introduce the two of you to see if he can make any suggestions to make things easier for you.'

Nathan looked between the two of them, as if trying to formulate a response.

'It's not charity,' she said, quickly. 'It's making the most of what you're entitled to. Jakub might be able to advise you on how your mum might get some help too.'

'I'm West Greenwich's answer to Citizens Advice,' said Jakub, placing his hands emphatically on his chest. 'Partly because I used to work at Citizens Advice, to be fair. And if I don't know the answers, then I can help you find them.'

'I don't know.' Nathan looked torn.

'Helping people is my job. You don't want to come between a man and his calling, do you? Just give me half an hour,' said Jakub. 'Angela is taking over the desk, and I've allocated the time. What have you got to lose?'

'Yeah, what have you got to lose?' Ella nudged Nathan with her elbow.

'And when we've finished, you can tell me where you got that magnificent shirt,' said Jakub, coming around to their side of the desk. 'Are you studying fashion? You must be studying fashion.'

'Yeah,' said Nathan, smiling at last.

'I'll leave you two to it,' Ella said. She paused on her way out, watching Jakub pluck leaflets from a stand and hand them to Nathan. There was a sensation in her stomach she didn't recognise. It was warm and light. As she walked down the steps and turned left towards home, she realised the feeling was the unfamiliar glow of selflessness. And it felt very good indeed.

Chapter Twenty-Five

Ella

Present Day

With the pasta bake already in the oven on a low heat and the salad in the fridge, Ella was feeling quite pleased with herself. She was a woman on top of things. She was contentedly reading *A Room of One's Own* in the sitting room when Verity arrived.

Verity thrust a bunch of purple, pink and white delphiniums towards her and grinned when Ella opened the door. They kissed on both cheeks. Ella smelt the familiar scent of coconut in Verity's hair and a gush of warmth and nostalgia for her old friend made her give Verity an extra squeeze.

'Thank you,' she said, taking the blooms and smelling them. 'Aren't we grown-up, making dinner and buying flowers?'

Verity followed her into the hall. 'Do you remember when we tried to have dinner parties when we were in sixth form? That curry!' She laughed.

Ella did remember. It was one of the occasions when she'd noticed her life was different to that of many of her friends. A group of six girls had taken it in turns to have dinner parties. Ella had been first, and she'd used one of Sally's many cookbooks to choose a recipe. Sally had helped her buy and prepare the food and the event had taken place in candlelight in the kitchen they were heading for now.

The evening was a glorious success. They'd drunk red wine and eaten Bendicks after-dinner mints, and as she had closed the door behind her last guest, Ella had felt like a sophisticated, consummate host.

Following that, the dinner parties went from bad to worse. The other girls didn't have the spare money for fancy ingredients, or parents who had the time or energy to indulge their daughter's middle-class fantasies. The spate of disastrous evenings ended had in Verity's parents' flat, where she had made a curry so spicy, it was inedible.

'That was rank,' Ella said with a laugh. She turned on the stairs. 'And I don't think I've used the word *rank* for twenty years, either.'

'I bring out the youf in you,' Verity said in an exaggerated South London accent. 'Something smells nice.' At the foot of the stairs, she closed her eyes and breathed in. 'I'm getting garlic and onion with fishy undertones.'

'Tuna pasta bake,' said Ella. 'With a sprinkling of chilli flakes.'

'Not a whole packet of Scotch bonnet?' Verity roared with laughter again.

'I thought I heard your voice.' Sally came down the stairs behind them and joined them in the kitchen. 'Good to see you, Verity.'

'Hi, Mrs H.' As she walked further into the room, Verity pointed at the picture of the library stuck to the fridge door. 'Aw, is that the room that was spoiled in the flood?' She leaned forwards to examine it more closely. 'It's so pretty. You must be gutted it was ruined.'

Sally nodded, looking deflated. 'Gutted is a good word for it. I sometimes feel like a fish with its insides removed when I think of what was lost.'

'It's drying out nicely, at least. After that's done, I'll clear it out and we'll decide on next steps,' said Ella, wanting to move the conversation in a more positive direction. She had already formulated a plan, but wasn't about to disclose it now. She took a vase from the cupboard and filled it with water. 'What would you like to drink?'

'Whatever you've got,' said Verity. 'I'm not fussy. I'm just excited someone's cooking for me for a change.'

'Do you do all the cooking at home?' asked Sally. 'You'll have to forgive me, it's rare I spend an evening with someone who was once in my class. I often wonder about my students, what their lives are like now.'

'I hadn't thought of that,' said Ella, placing the vase on the windowsill. 'It must be weird, to see the same faces every day for a whole school year, then for them just to move on.'

Sally nodded. 'It's a strangely intense and transient relationship. I suspect the vast majority don't give me a second thought, but each one has a little place in my heart.'

The memory of her father telling her she had to work harder, otherwise she'd end up as a teacher like her mother, crawled unbidden into Ella's mind.

'Of course, this was back in the day when you had time to spend with the children, rather than training them for tests and filling in forms. It was already changing when I retired, and I imagine it's considerably worse now.'

'Do you really remember all the children?' said Verity, accepting a glass of white wine from Ella with a smile.

'Memory is a strange thing,' replied Sally. 'I remember you sat next to Emmie Wilkinson on the square table next to the bookshelf and I can see your curly handwriting in my mind's eye, but ask me what I had for lunch today and I couldn't tell you.'

'A ham and cheese wrap,' said Ella, pouring wine into her own glass. 'With salad on the side.'

'Sorry?'

'That's what you had for lunch.'

Sally shrugged, seemingly unaware of the concerned look on Ella's face. 'Well, that sounds delicious. I wish I could remember eating it . . . And I've quite forgotten my original question.'

'You asked Verity if she did all the cooking at home,' Ella said, with a touch of unease. She wished she knew what was a normal amount of memory loss for someone Sally's age.

'I do,' said Verity. 'And everything else.' She took a gulp of wine. 'I've created a monster. I should have known not to marry a man who still lived with his mum at twenty-eight. He went from her doing everything for him, to me doing everything for him. I'm not sure he even notices.'

'Is he a good man, though?' It was a direct question and Ella was surprised to hear it coming from Sally's mouth.

'Define good.' Verity shrugged. 'I mean, he's a decent bloke, goes to work, comes home, goes to the pub. He's not harming anyone.'

'Is that the best we can hope for?' Sally sighed. 'Even in this day and age?'

Her mother's candid reaction seemed out of character. Ella shifted uncomfortably in her chair. She moved to a safer subject. 'Did you go to that art class at the library?'

Verity's face brightened. 'Yes! Oh my God, Ella, I'm so grateful you put me on to that. It was' – her eyes moved from side to side above their heads, searching for the right words – 'magical.'

'Magical?' Ella arched an eyebrow. 'High praise. What made it magical?'

'It was the feeling I got. I mean, I wasn't brilliant at it, or anything. It's not like I've suddenly turned into Tracey Emin, it's just that . . . I loved every minute – the learning, the watching, the trying things out. We did pencil sketching this week and we're going to try watercolour next time. The tutor, this brilliant artist called Phil, he's asked me to bring in some delphiniums from the shop next time and I can't wait. I'm literally counting down the days.'

They all turned to the flowers on the windowsill. Ella imagined trying to capture the clusters of frilly purple and white petals on paper. 'I'm so glad you enjoyed it.' She was, but a sliver of envy stopped her in her tracks. Verity's uncomplicated enthusiasm, the glow she had when she talked about the class – Ella realised it was something she couldn't remember feeling for a long time in her own life.

She took the salad from the fridge and put it on the table, then opened the oven. The room filled with the smell of garlic and hot cheese. The top bubbled as she transferred it to the table.

'Shall I be mother?' She squelched a serving spoon into the dish and held her hand out for Verity's plate. After serving the pasta, she passed the salad tongs to Verity. 'It's so good you've got the art bug again. Are you going to practise at home?'

Verity dropped green leaves onto her plate. 'Nah. There isn't room.'

'Is it a one-bedroom place?' asked Sally, her gaze on Ella's hands as she grappled with the tongs to capture a tomato before depositing it on Sally's plate. She mouthed a thank you before taking a fork between her thumb and little finger and spearing a piece of penne.

'It's two bedrooms, but Luke's filled the spare room

190

with his racing set-up.' She glanced up and saw the confusion on Sally's face. 'It's a PlayStation thing. He's got this chair rig that's like a racing car and it's got pedals and stuff. You'd be surprised how much room it takes up. With that and the sofa bed . . .' She trailed off.

'Do you have a room of your own?'

The wording made Ella look up. She knew Sally had read the Virginia Woolf book because she'd read and reread everything in the lost library.

'What do you mean?'

'Virginia Woolf says that a woman needs money and a room of her own if she wants to write fiction,' Ella said.

'Write fiction?'

'You could substitute painting for fiction,' Ella said. 'It's the same sentiment. Virginia Woolf was saying male and female creative experiences are worlds apart. A man can just get on with it because he probably earns money of his own and has a woman behind him doing all the practical life stuff, like cooking and bringing up the children. A woman in her day couldn't hope to write a book unless she had independent money and a room of her own. And things haven't changed as much as we'd like.'

'Do you have money of your own?' Sally leaned forwards as if it was a matter of urgency.

'Mum,' said Ella. 'You can't ask people things like that.' Ella couldn't believe Sally was being so intrusive. It was completely out of character.

'It's all right,' said Verity, looking from one to the other, her gaze settling on Sally. 'I've got a bit saved up. But I don't have a room of my own. You've got me thinking, though. It's not fair, is it? I pay half the mortgage, half the bills and everything, but I don't get half the space, and I do nearly all the house stuff.'

'It's not fair,' said Sally, more loudly. 'It's not fair at all.'

'All right, Mum.' Heat rose in Ella's cheeks. Verity might be an old friend and her mother's ex-student, but it didn't mean she could be told how to live her life when she came around for tuna pasta bake.

'You mustn't let him control you,' Sally said, her voice wavering as though she was on the verge of tears. 'Don't let him take your money.'

'Mum,' chided Ella.

'It's all right,' said Verity. 'I won't, Mrs H, I promise.'

Ella watched in horror as Sally started to cry. 'A woman needs to have money,' she whimpered. 'Her own money. And he shouldn't tell her what to do. He should be kind and honest. She doesn't deserve it. She doesn't.'

Ella's embarrassment turned to concern. She rose and put her arm around Sally's shoulders. 'Are you okay, Mum? What's going on?'

'A room of one's own,' Sally repeated. 'Money and a room of one's own.'

Ella felt Verity by her side. 'It's all right, Mrs H. It's all okay.'

They exchanged worried glances over the top of Sally's head.

'*Is this usual?*' mouthed Verity.

'She hasn't been herself since the accident,' Ella whispered over Sally's crying. She needed to call the doctor and speak to them directly instead of trusting Sally to do it. In truth, Ella was starting to suspect Sally may not have been her usual self for longer than that. The thought stung harder because she should have noticed. Maybe she would have done if she hadn't been so wrapped up in her own life and so full of misplaced bitterness and self-righteousness. If she'd been the kind of daughter Sally deserved.

Chapter Twenty-Six

Sally

Twenty-One Years Ago

'I don't understand. Could you say that again?' Sally rubbed the heel of her hand along the hard wood of the chair arm. It slid too easily. She wanted to be at home in her own chair, not in this modern office with its stark furniture and even starker news.

The solicitor looked down at the documents on his desk, then up at her. His face was serious, but then everyone's faces had been serious since Neil had died. Everyone's except Ella's. Hers was more a mask of pain. Sally pushed away the image of her suffering daughter and tried again to concentrate on what the man was saying.

'Given the situation, perhaps you need to consider selling the house,' he said.

'Selling the house?' That's what she thought he said the first time, but it still didn't make sense. 'Why?'

The solicitor shuffled in his seat. 'Since there's very little left after the debts have been settled, and the mortgage still has years to run . . .' He adjusted his glasses, his fingers fussing with the arm, then knitting together in front of him. 'I'm just trying to find a solution to . . .' He trailed off.

Sally sat, dumbfounded. Where had all their money gone? She and Neil had both worked full-time, apart from the five years Sally took off to care for Ella before she went to school.

The solicitor removed his glasses and wiped them on a silky cloth. 'Things could have been very different if the investments your husband made had paid off, but' – he put the glasses back on and gave an apologetic shrug – 'unfortunately they didn't. It was always a gamble. He preferred high-risk, high-yield investments, and, as I'm sure you know, your lifestyle isn't cheap.'

His lifestyle, thought Sally, *not mine.*

'Mr Harrison was a member of three private members' clubs, and since you always travelled first class, well . . . it all adds up.'

Sally had never even travelled business class and the private members' clubs were news to her. 'I can't sell the house.'

'On your salary alone, it's not going to be easy.'

'I'm not selling our home.' One of Neil's arguments for buying such an expensive house was that it would be a valuable inheritance for any children they might have. Sally baulked at the memory. She could see now it was a status symbol. Nothing more. 'I can't take that away from Ella too.'

The solicitor lifted his hands from the desk. 'What

you choose to do going forward is up to you, Mrs Harrison. I only wish I had better news for you.'

Sally hadn't seemed able to absorb information fully since she got the call that Neil had had a fatal heart attack in his office at work. Everything had a sepia tinge. Sound had to get through some kind of barrier to reach her.

She walked out of the solicitor's office and onto the pavement. The sound of traffic on Greenwich High Street buzzed over, around and through her thoughts. Everything was jumbled.

A memory pierced the barrier and appeared in shocking technicolour. It was of her and Neil lying in bed, soon after they'd moved to Circus Street. 'I've opened a new account,' he'd said. 'I think it's best we have all our money in one place from now on.'

'Why?'

'Things are going to be tighter now we have a house of our own to pay for, so I want to make sure we don't overspend. It's best we have both our salaries paid into one pot and I'll put—'

'Don't say housekeeping,' Sally had said. 'I don't want to be a kept woman with pocket money.'

He'd raised an eyebrow. 'All right, women's lib.' He had smiled that winning smile. 'We'll call it your wages, shall we? You choose the amount and I'll get it transferred monthly. Then I know exactly what we've got and can manage it more easily. That all right?'

He'd made it all seem so reasonable. Of course, he'd known she'd only ask for essentials, nothing extravagant.

He'd dealt with all the finances, paid the bills, and if she ever needed anything, she only had to ask. There never seemed to be a shortage, so she never worried about the arrangement. Amongst her friends, it wasn't unusual for the man to be in charge of the finances, so she didn't give it much thought.

And now it was too late to ask him where the salary she'd worked so hard for had gone, or what had happened to the savings they should have accumulated. And if she wanted to keep their home, she was going to have to pay the mortgage on her teacher's salary alone.

She arrived outside the house on Circus Street and imagined Ella inside. She'd hardly eaten since she'd been home from university, and her eyes were swollen slits in her gaunt face. None of this was her fault. Neil had been devious and flagrant. She had been a fool. But Ella was innocent. And, for all his faults, Neil had loved his daughter, and she adored him back. That's why Sally had stayed. Now she had all the information, she wondered whether that had been the right choice after all. However much Neil loved Ella, he hadn't chosen to put her first. That had always been Sally's job.

She decided to keep the meeting with the solicitor and the state of her finances a secret. What was one more on top of all Neil's other misdemeanours, all that Sally had borne for the sake of her darling girl?

She walked up the steps and slipped her key into the lock, vowing that, whatever it took, Ella would always have a home on Circus Street.

Chapter Twenty-Seven

Ella

Present Day

The next morning, after checking that Sally was still asleep, Ella explained what had happened at the dinner with Verity to Charlie. 'So I'll need to be off the phone by eight so I can call the doctor.'

'That's worrying,' he said. 'I'm glad you've got Verity there. It would be hard dealing with all that on your own.'

Ella thought about that, realising she hadn't felt lonely since the first few days in England. 'That's the thing, I don't feel like I am on my own here. All mum's friends have kind of scooped me up, and the place feels so familiar. Being back in Greenwich . . . it's like nothing has changed, but my attitude towards it has. Does that make sense? It's like I'm seeing it properly for the first time.' She paused. 'Do you ever get hankerings to live back in the UK?'

'Is that a leading question?'

Was it? 'Not really. It's just that I've been walking by the river, going to the market and the library. I never appreciated how grand and, I don't know . . . attractive it is. It's not just that it's a nice place to live. It feels homely.'

'Homely?' It sounded like a question, but Ella didn't have time to respond before he carried on, 'By the way, did Willow tell you she's got this really cute, dweeby new friend called Sasha? They don't seem like a natural fit to me, but she's happier than she was.'

'Yeah, she did. She seemed more herself when we talked. Sasha's dad's in the military, right? They seem to live quite an itinerant life. I'm worried she'll get attached, then Sasha will move on.'

'I know. Bloody Harper's got a lot to answer for. I wish we could make everything easier for Willow, but we can't choose her friends. I wish we could, though.' He laughed. 'Said every parent ever.'

'If I was Queen of the World . . .'

'Exactly.' Charlie laughed. 'I got to the end of *The Great Gatsby*, by the way. Loved it. Did you?'

Ella remembered the conversation with her mother and blanched. 'You should have heard what Mum had to say to me about that one. She eviscerated me. Honestly, it was a smack in the teeth. The worst thing was, I couldn't even argue with her. Too much to tell you now. I'll email you later.'

'Now I'm intrigued. What's the next book?'

'*A Room of One's Own* by Virginia Woolf. The one that started Mum off last night. It's another short one. We're getting through them, aren't we?' She looked at the time on the top of the phone screen. 'Can you put Willow on? I've only got a few minutes.'

'Yep.' He shouted for Willow, his voice sounding very far away. 'Love you. Speak in the morning.'

'Love you too.' She tried to remember when they'd stopped saying that to each other in everyday life. Too long ago.

Willow was breathless when she got to the phone. She asked Ella to switch to FaceTime, then looked earnestly into the screen. 'I only came second in the science quiz.' Her mouth drooped and Ella so wanted to hold her.

'Second is good. Well done.'

Willow eyed her with suspicion. 'You usually ask who came top.'

Ella knew that was true. Ordinarily, if Willow didn't get the highest mark, she checked out the competition before saying anything about how well she'd done. Just like her father had with her, she thought now. It didn't feel good, but it had made her strive to be the very best the next time, and the time after that.

'Sasha says that it's not how well you've done that matters, it's if you've done your best.'

'Sasha sounds very wise,' said Ella, smiling back at her daughter on the screen. An eight-year-old girl was better at supporting her daughter than she was. 'I'm looking forward to meeting her when I get home.'

Willow still looked confused about this change in Ella. Ella imagined her saying: *Who are you and what have you done with my mummy?* 'I can't wait to see you. Will Grandma be coming with you?' Her accent sounded astonishingly strong.

'Afraid not. Just me, but maybe we could plan a trip for all of us to visit Grandma soon.'

The phone screen jigged, and Ella could imagine Willow kicking her legs like she did when she was excited. 'I'd love that! Sasha's been to London, and she thinks it's ripper that Grandma lives there.'

'It is ripper.' Ella laughed at how Australian the word sounded. She saw the numbers at the top of the screen turn to 7.59. 'I'm sorry, lovely, I've got to go. I need to make a call at eight.' If she could pull Willow through the screen and hold her, she would. 'I miss you so much. Love you.'

'Love you too, Mummy.'

'Love you,' Charlie yelled from the background. 'Speak to you later.'

Willow blew kisses, then the screen went blank.

Ella tried to keep the image of Willow in her head, rather than her father's voice, which echoed in her mind. She could hear him telling her to aim for the top, where she belonged. The phrase 'it's lonely at the top' occurred to her and caused her breath to falter.

She tapped out the number for Sally's doctor's surgery and pressed the call icon. First, she listened to an automated message for what seemed like forever, then Vivaldi's *Four Seasons* for eighteen interminable minutes, leaving her to ponder whether she really was someone who valued what they had over who they were. She didn't want to be. She knew that much.

'Hello, surgery,' a voice said, eventually.

'Hi, yes. Can I make an appointment for my mother please?'

'Is it an emergency?'

'Not an emergency, no, but I would like her to—'

'I've got an appointment on the ninth of June, so can you give me her name and—'

Ella stiffened. 'I was hoping to be able to come in with her. She's a bit forgetful and I live in Austra—'

'It's the first available, I'm afraid.'

'Is that really the best you can offer?' Ella couldn't keep the derision from her voice.

'Do you want the appointment?'

'All right, thanks.' If she was Queen of the World, doctor's receptionists would need to take an extended course on bedside manners before they were allowed near a telephone. She gave her mother's details and made a note of the time and date. At least Glenda would be back from Antibes then, so perhaps she could go along with her. She didn't like the thought of relying on neighbours to look out for her mum, but if Sally did have a memory problem, she could hardly ask her to remember an appointment, what to ask when she got there, and report the whole thing back verbatim. She needed to come up with a better solution, but until she did, she decided to keep the appointment to herself and monitor Sally closely so she had a clearer view of what might be happening.

She heard the post slap onto the tiles upstairs. She trudged up from the kitchen to collect it, then went up the next two flights to her mother's bedroom. Sally was sitting up in bed. She looked perfectly content, all traces of last night's upset gone. Ella thought about bringing it up, but Sally looked serene and rested, so she decided to let it go.

'All right if I open this mail?' she said, fanning it out for her mother to see. Sally nodded. They were all junk, except one from Lewisham Hospital Outpatient Department. Ella scanned the letter. 'You've got an appointment to get your fingers looked at the day after tomorrow,' she said. 'I expect they'll say you only have to wear the splint at night after that, if they've healed okay.'

'That'll be a relief,' said Sally. 'It will be a step up to only wear one arm condom in the shower.' She grinned. 'That's not a sentence I ever thought I'd say.'

That was the usual Sally. Maybe there wasn't anything wrong at all.

Ella helped her to get ready for her shower. She no longer noticed how thin Sally was, and neither of them was awkward or bashful about the process like they had been when Ella had first arrived.

'Coming to the market with me?' Ella asked after she'd dried Sally's hair at the dressing table in her bedroom. She watched her mother's face in the mirror. She seemed to be battling with something.

'I don't think I've got the energy,' she said. 'It takes it out of me, just getting cleaned up.'

'It will be easier when the splint's off those fingers.' She hoped that was true. Sally was more listless these days than Ella expected someone of her age to be. Or were her expectations too high? She was in her seventies. 'Mind if I pop out for an hour?'

She didn't want to miss an opportunity to go into the village. Ella felt the time she had left in Greenwich was spiralling away from her. When she had booked her flights, a month had seemed like an age. She had seen the days and weeks spreading before her like a lifetime of stilted conversations and duties.

But it hadn't been like that at all. The time had sped by. There weren't enough hours in the day for all the books she wanted to read and talk about with her mum, all the places she wanted to revisit, all the people she had discovered and rediscovered since she'd been home.

Home. She repeated the word in her head. What constituted a home?

Ella thought about their house in Sydney. She didn't get the warm feeling of home until she visualised Willow barrelling through the door, followed by Charlie. She glanced around her mother's bedroom, once again feeling the loss of her father when she saw his empty bedside table. But looking back at the mirror and seeing her mother's lined face in the glass, the feeling of home returned.

Home is where the people you love are, she decided.

'I'm on the lookout for *The Five People You Meet in Heaven* today.'

'I adore that book.' Sally smiled at her reflection. 'Say hello to Hannah for me. Tell her I'll pop down to see her soon.'

* * *

Ella bought the coffees before going to Hannah's stall. She mused at how strange it was that little over a fortnight ago, she'd forgotten this woman existed, and now they had a ritual together like old friends.

'Today's challenge is *The Five People You Meet in Heaven*,' said Ella. 'And, go!'

'Mitch Albom. A for Albom.' Hannah started to pick through the spines of books in the middle of the table. Less than a minute later, she threw a book with a blue cover with a small illustration of a Ferris wheel on top of the others on the stall.

Ella laughed and handed over the cappuccino. 'How much?'

'Not a cent. I'm still up on the deal,' Hannah said, holding her coffee aloft.

'Thank you.' Ella picked up the novel and turned it over in her fingers. 'I wonder what Mum wanted me to learn from this one,' she said. 'Hope it's not too brutal.'

'Your mum's never brutal,' said Hannah. 'She's got a heart of gold, that one.'

'You wouldn't want to get on the wrong side of her.' Ella slipped the book into her bag. 'She's fair, but she's definitely firm when she wants to be.'

'Ha! She's not a pushover, no, and that's a good thing

in my book. You know that when she says something, she means it; there's no bullshit. It's a rare quality. She's authentic; I think that's what it is. The world needs more authentic people.'

'You're not wrong.' Ella considered the word. It did describe her mother. She realised she'd like it to be a word people used to describe her too. 'I'm doing a little project for her, and hoped you might help,' she said. 'You gave me the idea, actually. How do you feel about choosing a book for Mum's new library? Something you think relates to her.'

'I don't remember having that idea, but I'm dazzled by my own brilliance.' Hannah scanned the heaving stall in front of her. 'How on earth will I choose?'

'Yeah, I think you and Jakub at the library have got the hardest job of everyone I'm asking. You've got too much choice. That's what you get for being literary oracles.'

'I'm going to get a new sign with that on,' said Hannah. 'Second-hand bookstall doesn't have the same ring as Stall of the Literary Oracle, does it?' She raised her hands and mimed a banner overhead.

'You should. It's catchy. Would you write something in the front of the book? Doesn't have to be long, just something personal.'

Hannah agreed and Ella was feeling pleased with herself as she set off back towards West Greenwich. Outside the Picturehouse, she saw Pru walking towards her in the direction of the town centre.

'Hello, Pru,' she said, when they drew close. 'I'm glad I bumped into you.'

Pru stopped but didn't smile. 'Oh, hello, Ella.' She tucked an escaped strand of hair behind her ear with a brisk gesture, as if even her own hair had to be dealt with quickly and efficiently.

She didn't look pleased to see Ella at all. 'You look well,' Ella said.

'Do I?' The words seemed to be said as a challenge, which made Ella regret trying to be nice. Pru could do with some of her mother's authenticity. Everything she said seemed to have a subtext that Ella had to dig around to find. 'I was disappointed not to see your mother at book group last night,' Pru scoffed. 'It's a bit of a blow to host an event and go out of my way to deliver the book when the supposed attendees don't show up or send their apologies.'

Ella started. No subtext there. Straight in with the blow. 'Oh. Sorry. I didn't know it was on last night.' She tried to remember if Pru had mentioned the date when she came around. 'I don't remember you telling us when it was.'

'Huh,' Pru huffed. 'I didn't think it necessary since your mother has been attending on the same day of the same week for over seven years. But I'm sure you're right – it was remiss of me not to send her a personalised, handwritten invitation.'

Ella wanted to tell her to wind her neck in, but, instead, said, 'Sorry. We had a guest over. My fault. I didn't check if Mum had a prior arrangement.'

'Yes, well.'

Yes, well, what? thought Ella, moving out of the way of a man in a wheelchair with a small dog on a lead.

'I need to get along. Have a good day.' Pru started to march away, leaving Ella wondering how she made *Have a good day* sound like a threat. Her head handed it back to her in the voice of The Terminator: *Have a good day, or else.*

'Sorry, hold on.' Ella caught her up. 'I was going to ask you a favour, actually.' Pru stopped, her mouth pinched in a tight line. 'I was hoping you could help with a project I'm doing.'

'I have little time for other peoples' projects,' said Pru. 'I have enough projects of my own to be getting on with.' She said 'projects' as if it was a filthy word.

'I'm hoping Mum's friends will each choose a book and write an inscription inside to help rebuild the library she lost in the flood.' Ella spoke fast, unable to shake the feeling that she was wasting precious seconds of Pru's time, and Pru was counting.

Pru shook her head. 'Typical.'

'What?'

'For a start off, it wasn't a flood. It wasn't some act of God in which innocent people lost their homes. She left the bath running.'

Ella was taken aback. 'Oh, yes, I suppose—'

'And I wish I had enough spare time to spend it thinking about which pretty words I could use to make your mother feel universally adored, but I don't. I'm sorry, but I won't be adding to your little library. I have too much to do at the actual library, the one that helps underprivileged people; those in actual need.'

She set off walking again. Ella was too stunned by the harshness of her words to do anything but watch her hunched shoulders disappear off down the road.

Chapter Twenty-Eight

Ella

Present Day

The time for Sally's hospital appointment had come and gone and the waiting room was getting fuller rather than emptier. A young man with a plastic boot on his right ankle sat heavily in the seat next to Ella, almost knocking her phone from her hand when he tried to balance a pair of crutches against his thigh. He apologised and Ella told him it was fine, not least because his citrus aftershave scent masked the smell of body odour that had filled the room before he arrived.

Ella looked back at her phone, peering at the photograph of the lost library. 'This copy of *Persuasion* looks old,' she said, leaning towards Sally. 'It's so strange how the title is split and hyphenated like that, instead of written along the spine.'

She enlarged the picture and Sally's gaze followed to where she pointed. Her face fell. 'That was a very precious book,' she said, her voice little above a whisper. 'I can't believe it's gone. It meant so much to me.' She paused, her lips tight as though trying to hold back tears.

'Anne's one of my favourite characters in literature. Such a wise girl, so full of love, always trying to do her best.'

Ella hoped the book was in her mother's collection because that's what Sally once thought of her. Maybe, one day, she would again.

'I have to admit,' said Sally, 'that wasn't one I bought for you.'

Ella swallowed down her disappointment. Served her right. Hubris never ended well. She should have learned that by now.

'I kept my most special books in that room. Familiar stories can become old friends after a while. That one was a present from a friend. Such a thoughtful gift. That version was published in nineteen fifty, you know.'

'The year you were born,' said Ella. A knot formed in her stomach. She hadn't worried too much about the covers of the books she'd replaced so far because she'd presumed it was the content that was important, but since this book was a precious gift published in that significant year, she should try to replace it like for like.

The young man's name was called, and he struggled to his feet, letting the crutches crash to the floor. Ella collected them and handed them to him and was rewarded with a grateful smile. Watching him clomp away, she couldn't help looking at the clock on the opposite wall, wondering why he was being seen before them. Perhaps it was a different doctor. One with fewer patients or better timekeeping. If she was Queen of the

World, patients would be teleported into the doctor's treatment room from their own homes at the moment the doctor was ready. Although, even she had to admit that one might be problematic to action.

After another half an hour, they were finally called through to the curtained-off area. After some examination, the nurse said, 'You only need to use the splint at night-time for the next two weeks, but don't try to do too much. You'll need a lot of physio before you're back to full movement, but we'll talk about that on your next visit. Okay?'

'Righto,' said Sally.

Her fingers were swollen and bruised, and Ella winced when the nurse asked Sally to move the joints. She could tell her mother was trying to be brave. She had the urge to wrap her in her arms and kiss the top of her head. She hardly recognised herself. She imagined Charlie saying, *Who are you and what have you done with my wife?* in an upper-class British voice.

These urges of protectiveness towards her mother were new. Sally was a capable woman. She'd never seemed to need much from Ella, even when she was younger. As Sally thanked the nurse and carefully pulled her cardigan sleeve over her fragile fingers, Ella understood it wasn't that Sally didn't need anything from her, it was more that she had given Ella the freedom to choose what she gave. She never asked for a hug. She didn't demand a phone call at a specific time. She didn't emotionally blackmail her into more contact.

She took what was offered without complaint and she gave her time, attention, warmth and love without the expectation of any of it in return. And Ella really hadn't given much in return. The knowledge of that made her want to slap her own face.

***

Back home, Ella tucked her legs under herself on the sofa and scoured the internet for a copy of the sage green, cloth-bound edition of *Persuasion*. Her heart lifted when she found one on a site called *Country House Library,* but when she clicked the button to put it in her shopping cart, a message popped up telling her it was sold out. She growled at the screen, and tried again, using all the search terms she could think of. Half an hour later, she was ready to throw her phone against the wall.

One last attempt led her to an edition in a private collection in Canterbury. It was on the website of a university professor who had a blog about his favourite books. Ella read what he wrote about *Persuasion* and found it incredibly moving. She'd never read the novel herself, but the professor's eloquent description of the love between Anne and Captain Wentworth made it clear this book meant a lot to him.

At the foot of the webpage there was an email address for Professor Walker. Canterbury was only about an hour away, and Ella thought she'd like to talk to the man who loved this novel as much as her mother clearly did. She knew his copy of the book wasn't going to be for sale, but he might know where she could get hold of another, and at the very least, she might learn more about what made the story special to Sally and, perhaps, get a little insight into her world. She'd neglected and dismissed her mother for far too long. Now she wanted to find out what made her tick.

She tapped out an email, asking if he'd possibly have the time for a conversation about the book, pressing send as Sally came into the room, followed by Hadron. Ella waited for the cat to clock her and growl, but she just padded across the room and curled up next to Sally's chair. No bum display, either. That was a first. Ella caught herself feeling grateful she hadn't been effectively flipped off by a one-eyed cat. How had it come to that?

'Have you seen my copy of *The Alchemist*?' Sally said. She held her hand against her stomach as if protecting the fingers now they weren't safely kept in place by the splint. 'It's book group tonight and I feel like I ought to go after Pru made the effort to bring the book.'

'Ah, I bumped into Pru the other day.' Ella cringed at the memory. 'Afraid you've missed book group. It was the night Verity came for dinner. I didn't realise it was that evening. Pru was a bit snotty about it, actually. I'm not a fan of that woman.'

'No,' said Sally, her brow furrowed. 'Book group is tonight. It's the third Monday of the month. It's always the third Monday of the month.'

'It's Thursday today, Mum. Remember, Verity came over on Monday and the hospital appointment was today. It's Thursday.'

Sally stared at her, patting her fingers on her abdomen nervously. 'It's Thursday?' Her voice wavered. 'I thought it was Monday.'

'Time flies. Don't worry, all the days blur for me as well,' said Ella, lightly.

Sally's troubled expression made her heart beat quickly. The fact she was visibly upset by her mistake made it worse. Questions crowded Ella's head, but now wasn't the time to quiz her mother. She needed to proceed cautiously so she had a clearer view of what the doctor needed to know when the appointment finally arrived.

But she would be on the other side of the world when that happened, she remembered. Ella watched as Sally sat down in her armchair, the heel of her hand rubbing slowly back and forwards along the fabric. 'Everything all right, Mum?' she asked, her voice gentle.

'Yes, love,' said Sally, giving her an unconvincing smile. 'Everything's fine.'

***

'I'm really sorry to do this, but I think I need to extend my stay for a couple of weeks,' Ella said to Charlie over the phone in a hushed voice. 'I feel awful about it, especially since Willow is having friendship issues.'

'Willow's fine. She and Sasha are joined at the hip

these days,' said Charlie. 'Two weeks, did you say?'

'Yeah. Willow did say she's getting on well with Sasha. Is she really all right or are you both just putting on a brave face for me? Tell me if it's not okay for me to stay. I know it's a lot to ask, but I'm worried about Mum.' She was speaking quickly. She didn't really know if she was doing the right thing. The guilt about Willow was competing with guilt about leaving her mum when she didn't know what was going on with her. Nobody told you that having any kind of family meant never being sure if you were doing the right thing.

'Please don't worry about Willow. She really is doing okay. I promise. Did it go badly at the hospital, then?'

Ella thought back to when Sally's hands were all they had to worry about. Simple times. 'It's not that. They took the splint off her fingers. They look really painful, but she's not complaining. It's her memory. Actually, it's loads of stuff, like that weird evening with Verity. Mum's told me that she's had tests and got the all-clear, but I can't help thinking she's hiding something. I couldn't get her a doctor's appointment until the ninth of June, and I really think I should be here for it. I'm quietly collecting evidence, which seems sneaky, but I want to be as clear as I can about what's going on, so when I come back to Oz, there's a plan in place. I just don't think I could settle if I come home without knowing for certain she's fit to be left on her own.'

'Is she that bad?'

Ella thought she heard a noise and paused, but it was

216

only Hadron banging into the ottoman. She switched position on the sofa so she could keep an eye on the door. 'I'm just not sure and I feel horribly guilty about that. It could be that she's just not as sharp as she was and that it's been a gradual, normal deterioration, but I've been away so long that I don't know. Isn't that terrible?'

'Well, we're fine here. Don't worry about us. Is work okay with you taking more time off?'

Ella noticed Charlie didn't reply to her question. It stung that she knew they would manage perfectly well without her. She had no right to feel sad about not being missed when she ordinarily spent more time at work than at home. 'Fuck work.' She smiled when Charlie audibly spluttered. 'But, yeah, they'll be fine. I'll take it as unpaid if I have to and tell them I'll do what I can on email.'

'I never thought I'd see the day . . . This has been an eye-opening trip for you, hasn't it?'

'And some. Wish I'd done it years ago.'

'There's a right time for most things,' Charlie said. 'This is happening now for a reason.'

'Funnily enough, our next book deals with that very thing. It's *Persuasion* by Jane Austen.'

'Okay. I'll get it from the library tomorrow.'

'Pop in and take a pic of Willow sleeping for me, will you? I miss sticking my head around the door and watching her gorgeous face when she's asleep. The thought of not seeing either of you for even longer hurts my heart.'

'I'll do that now. For what it's worth, I think you're doing the right thing. Love you. Bye.'

Doing the right thing? Ella thought about that when she lay in bed that night. She had been trying to do the right thing when she came to England, but now it felt like so much more than that. Now she was acting out of love.

Chapter Twenty-Nine

Ella

Present Day

It was a bright and sunny morning. When she was in Australia, if she imagined London, it was sheathed in drizzling rain, but since she'd been back, it had only rained three times. Another thing to add to the *fabrications for justifications* list she'd started in her head.

'Fancy a walk in the park, Mum?'

'I'm all right here, love, thank you.'

Ella gave her a sideways glance. Sally had always been an active woman. This reticence was definitely out of character. 'Please come with me. I'll be lonely on my own.'

After ten minutes cajoling, she managed to get Sally into her trainers and out in the sunshine. Nathan was in his usual spot on the front step, a plume of smoke spiralling up from his thin cigarette. He jumped up when he saw the two of them, a grin splitting his face. 'I was coming to see you when I'd finished my smoke.'

Ella was surprised to see he was talking to her, not Sally.

'I'm so bloody grateful to you.' He grimaced. 'Sorry for swearing, Sally.'

'Don't mind me,' said Sally. 'What's my daughter done to earn your gratitude?'

'She took me to the library,' he said. 'And introduced me to that Jakub fella.'

'Ah, lovely Jakub.' Sally smiled. 'We really must go and see his act again. You'll come along, won't you, Nathan?'

Nathan looked confused. 'What act?'

'Bridget Bard-Oh,' said Sally, as though that was self-explanatory.

Nathan's freckled nose scrunched. 'What are you on about?'

'He has a drag act called Bridget Bard-Oh,' clarified Ella. 'He performs comedy poetry.'

Nathan nodded, as if things were only marginally clearer.

'Anyway, tell me what Jakub said,' Ella said.

'He was brilliant; he rang my mum. Can you believe it?' He shook his head, a huge smile on his face. 'He told her exactly what she was entitled to, where to go for support in Manchester . . . just loads of really helpful stuff, and he's rung her every day since to get updates and keep her, you know, moving forwards. The man's a legend.'

His delight was infectious. 'And what about you?' Ella asked, aware he'd immediately thought about helping his mum, with no mention of himself. 'Has he managed to get you any help?'

'Yeah!' Nathan's eyes were wide. 'There's this bursary at uni that I didn't know anything about, and he's helped me apply for a SIM card for my phone and there's loads of stuff . . . I can't remember it all, but he's helping me keep track too.' He blinked. 'Oh, yeah, and I didn't know I could get support because of my ADHD as well. I've got an appointment with the disability something or other at uni next week. I think they give you programmes for your laptop and that, to make things easier, you know?'

Ella was swept up in his enthusiasm. 'Who said libraries were just for books, eh?'

'I know, right?' said Nathan, shaking his head again. 'I didn't have a clue. I wouldn't ever have thought of asking in there if you hadn't got me organised.'

A flood of affection washed through Ella. She held her arms out and he moved forwards to give her a hug. He was warm and kind and lovely, and Ella was so very pleased to have had some small part in making his life better. She wondered if this was how Sally felt every time she did a good deed. What a fantastic way to spend a life.

'Don't leave me out,' said Sally, opening her good arm wide and wrapping it as far around the pair as she could.

'Fancy a walk?' Ella said to Nathan when they released each other, still grinning.

'Thanks, but I've got to finish these.' He pointed at the pinned turn-ups at the bottom of his bottle-green trousers. 'Need to get the stitching done, then write my analysis before tomorrow.' He stubbed out the cigarette he'd left in a ramekin and climbed the steps to his house. 'See you later, people.'

They walked along Gloucester Circus, Ella admiring the majestic terrace on her right and the trees surrounding the private garden in the middle. She let out a contented sigh and hooked her arm through Sally's as they crossed Crooms Hill and entered Greenwich Park. They paused to let a little girl wobble past on a bike, her father following behind, one arm extended as if ready to catch her at any moment.

'How do you feel about me staying on for a couple of weeks?' said Ella, watching the little girl's wheels spin faster, her dad picking up the pace. She remembered her father teaching her to ride a bike in this very park, but when the memory came, it brought a shadow of fear with it. She recalled his voice, sharp and demanding, insisting she climbed back on the bike when she'd fallen off. The memory of the pedal smacking into her shin, making a lumpy purple bruise across her bony leg and her dad telling her not to be a crybaby and get back on. *Get back on now.*

'What about Willow?' said Sally. 'And work? You've got commitments at home, love.' She lifted her hand. 'And it's so much easier now I've got the use of my fingers back.'

'Willow's fine. She's happy that I FaceTime her after school every day and, to be honest, I don't usually see her much in the week when I'm at home. Of course I miss her, but technology makes it easier.'

'It's lovely, seeing her little face.' Sally grinned. 'She's such a gorgeous girl. I could eat her up.' Ella had started to make sure Willow and Sally had a chat in the mornings after they'd filled each other in on their days. She couldn't believe that, before her accident, Sally only saw Willow on a screen once a month. How cruel it had been on both of them that Ella had denied them time with each other. Sometimes, the guilt made her leave the room when Sally and Willow were chatting and giggling together. She would never make that mistake again. 'What about work?'

Ella flapped her hand dismissively. 'They'll survive. They can email me if they get desperate.' When her boss had replied to say it was fine for her to take unpaid leave, she'd been ashamed of how disgruntled she'd felt. Before coming back to England, she'd told herself she was indispensable. That had been her excuse to herself and to Charlie for the long hours she worked and all the time she spent on her computer at home.

Yet when she took six weeks off, nobody died. Nobody even blinked an eyelid. What did that tell her? More than she wanted to admit.

'Well, if you're sure,' said Sally, as they fell into step along the path. 'That would be wonderful – really, really wonderful.'

'I'm sure,' said Ella.

An email alert buzzed on her phone. She unhooked

223

her arm from Sally's and took it from her pocket. The email was from Professor Walker, the man with the special copy of *Persuasion*. He was inviting her to his office at the university to see the book and discuss it. That was much more than she'd hoped for. The thrill of anticipation put a bounce in her step.

'Fancy a trip to Canterbury tomorrow?' she said, breezily. It might be a nice surprise for her mum to meet someone else who loved the book as much as she did.

'Canterbury?' asked Sally, turning to her with a frown.

'Thought it might be nice to have a day out.'

Sally shook her head. 'I don't think so.'

Ella was confused. 'It's meant to be beautiful, especially if the weather's like this.'

'No thank you.' Sally picked up the pace, marching up the path towards the observatory.

'Why not?' Ella took long strides to keep up.

Sally stopped. She closed her eyes. 'I think I'll go back. I'm feeling a bit tired.' She did an about-turn and walked back down the path towards home.

'You okay?' Ella had to raise her voice to reach her mum, who was now marching away. This sudden mood change was similar to the one when Verity came for dinner. Ella made a mental note to add it to the list she was keeping in her bedroom.

'Just tired,' said Sally.

She went straight to her room when they got home, leaving Ella to wonder what on earth had caused such an odd reaction. She decided not to mention her trip the following day again, since it seemed unlikely to result in her finding a copy of the book to buy. Instead, she called Hannah, who seemed delighted at the request to keep Sally company while Ella took the train to Canterbury on her own.

Chapter Thirty

Sally

Twenty-One Years Ago

The last funeral Sally had been to, everyone had been asked to wear bright colours. But that was a memorial for Elaine, one of the early members of The LCG and she'd lived a long and fulfilled life. The funeral was a celebration of ninety well-lived years, and there had been a kind of joy when the congregation sang 'All Things Bright and Beautiful', and toasted Elaine with champagne at the wake.

This was different. Nobody could say Neil had lived a long life. 'He was taken too soon' was the phrase Sally had heard over and over again. It seemed only right to wear black. It certainly matched her mood. She felt black inside and out. The only colour left in her crumbling world was brought by Ella.

She checked her watch, then walked to the foot of the stairs and called up, 'The car will be here soon. Come on, love. We don't want to be late.' She waited, but there was no reply. 'Ella,' she called. 'Are you ready?'

She listened, and thought she heard crying. Her heart

dropped even further. She didn't know how she was going to get through the day, so had no idea how Ella would cope. Sally had been numbed by all she'd learned about her husband in the days since he'd died. Ella's grief was sitting on her skin like exposed nerves.

When she poked her head into Ella's bedroom, she expected to find her on her bed, sobbing into her pillow, like she had so many times since she had arrived home, but the room was empty. Sally went to the foot of the stairs leading up to her own bedroom on the third floor. The sound of sobbing drew her up.

'I'm sorry, love,' she said, as she approached the bedroom. 'I know this is hard, but we've got to go.' The sound of gasping sobs made her heart contract. 'Oh, darling.' Ella was sitting on the floor with her back to her. Her shoulders bounced with juddering breaths. 'Ella, love—'

Ella spun around. She jumped to her feet. Two angry red spots burned on her cheeks; the rest of her face was grey. 'How could you?' she screamed, making Sally jump back. 'How could you do it to him?'

Sally didn't understand. She took a step forwards, but Ella recoiled.

'Don't come near me.'

'What's happened?' Sally scanned the room, looking for anything that might explain this astonishing outburst.

'I was looking for that book of poems you said I'd find comforting. You said it was next to your bed. But I found that instead.' She pointed to the floor. Next to

Sally's bedside cabinet was a piece of paper. From where she stood, frozen by the door, Sally could see the wet imprint of tears like pockmarks on the letter. She saw the headed paper. The writing. The words she'd read over and over again to sustain herself when nothing else could.

And then her world tipped.

Chapter Thirty-One

Ella

Present Day

Ella walked from the station to the city-centre campus, then followed the directions on the email until she came to the red-brick Creative Arts building. On the second floor, she found Room Two and knocked.

'Ella Harrison?' A tall man with white hair and kind eyes opened the door and held out his hand. 'How wonderful of you to come. I trust you had a pleasant journey?'

'Yes, lovely, thank you. It's so nice of you to make the time to see me, Professor Walker.' Ella shook his hand and smiled back at him. His eyes searched her face with an intensity that was unnerving.

He released her hand and gave a brief head shake, as if waking from a trance. 'Please, come into my office.' He led her into a modern, square office, which was lined with shelves and shelves of books. An incongruous dark wood desk sat to the left and on it she saw the sage green book.

Professor Walker gestured for her to sit in one of the

small armchairs under the window. He picked up the book and sat in the other. 'You said in your email that your mother's copy of *Persuasion* was damaged in a flood?'

'That's right.' Pru's words replayed in her head, but she resisted the urge to minimise what had happened to Sally's little library. 'Unfortunately, all the books were waterlogged. She'd spent years building it up. It wasn't valuable or anything, just precious.'

'Precious beats valuable in my book,' said the professor, then gave a quiet laugh. 'In my book. Ha.' He shook the book in his hand for emphasis.

'I agree,' said Ella, scanning the walls of books. 'You have an impressive library here.'

The professor's eyes followed hers. He let out a sigh. 'All special,' he said. 'Although, what book isn't precious? Each one contains someone's thoughts and feelings, doesn't it? And if you believe every individual's life matters, and I do, then to have captured something of someone's inner world in the pages of a novel' – he let out a long breath – 'it's like holding the magic of their soul within those pages for time immemorial.' He cocked his head to the side and grinned. 'And that's before we get to the beauty of language, the characters and the stories we can learn from.'

For a second, Ella was eighteen again, trying to decide what to study at university. Sally had encouraged her to study literature, saying similar things to what the professor said now. But her father's voice was louder and more persuasive. *Money makes the world go round,* he'd said. *Any fool can read a book.* So, she'd chosen law instead. She turned back to the professor, painfully aware it wasn't just her father's insistence that had influenced her, it was the fact she respected him more. She wanted to please him and make him proud.

Now she accepted what she'd always known deep down – her mother was already unwaveringly proud of her, and Ella hadn't valued that unconditional love and acceptance at all. She'd denied herself all those books with their unique and magical thoughts, characters and enriching stories, for what?

'Is this a bad time to admit I haven't read *Persuasion*?' she said, grimacing.

He raised his eyes to the ceiling. 'Oh, how I envy you. What a joy you have in store!'

Ella loved that response. She'd been nervous he'd judge her for wasting his time, even though she'd explained in her email that she wanted to discuss the book because of her mother.

'Would you mind telling me about the novel?' she said. 'I've read your blog, but . . .' She paused. His warm eyes watched her, giving her the confidence to be honest. 'I've been estranged from my mum . . . well, distant at least, for a long time, and now we're in the process of repairing the damage. I got the impression that this book, in particular, meant a great deal to her. I feel like, if I heard about it from someone else who's passionate about it, I might learn something more than if I read it myself, and I might be able to understand Mum a bit better.'

'How thoughtful,' he said. 'I'm sure she's incredibly proud of you, and always has been, whatever the distance.'

Ella looked down at the carpet, scuffing her shoe on the wiry fibres. 'I'm starting to suspect that's true.'

'"Pride is one of the seven deadly sins; but it cannot be the pride of a mother in her children, for that is a compound of two cardinal virtues – faith and hope."' His voice had a sing-song quality that made her look up at his face.

'Faith and hope,' she said, thinking of how that sentiment applied to Sally and how true it was of her own feelings towards Willow. 'That's a great quote. Is it from *Persuasion*?'

'Sadly not. It's Charles Dickens, but he knew a thing or two about what motivates people.' He smiled, his laughter lines deepening. They were more pronounced than his frown lines and his eyes had a softness that made her feel strangely safe. Ella assessed he was a similar age to Sally and felt sorry she wasn't there. She suspected they'd get on. 'What do you want to know?' He opened the cover and flicked through the pages.

'Erm . . .' She wished now that she'd noted down questions. 'Why is it one of your favourites?'

He rested his hand on an open page and looked up, as though absorbing his answer by osmosis. 'I think it's actually my favourite book of all time,' he said, 'and

I've read a few.' He took a deep breath. 'First, there's the social commentary about class and social mobility. As I've already said, I believe each individual has equal worth, so the fact Austen is subtly subversive about her support for change in societal structures appeals to me. Neither of us is revolutionary, but we believe in social flexibility.'

Ella nodded. She thought of how Sally treated everyone the same, from Malcolm, the man in the library who trundled his worldly possessions around with him in his shopping trolley, to Glenda next door who spent each May at her house in Antibes. She treated everyone with respect, without exception. Ella couldn't say the same about her father. He would bark orders at waiting staff. She remembered how embarrassed it had made her when she was a teenager. Not that she'd dared say anything to him.

'I also enjoy the question Austen poses about duty.' Professor Walker's face turned serious. 'It's something I discuss with every cohort I teach. To whom do we owe duty? Is it to ourselves, or our parents, spouses, children, society as a whole? Who teaches us our duties, and are they worthy of such responsibility? Should we be persuaded by people we respect, or should we only take our own counsel?'

'And what have you decided?' It was a fascinating question and Ella was interested in this intelligent man's answer.

'Oh, how long have you got?' He slapped his hand

down on the book. 'First, we'd have to define duty. Is it simply a social construct, or do we include what's instinctive, like the mother's instinct to protect her young? In the first instance, it's complicated – like when you're told to put your own oxygen mask on before helping anyone else if a plane crashes. Would we? Should we? Isn't it our duty to protect those who are weaker or less able? But then, if we are impaired, how can we help others?

'Also, I think the duty of a parent to a child is more straightforward than that of the child to the parent. Mostly, a parent has chosen to bring a child into the world. A child does not elect to be born. But sometimes parents fail to do right by their children, and if you look at what society perceives as a mother's duty in comparison to a father's, that's a whole new discussion point.'

Ella smiled. 'That's a can of worms, right there.' An image of Charlie comforting Willow after a tumble appeared in her mind and she felt a surge of gratitude to him for being brave enough to break the traditional mould.

'Indeed,' said the professor. 'But what I love most about this book is the love story of Anne and Captain Wentworth.'

'I wish I'd read it before I came,' admitted Ella, feeling foolish she didn't know what he was talking about.

'I find it a hopeful love story,' he continued, a wistful look in his eye. 'They were parted because of circumstances, and because Anne thought she was doing the right thing – what she was persuaded was her duty.'

'But they had a happy ending?' asked Ella, hopefully.

'Eventually.' Professor Walker smiled sadly, and Ella wondered what was behind that smile. He held the book up. 'I'd like you to take this.'

Ella blinked. 'No! I mean . . . that's not why I came . . .'

He pressed the book into her hand. 'I wouldn't offer it if I thought you had. I want you to take it because you came here for someone else. You want to repair your relationship and understand your mother. And you want her to be happy.'

Ella tried to hand the book back, but he raised his arms and stood.

'I'm afraid I have a lecture in a few minutes, so I really must get along.'

'But . . . can I at least pay you for—'

'Absolutely not. Please do me the favour of emailing me your thoughts on the book – that, and the thought of your mother's smile, will be payment enough.' He walked to the door and held it open.

Ella was lost for words. The cloth book jacket felt rough under her fingers. She walked to the door, wishing she could think of some way to adequately express her gratitude. 'I will let you know. I'm sure I'll love it. Mum will be so pleased. Thank you.' She stepped over the threshold to the corridor and turned back. 'Thank you again. It was lovely to meet you.'

'It's been my pleasure,' he said, his voice cracking, as he turned abruptly and closed the door.

Chapter Thirty-Two

Ella

Present Day

Hannah left ten minutes after Ella got home from Canterbury and much as Ella would have loved to sit down and start to read, she hauled her weary self down to the kitchen to start making dinner.

'Come and chat to me while I make the stir-fry,' she said to Sally.

It was strange Sally hadn't asked how she'd got on. When she was younger, Sally always asked about her day as soon as she got in. It had been one of the most irritating things about her when Ella was a teenager, as if Sally was trying to keep tabs on her, interfere with her life.

Now Ella was a mother herself, she understood that need to know more about a child's life when they were out of sight. She craved information about Willow's day. The fact her daughter was at school more than at home felt like a gaping hole of time where Ella couldn't access her. If she was Queen of the World, schools would have webcams so parents could watch their children during the day. She paused the thought. That would probably cause more problems than it solved . . . and be slightly weird. Her Queen of the World ideas used to be a comfort. Now she was starting to see that there was rarely a clear-cut right or wrong in any situation.

In the kitchen, Ella poured them both a glass of wine, taking a big glug of hers. It was cold and fruity and delicious. She took another gulp and refilled her glass.

'Can I help?' asked Sally. 'Now my hand is free?' She waved her hand regally.

'Aren't you meant to rest it?'

'I could chop things if they weren't too tough,' she said, 'and if the knife's sharp enough. Give me that little paring knife and I'll slice the mushrooms.'

Ella hesitated by the cutlery drawer.

'Come on,' said Sally. 'I'll stop if it hurts. Promise.' She winked.

Wondering when this strange role reversal had taken place, Ella washed the mushrooms and put them in a bowl, along with a chopping board and the knife on the table in front of Sally. She got the rest of the ingredients out of the fridge, and they worked in companionable silence until Sally said, 'Voilà.'

Ella saw all the neatly sliced mushrooms and grinned. 'Get you, master chef,' she said.

'Pass me the coriander,' Sally said. 'I'm unstoppable now.'

'Don't overdo it.' Ella swooped the mushrooms back into the bowl and put the fragrant bunch of herbs on the board. 'Stop if you feel so much as a twinge.'

'Yes, boss.'

The smell of hot olive oil made Ella turn back to the stove and slide the thin slivers of chicken breast into the pan, drawing her hand away as oil spattered out, stinging her skin.

Over the sound of sizzling, she heard Sally laughing quietly behind her.

'What's funny?'

'Oh, I was just remembering how what was meant to be a romantic meal went horribly wrong when the chef put coriander on Andrew's meal when he'd expressly told him he shouldn't. He always said it tasted like soap. You should have seen his face. It really was as if someone had washed his mouth out with Fairy Liquid.'

Ella stilled, a pressure building inside her head.

'He hated the stuff,' Sally added.

Ella watched the chicken strips sizzle and brown, her pulse thundering in her throat. 'Did you two have a lot of romantic dinners?'

'Only when we could fit them in. Things always seemed to get in the way.'

'I'm sure they did,' Ella said through gritted teeth. Sally seemed so oblivious to her mistake, it would have been laughable, if it wasn't for the fact it was clearly Ella and her father who had got in the way. 'So, this romantic dinner,' she continued, 'when was that?'

'I expect you were about six or seven. I can't remember exactly.'

Ella turned, astonished to see Sally was smiling. 'When I was six or seven?'

'Yes.' Sally looked up. 'What's the matter?'

'Are you kidding me? You glibly throw in a story about a romantic dinner you had with Andrew and you're asking me what's wrong?' She shook her head. 'I knew I shouldn't have believed you. I knew I was right about that letter. You were having an affair all that time and now you're just acting like it's no big deal?'

Sally dropped the knife. 'I don't know—'

'I can't believe I took it all in,' Ella said, her mind returning to all the times she'd berated herself for condemning Sally without knowing all the facts. 'You really made me believe you.'

'Ella, no—'

'Don't try to deny it now.' She calculated the years of betrayal in her head. 'So, if you were having romantic dinners with Andrew when I was six, and I didn't find the letter until I was twenty-one . . . Jesus!' She threw her hands up in the air. 'It was pretty much for the whole of your marriage, the majority of my life.'

The smell of burning made her turn back to the hob. She switched it off. 'Don't want to burn the house down, do we? Or you might have to get me back here again to look after you; because that's what this has all been about, isn't it? You needed me to look after you and you were willing to lie and manipulate me to get what you wanted. This kind old lady act is just that. It's an act, and I fell for it. Everyone around here did.'

Tears streamed down Sally's face. 'I didn't mean to say Andrew.'

'What?'

'If I said Andrew, I'm sorry—'

Ella gasped, feeling a new betrayal open up the old wound. 'I don't suppose you did mean to say it. It doesn't fit with your story, does it? But lies will come out, won't they?' She couldn't bear to see the tears of self-pity running down Sally's face. She left the pan, the chicken limp and greasy, and marched from the room.

Chapter Thirty-Three

Ella

Present Day

Ella's heart was still racing from the confrontation with Sally when she heard a tapping on her bedroom door. When she opened it, her mother was standing on the landing, a piece of paper in her hand. Her senses heightened by distress, Ella was aware of the low hum of the dehumidifier from the room across the landing, like the collective voices of characters from the ruined books, all judging her.

She nodded at the paper. 'What's this, a sworn testimony?'

'I'm sorry you were hurt by what I said, but I swear on my life, it was a mistake. It was Neil who didn't like coriander. It was Neil I was eating with that evening. I don't always find the right words . . .' Sally's eyes were rimmed with red. She held the paper out. 'I should have shown this to you before. I can see that now. I've been an idiot.'

Ella huffed. 'More secrets? Great.' She walked past Sally and went downstairs. 'I need a drink.'

241

Ella glugged wine into her glass, not looking up when she heard Sally's slow footsteps follow her to the kitchen.

Sally put the paper on the table and unfolded it. She flattened it with a shaking hand. 'I hope this will explain how I made such a stupid error.'

There was a blue box at the top of the paper with white letters spelling out NHS. Ella glanced up at her mother's worried face. 'What's this?'

'I had some tests, before you came, before I flooded the bathroom. I got the results that day I went to the doctor's.'

Ella's knees weakened. She looked at the letter but only got as far as *Lewisham and Greenwich NHS Trust* before her eyes seemed to film over.

'It was a memory test. I think it's called the memory clinic, but I'm not sure. I'm not too sure of anything anymore,' Sally confessed.

'But you said . . .'

Sally shook her head. 'I know. I'm a stupid, stupid woman. I didn't want to face it. I didn't want you to worry. I don't know what I was thinking.'

'So it's . . . Alzheimer's?' Ella's voice shook.

Sally sat, smoothing her hand across the paper. 'That's not certain yet. I've got to have an MRI on my brain and more tests, but it's some kind of dementia, yes.'

'But you said . . .' Ella still couldn't grasp the enormity of it. Her head swam. 'You said it was a urine infection making you forgetful.'

'I did have one of those, when I went into hospital. I

242

wasn't lying about that. But these memory lapses have been going on for quite a while. I'm so sorry I kept it from you. I thought I was doing it for the right reasons, but I can see I've just made things worse. When I got the test results, I suppose I wanted to let it sink in, try to decide what to do for the best. You were only here for a short time, I didn't want to ruin it with more bad news, and I didn't want you to have to worry about me when you went back. I shouldn't have lied. It was stupid of me.'

'But you're only seventy-two,' said Ella, knowing it was a pointless thing to say. She wanted to say: *It's not fair, it can't be right. I've only just found you again, I can't lose you. I can't watch you disappear when you're still here.*

'I'm sorry, love. I didn't want to put you through this.'

The sincerity in that apology made Ella's heart break. Ten minutes ago, she'd been convinced her mother was a manipulative, deceitful charlatan. Now, Ella could see she was distressed and suffering, and it was all too much to bear.

'I'm sorry, Mum,' she said. 'I'm sorry I doubted you. I should have learned better by now. And I knew Dad didn't like coriander.' It seemed like the most ridiculous and futile thing to say, but she didn't have any more words. Her thoughts were filled with the enormity of it all. Her mum had an incurable condition that would eat away the essence of her. She cloaked Sally in her arms, and they sobbed together for all they had lost and all the loss to come.

***

After ten minutes, Sally wiped the tears from Ella's face with her swollen finger. 'My lovely girl. I wish I could have protected you from this.'

'I wish you'd told me. Things would have made more sense.'

Sally sighed. 'I was going to, but it hadn't been confirmed when you first arrived. I was in denial, I suppose. I'd been hoping it was . . . I don't know. Not this. Then, we were having such a lovely time, I didn't want to ruin it. It's such a burden to put on a child.'

'I'm forty-two.'

Sally fixed her with a firm look. 'You'll always be my child.' She folded and unfolded the letter. 'And now there's so much to unravel. The house is a mess and—'

'We don't need to worry about that,' said Ella. 'I once heard somebody say if it can be fixed by money, then it's not a real problem. I don't know who it was, but I agree with them right now.'

'What money?' said Sally.

'Well, I know you don't have insurance—'

'I'm so sorry about that.'

Everything was falling into place in Ella's mind: the lapsed insurance, Sally's unwillingness to leave the house. 'It's not your fault.'

'It is, though, isn't it? If I hadn't let the insurance expire, they'd be dealing with this.'

'We don't have to talk about this now.'

'Do you mind if we do?' Sally said. 'I feel like I've been

244

keeping things to myself for so long and . . . well, I don't know how long I'm going to be lucid for. Sometimes I wake up with a sense of dread, like I know something awful has happened, but I can't pinpoint exactly what.'

'Oh, Mum.' She stroked the back of Sally's hand and felt it tremble.

'I think I'd like to get a start on things while I still can.'

'Okay. I can take over all the—'

'No thank you.' Sally took a gulp of air. 'It's important to me I still feel useful and as normal as possible for as long as I can. I'd like to be involved, but I do need you to know the truth. All of it. I think that's the only way we'll get through this together.'

Ella nodded and stayed quiet.

'For a start, the house is a constant worry, and I don't know what to do about it. It's a listed building. It's all got to be repaired in accordance with the rules.'

'So . . .' Ella said, not quite knowing how to broach the subject of how much money Sally actually had. 'Did Dad leave enough to . . . ?'

Sally gave her head a brief shake. 'We still had a mortgage when your dad died. He'd made some bad investments, and had an expensive lifestyle apparently, so there wasn't really any money to leave.'

'What?' Ella was confused. She hadn't received a penny from her dad's will and she'd presumed he'd left a significant amount to Sally.

Sally scrunched her eyes tight. 'I know how much you

245

loved your father, so I didn't want to have to tell you any of this, but in the current situation . . .' She paused. 'And he loved you. What I'm going to tell you doesn't change that. He always loved you – you know that?'

'I know.' Ella's throat constricted. She swallowed. 'Go on.'

Sally took a breath. 'It turned out your dad was living beyond his means. He spent a lot of money on . . . his mistresses.'

'Other women?' Nausea flooded her mouth with saliva.

'I knew he had affairs,' said Sally, quietly. 'It was Andrew who told me about his first one, or the first either of us knew about. That's why the two of them fell out. Andrew thought I had a right to know.'

'Dad had affairs?' The memory of her father Ella kept in her head was of a God-like man who did no wrong. Who was wronged by her mother. That image seemed to swoop and dive as she tried to take it all in. 'And Andrew told you?'

'About the first one, yes. After that, I discovered things myself. It's a cliché really. Dinner receipts, presents meant for someone else. Later, he got brazen – holidays in exotic places, things like that. I found out about the first-class travel and private members' clubs soon after he died.'

'Oh, Mum.' Ella's heart yearned for the imaginary father of her memories, but, in truth, she knew deep down everything Sally said was true. 'That's why . . .'

246

'That's why Andrew and I communicated in secret. He was a rock to me. I hope you understand now why I needed the support. It truly wasn't an affair, Ella. I promise you that.'

Ella believed her. A part of her wanted to think this was a symptom of the dementia, but pieces of the jigsaw of her childhood she'd ignored started to slot back together: her father's long absences, the hushed arguments, the change in her mother when she stopped dancing in the kitchen and spent more time than usual escaping into novels.

Sally continued, 'In the end, I didn't even mind that much about the affairs. It meant he wasn't here, treating you like a performing monkey, demanding you came up to his ridiculous standards.'

'He didn't . . .' Ella stopped. Another long-buried vision of her father standing over her appeared in her mind. He was red-faced and angry, telling her she wasn't trying hard enough, that she'd end up as a teacher like her mother if she didn't put in more hours of studying. 'So, the money he left . . . ?'

'There was very little.'

Ella tried to process all this devastating information. 'I'm so sorry, Mum. I can't believe you've held all of this inside.'

'I wouldn't be telling you now if the situation was different. A mother shouldn't burden her child unnecessarily.'

'But . . .' Ella closed her mouth. Her mum knew how

she idolised her father. If she hadn't spent this time with Sally, she may not have believed her even if she had opened up sooner. 'I'm sorry you couldn't tell me. I'm so sorry he did that to you. He was a fool if he couldn't see how lucky he was to have you.' The words didn't begin to express the anger she felt towards the man she had revered. How dare he treat her wonderful mother like that? How could he betray them both?

She wanted to go to her room and absorb the shockwaves that were crashing through her, but she wouldn't abandon her mother when she needed her. It was her time to step up. She tried to get back to the problem in hand. 'So, you don't have pots of cash stashed away?'

Sally shook her head. 'If I'd been well off, I'd have been able to give some to you, so you didn't have to work so hard.'

More guilt blindsided Ella. It wasn't money that motivated her to work such long hours, but right at that moment, she couldn't remember what her motivation was. Probably some misguided notion that it would have made her father proud. Now it felt like she was filling a hole, plugging something empty inside by working so much she never had to address it.

'We're okay,' she said. 'And Charlie told me he'd like to go back to work now Willow's more independent, so don't worry about us.'

'You must've wondered why I worked until retirement, if I was a wealthy widow? I wanted to keep the house in a decent state, so you had the inheritance you deserve.' Sally looked at the crack in the plasterwork above the kitchen window. 'But I've made a poor job of that, and now those ruined rooms . . .' Her eyes filled with tears again.

Her dad had left her mother without the means to pay for the house he'd wanted as a bloody status symbol. Ella's brain couldn't reconcile the image she'd carried of her dad since she was a child with the one her mum was describing now. Although . . . she could, couldn't she? She knew now she'd idolised her dad, partly because he was so rarely there. She'd built an image of a man who was successful, elusive and exacting. She had craved his attention, his approval and his love. All were hard won, which made them all the more valuable to her, while the woman sitting across from her now had been a calm and constant presence throughout her early life. Love in abundance, freely given, didn't seem worth half so much. What a fool she had been.

'God, Mum, I'm sorry. I had no idea.'

'That's what I wanted. I tried hard to keep it that way. I knew how much it would hurt you.'

A new grief clutched her heart, stronger than that for her dad, which she'd held on to so doggedly. She'd lost twenty-one years of loving and being loved. Her selfless mother had chosen to suffer her rejection rather than hurt her with the truth about the man she worshipped.

Sally looked into her eyes and Ella saw the same love there she always had. 'The first affair, I admit, it almost broke me. I suppose I worshipped him too, at the start. He was charismatic, and so clever. I adored him. I couldn't believe he'd picked me out of everyone. We were like the golden couple at university. He seemed to glow, and I basked in his light. Hubris is a terrible thing.'

'I would never accuse you of that.'

Sally smiled. 'I don't know. There's vanity in wanting to be the popular one, even if it was by proxy. I made a choice to marry him, despite knowing his faults. I knew he could be bombastic and selfish, but, to some extent, I thought he deserved to be. He seemed to be brilliant at everything he tried. I admired his confidence. But if I'd known he'd be the kind of father he was, I would never . . .' She looked at Ella for a long moment. 'But he did love you. I know I'm repeating myself, but I want you to know he really did. And our marriage wasn't all bad. We had some great years together, before . . . Well, they say power corrupts, don't they? I believe that's what happened to Neil. What he allowed to happen to him.'

Up until recently, Ella would have said her father had loved her more than her mother did. Now she could see how distorted her view had been; how naïve and foolish. She enfolded Sally in a hug and held her as tightly as she dared. 'I can see why you said I'm just like him.' She was glad she couldn't see her mother's face.

'I was angry when I said that. I didn't mean it.'

Ella felt the fragility of her mum in her arms and hated herself. 'I've been so selfish. I should never have been distant. I was punishing you; I suppose. And now I

250

can see you didn't deserve that. I'm so sorry I chose his memory over you. It was built on lies I told myself. I'm so sorry.'

'It's not your fault. Maybe I should have tried to tell you before, but we can't rewrite the past, however much we'd like to.' There was so much warmth in Sally's voice and Ella loved her even more. 'There's one more thing I need to tell you,' said Sally, the concerned expression returning. 'I told you that I never sent another letter to Andrew after you went to Australia.'

Ella tensed. This was all too much to take in. Her emotions were pitching in too many directions.

'And that's true,' Sally said.

Ella let go of her breath.

'But he still wrote to me, every few months, for years. Almost a decade. And, although I didn't put them in the post, I did write letters in return. It felt like catharsis, like I was talking to someone who would understand, even if he never got to read them.' She gave a small, nervous smile. 'Will you forgive me for keeping things from you?'

Ella viewed the tiny, frail woman in front of her and knew she would forgive her for anything now. But herself? After so many years, that was a different matter altogether.

Chapter Thirty-Four

Ella

Present Day

At last, the dehumidifier had dried out the library enough for the real work to start. To keep costs down, Ella was clearing the room out ready for Bill the Builder to begin the following day. It was heartbreaking to pick up more of her mother's precious books, only for the dried-out, brittle pages to disintegrate and fall from her fingers. She filled another black sack and dumped it on the landing, standing back to assess what she should do next.

The sash window was open, flapping the blue curtains above the armchair. She gripped the arm of the chair and heaved it across the floorboards. The legs scraped, then stopped. She tugged the other and shifted it from side to side until she got to the door. She leaned her back against it and rested. On the floor where the chair had been, she saw an open book, its pages fluttering in the breeze from the window. It was probably the last book Sally had read in here. It must've dropped under the chair.

Ella imagined the book falling from her mother's fingers as she fell asleep. Another image appeared of Sally letting the novel drop as she cried alone. Ella picked up the miraculously undamaged book and closed it to see the cover. Her heart lurched. *Little Women.* The sight of Meg, Jo, Beth and Amy instantly took her back to her eighth birthday. She was lying in her bed in this house, her mother by her side. She could smell the chlorine in her hair from the swimming party and feel the pages of this book in her fingers as she took it from her mother's hands.

She held her breath, hardly daring to hope the inscription was intact. The book was dry. It must've been protected from the flood by the chair, so there was no reason for the words her mother wrote to her all those years ago to be lost. But so much had been lost: books, carefully written notes . . . years. How long until Sally's memories were lost too?

Ella opened the book, turned to the inside page, and read.

My lovely Ella,

I'm even more proud of you than Marmee is of her girls. I hope this book always reminds you of that, and gives you the courage to follow your dreams. I see a little of all the March girls in you, but I think you're most like Jo. Like her, you prefer 'good strong words that mean something' and that's an admirable quality to have.

When Amy says, 'I'm not afraid of storms,
for I'm learning how to sail my ship,' it reminds
me of your growing confidence and strength of
character. You're already on course for a bright
future, my precious girl. I can't wait to see what
adventures are in store for you.
All my love, forever,
Mummy

Ella closed the book and held it to her heart, tears falling from her chin. There was so much love in those words, so much hope. And what had Ella given in return? She'd turned her back without knowing the whole truth. She'd judged and condemned a woman who always put her first: a woman who built a library out of love, just for her.

***

'Remember this?' Ella washed away any evidence of her crying before taking the book to the sitting room to show her mother.

Sally's eyes lit up when she saw the copy of *Little Women*. 'Be worthy, love, and love will come,' she said, holding her hand out for the book.

Ella dug her fingernails into her palm to stop new tears from escaping. 'You always loved that phrase.'

'Where did you find this?' Sally was turning the pages with an expression of awe.

'It was under the chair. The velvet must've absorbed all the water.'

Sally stopped at the inscription. She smiled up at Ella. 'A lifetime and five minutes ago,' she said.

Ella nodded. She sat on the sofa, leaning forwards with her elbows on her knees. 'Mum, I've been thinking about what we should do going forwards.'

Sally's smile fell. 'Oh. Righto.' The heel of her hand worked back and forth along the chair arm.

'I wondered if it might be a good idea to tell your friends about your diagnosis.'

'Oh.' Her face brightened. 'I thought you were going to suggest I went into a home.'

Ella sat back. 'What? No, of course not.' Did her mother think she was completely heartless? What kind of person suggests that so soon after they find out about a dementia diagnosis? 'Not at all . . . unless that's what you want?' Perhaps Sally would feel safer in a home. Maybe she would actually be safer. God, there was so much to think about.

'Not now, but it is something we'll have to talk about later,' said Sally, her chin trembling as she spoke. 'I might not be able to manage here, when it gets worse, I mean.'

'There's a long way to go before we have to think about that,' said Ella, her voice firm. She wished she was as certain as she sounded. 'But I do think getting a bit of support is a good idea. We've got the doctor's appointment booked and I'll still be here for that, so we'll know more then. How do you feel about telling people about your diagnosis, so your friends know what's going on?'

'I don't know that I can,' said Sally. 'I still get a bit emotional when I talk about it. I don't want to cry and make everyone feel sorry for me.'

'Do you want me to do it?'

Sally put her fingers to her quivering lips and gave a tiny nod. Ella sat on the chair arm and held her mother, knowing it was something she should have done a million times before.

Chapter Thirty-Five

Ella

Present Day

Ella sat at the circular table under the library's first blue dome, feeling like a doctor about to deliver bad news. Her stomach had been churning since Sally had told her, and now she was sharing the diagnosis with other people who loved her mother. She wasn't even sure she was doing this the right way. Was there a right way to tell people about a degenerative condition? Round robin letter in a Christmas card? Text? She was relieved when Jakub checked out the last of the library's clients and came to join her.

'Now we're officially closed, are you going to tell me the reason for this clandestine meeting?' He waved his hands over the table as though conducting a seance. That was not an image Ella wanted to dwell on.

Before she could answer, Pru marched from the entrance towards them wearing a smart trouser suit. She was followed by a smiling Mina, like sunshine after rain.

'I hope this won't take long,' said Pru, tugging at the

hem of her jacket before sitting down. 'Some of us are busy.'

'You can take as long as you like,' said Mina. 'I'm getting out of bath time with my three. Hadi can deal with the splashing and moaning when they get soap in their eyes.' She sat and let out a satisfied sigh, ignoring Pru's quiet tutting.

Verity was next to arrive. She looked stunning in a yellow linen dress and matching headscarf. She stopped before she got to the table, her mouth dropping open, her eyes on the wall behind them. Ella turned to follow her gaze and found a series of watercolour paintings showing a vase of delphiniums from various angles.

'Oh, my days,' said Verity. 'I can't believe it.'

'Is one of those yours?' asked Ella, standing and moving to look more closely at the paintings. 'They're gorgeous.'

'They're all mine,' said Verity, her voice breathless, as if she truly couldn't believe her eyes.

'What! Wow, Verity.' Ella was amazed at the professional-looking paintings. 'You're even more talented than I remember.'

'Phil asked if I was happy for him to display them, but I thought he'd asked everyone in the class. I thought it was going to be like when the teacher puts up the kids' work at the end of term.'

'So, this is your exhibition?' said Jakub, joining them. 'I've had at least five people ask me if they're for sale.'

Verity spun around. 'You're kidding?'

'I assure you, madam, I am not.' He grinned.

'Are they for sale?' Ella inquired as she gestured towards a striking close-up featuring vivid purple and white hues. 'Because I think that one would look gorgeous in Mum's kitchen.'

'Stop it,' said Verity, hands on her face, squishing her cheeks, still the image of astonishment. 'If Mrs H wants one of my pictures, she can have it for free.'

They turned at the sound of an irritated cough from Pru. 'Can we please get on?'

Miserable bat. Couldn't she see they were having a moment? Or maybe she could, and that's why she wanted to ruin it.

Hannah and Nathan bustled in then and soon everyone was seated at the table. Ella became the focus of inquisitive eyes.

'Thank you all for coming. I really appreciate you giving up your time.' She looked at Pru and smiled, despite being met with a stony stare. 'The first thing I wanted to do was to thank you all for welcoming me back to Greenwich. If I'm honest, I'd let my memories of the place fade, and I thought I'd made Sydney my home.' She looked up at the graceful dome above them. 'But you always have a fondness for where you were raised, don't you?'

'I'm never going back to Moss Side, and you can't make me,' said Nathan, crossing his arms and enjoying the laughter from around the table.

'I bet you still get misty-eyed when you go home,'

Ella said.

He shrugged. 'Only when I see my mum.'

'Aww,' said Verity, giving him a nudge. 'Aren't you a sweetheart?'

Nathan blushed, and Ella loved him a little bit more.

'Very good point,' said Ella, 'and that's really what I wanted to talk to all of you about. Another thing I've realised since I got back to the UK is that it's the people who make a home.' She looked around the building with its ornate plasterwork and shelves of books. 'Without Jakub at the front desk and Mina working away in the far room, even this beautiful building would lose its charm.'

They all followed her gaze from the huge front window, up the white columns to the blue dome.

'And the market wouldn't be the market without Hannah, or the florist without Verity.'

'So, you're saying I made Circus Street what it is today?' remarked Nathan, nodding seriously, then collapsing into giggles. 'I'm not sure whoever designed those fancy houses planned them with a skint Mancunian fashion student in mind.'

'You're part of the rich tapestry of the street,' Ella assured him. 'And, anyway, who wants to live in a world where everyone you come into contact with is a carbon copy of you?' She noticed Pru was glaring down at the table and scrabbled around to find something positive to say about her. It wasn't easy. 'And I bet people around here are thrilled to have the opportunity to speak Spanish, Pru.'

It was a weak gambit and Pru's impassive face told her as much.

Ella decided to get to the point. 'I've brought you all here today to tell you that, unfortunately, Mum's not well.'

She waited for the mutters of sorrow at the news to die down.

'She's known for a while something's not quite right, and when I got here, a few of you had noticed she hasn't been around and about as much as usual.' She cleared her throat to fight back the collecting tears. 'And she's had some tests that have confirmed she's got some form of dementia.'

'Oh no,' said Verity. 'She's not old enough, surely?'

'From what I've read, it's not considered early onset unless you're diagnosed before you're sixty-five.' Ella had made herself stop reading about dementia. It was too frightening. Her mind always went to the worst-case scenario, and, until she had more information, that wasn't productive for her or for her mum.

'Bless her. I did wonder,' said Jakub. 'She hasn't been herself for a while, poor lamb.'

'Apparently it's quite common for people to become more introverted and a bit depressed,' explained Ella.

'The flood . . .' said Pru, suddenly.

'Yes, it makes more sense now, because she would never have forgotten something like that before,' Ella agreed. She wondered if Pru remembered sniping about how it wasn't a flood, it was a silly old woman leaving

261

the bath on. Half of Ella wanted the memory to sting the tight-faced woman across the table, but when she saw the pained look in Pru's eyes, the feeling subsided.

'What can we do?' asked Hannah. She leaned forwards, gripping her hands together. 'I'm a fixer. I need to feel like I'm doing something when I hear bad news. Give me a job, for my sake, if not for Sally's.'

The nods around the table filled Ella's heart to bursting. 'Thank you,' she said. 'I've only got ten days left until I'm meant to fly back. It's not much time, and I'm feeling quite overwhelmed, so I can't imagine how Mum feels. We're doing what we can with the house, so that's in hand. I'm looking into getting some support for her at home, and before I go back to Sydney, I'll talk to Mum and my husband and work out what we need to do.'

'Do you think Sally would mind the kids coming with me if I pop in now and again?' asked Mina, her face full of concern. 'They could help her keep up with her signing.'

'I think she'd love that,' said Ella.

'I can bob in every day, even if it's just for a bit,' offered Nathan.

'We could do a rota,' suggested Jakub.

'You lot are amazing,' said Ella. 'Thank you so much. At the risk of sounding ungrateful, Mum only said I could tell you all today. She wanted you to know but thought it would be too upsetting to go through the explanation herself. I'll need to see what she wants to do about everything else before we start to organise her life for her. She's been independent for a long time. I think it's only right she stays in control for as long as that's possible.'

'And she could be all right for years yet,' said Hannah.

Everyone murmured their agreement.

Ella held up crossed fingers. 'Exactly. And since I'm only here for a little longer, I've got a project of my own I was hoping you might all be willing to help me with.'

The group huddled together while Ella explained, and she was delighted when they came up with more ideas to make her plan happen. Fifteen minutes later, they'd decided on who would do what, and then they were outside on Greenwich High Street, hugging and saying their goodbyes.

'Do you have time to pop to the pub?' said Verity, when only she, Ella and Pru remained.

'Yeah, I could murder a drink,' said Ella. Pru was hovering. 'Fancy joining us?' Ella asked, out of politeness.

'No, thank you, but could I have a quick word?'

'I'll see you in The Gypsy Moth,' said Verity, and set off towards town, attracting admiring glances from passing motorists, which she didn't appear to notice.

Ella turned to Pru. 'What's up?'

Pru looked down at her court shoes. 'I wanted to apologise for being uncharitable before.'

Ella shrugged. 'We don't know what we don't know.' Tempting as it was, she didn't see the point in making Pru feel worse.

'That's generous, but I think we both know I was holding some kind of silly grudge against your mother, and now I feel rightfully ashamed.'

A truck trundled past noisily. Ella watched it disappear down the road towards Deptford. 'What was your grudge about?' she asked. 'I wondered what was going on there, because everyone seemed to love Mum, except you.'

'I suppose that was my problem.' Pru looked behind them at the lintel over the library door. 'She's always been treated like some kind of deity in here.'

'And you felt overlooked?' Ella tried to understand.

'It wasn't that so much,' said Pru, 'as the fact that it all seemed to come so easily to her. It was like she didn't have to try. People loved her automatically. She never had to work for it like it I did. I can see now I resented her for that . . . and everything else, if I'm honest.'

'What do you mean, everything else?' This insight into how Sally was perceived was fascinating. She'd only just learned to see her mum as an individual outside her role as her mother. Hearing how someone else saw her added another dimension.

'Where do I start? The big, fancy house on one of the best streets in Greenwich. The marriage, and yes, I know losing a husband so young is tragic, but at least she was loved.'

Ella went to interrupt but stopped herself. That wasn't her information to divulge.

'She went to university and became a teacher; she has

a daughter she adores and a granddaughter she dotes on. And it all seemed to be handed to her on a plate.' Pru stopped and pursed her lips. 'Comparison is the thief of joy. That's what they say, isn't it?'

Ella nodded, unsure how to respond. She could burst every one of Pru's theories about Sally but wasn't sure she should. Would Sally prefer to be idolised or pitied?

Pru continued. 'My parents couldn't afford for me to go to university. I would have loved to. I wanted to study modern languages and travel and . . .' She sighed and sadness seemed to seep from her. 'Anyway, none of that ever happened.'

'But you teach Spanish now.'

Pru shook her head. 'I kid myself I do. It's a Spanish conversation session Jakub helped me set up. There's only ever four people there and I spend half my spare time on Duolingo trying to keep one step ahead.'

'Fake it 'til you make it,' said Ella, smiling at this new, candid version of Pru. 'You know Mum's life hasn't been the dream you've created in your head?'

'Nobody's ever is, is it?' replied Pru, her eyes lowered. 'It's easy to pretend everyone else is lucky and you've been dealt a bad hand. It stops you having to address your own shortcomings.'

'I hear you loud and clear,' said Ella. She reached out and rubbed Pru's arm. 'Thank you for talking to me.'

'Thank you for not appearing to hate me.'

'I don't hate you,' said Ella. 'Glass houses, and all that.'

Pru's eyes were soft for the first time since Ella had met her. 'I still think she's very lucky to have you. And please, don't hesitate to let me know what I can do to help. And, if it's all right, I would like to choose a book for Sally, for her lost library.'

'That's great, thanks,' Ella said. She was surprised when Pru pulled her in for a quick hug, before turning and walking away.

Chapter Thirty-Six

Ella

Present Day

Verity was sitting in the beer garden of The Gypsy Moth with two pints of cider on the table in front of her when Ella arrived. 'What was that about?'

'She just wanted me to know she was there if Mum needed her.'

'Aw, that's sweet. Wouldn't kill her to crack a smile, though.'

Ella shrugged. 'We're all different, aren't we? And I suppose none of us know what's going on in someone else's head.' She was more aware of this fact than she ever had been. It occurred to her that, if she'd had this insight when she was younger, her life may have turned out differently. But insight came with experience, she supposed.

Verity pushed one of the drinks towards Ella. 'Thought we should have a drink after that. Must've been hard to face up to Mrs H being ill. Telling everyone must've been tough too.' She reached out and squeezed Ella's hand. 'I bet you wish you were eighteen again, don't you?'

Ella smiled and took a sip. She did wish she was eighteen again, but not so she still had firm thighs and more than half her life to look forward to, but because she wished she could make better choices. Given her time again, she would have appreciated her mum. She would have tried to see her dad as the flawed man he was, and supported Sally instead of blaming her for something she didn't do and fleeing the country.

She realised, even if she was Queen of the World, she wouldn't make a different choice about marrying Charlie. He was a special man and it had taken her this long to fully understand that. If she was honest, she'd sometimes been frustrated that he wasn't driven and ambitious like her dad. On reflection, she suspected, on some level, she'd chosen him precisely because he was nothing like her father. He had more of her mum's traits, and she vowed to cherish that. She imagined how she'd feel if he walked across the beer garden now and the thought of holding him made her eyes fill with tears.

'Aw, don't cry,' said Verity. 'We'll all help with your mum. You're not on your own with this.'

'Actually,' said Ella, grimacing, 'I was thinking about Charlie. I miss him so much more than I thought I would. I really want a cuddle.'

Verity moved around to her side of the table and gave her a bear hug. 'That better?'

'Much,' Ella lied. It was nice to have Verity, but she wanted Charlie and Willow. She wanted to lie down

268

with them in her bed at home and bury her head in their hair. She wanted to sit with them and just listen to them chatter and laugh. Why didn't she do that more when she was in Sydney? Why was she always rushing to work? She was running away, she thought. Always running away.

'Me and Luke are splitting up,' said Verity, going back to her seat. She took a gulp of cider and raised her eyebrows.

'What?' Ella tried to read Verity's expression to gauge how she should react, but her face was neutral. 'Are you okay?'

'I am,' said Verity. 'Mostly.'

'Your turn for a hug?'

'Nah, honestly, I'm all right. I have the odd wobble because it feels like I've failed, and I'm scared of living on my own and stuff, but, to be honest, I think I'm mainly relieved.'

'Tell me everything.'

Verity took another drink. 'Well, you know that night your mum cried?'

'Yeah.' The memory had new, painful significance now Ella knew about the dementia and her father's betrayal.

'I went home that night and told Luke I needed a room of my own, for my artwork.'

'Okay . . . And what did he say?'

'He told me to get over myself.'

'Oof. How did that go down?'

269

Verity laughed. 'I think you can imagine. Anyway, when I came down off the ceiling, he was looking at me funny and then he said, "What's this really about, babe?" and I said, "Do you love me?"'

'Bloody hell,' declared Ella. 'And?'

'He said he did, and I said, "But are you in love with me?"'

Ella nodded. She was in love with Charlie. She knew it in her bones and felt intensely grateful for that.

'And after I explained what I meant about a thousand times, we both agreed that, actually, we're not in love with each other anymore. He thinks I'm nice and funny and I think he's decent, but that's not enough, is it?'

'Oh Verity,' said Ella, unsure of what she was meant to say. 'So, what happens now?'

'I've been to the bank, and they've agreed a remortgage so I can buy him out. He's moving in with his mate.'

Ella spluttered on the slurp she'd just taken. 'You don't mess about.'

Verity shrugged. 'The house has gone up in value and I can still afford the mortgage on my own, so I thought, why not? We only get one life, best make the most of it, right?'

'Right,' said Ella. The words repeated in her head. *We only get one life, best make the most of it.* Was she making the most of hers? She didn't think she was. In fact, she'd been unhappy in Sydney for longer than she cared to admit. She'd blamed Charlie, but now she was away from him, she understood he was not the problem. And if wasn't him, then it had to be her.

'So, I'll have money – well, enough to get by on – and a room of my own.'

They clinked glasses and Ella viewed her friend through fresh eyes. 'I'm so impressed you saw a problem and fixed it. I'm so proud of you.'

'Wouldn't have even thought about it if it wasn't for you and Mrs H. I would have kept plodding on forever, never giving myself the chance to be truly happy.'

'Do you think you'll be happier on your own?'

Verity lifted her palms. 'Who knows. But I'm going to have a cracking time finding out. I'm going on the dating apps.' She guffawed. 'I'm going to see what's out there.'

The thought of dating apps made Ella shudder. 'You're brave.'

'I suppose I am,' said Verity, patting her hair with a proud smile. 'I could have stayed with Luke, but I'm too young to settle. I want it all, and if I can't have it all, I'll have fun trying.'

'Cheers to that.' Ella lifted her pint and drank.

'Seriously, though. I want another chance at love.' Verity's voice was quiet. 'I deserve to be with someone who notices when I enter a room, someone who puts me first. Hell, I want a man who writes me love letters.' She lowered her lashes. 'Do you think I'm asking too much?'

Ella thought of Andrew writing to her mother for almost a decade despite never getting a reply after her father's death. 'No,' she said. 'I think there are men out there who would do that for a woman they love.'

And perhaps those men deserved a reply.

Chapter Thirty-Seven

Ella

Present Day

'Mum,' said Ella the following morning as they ate breakfast at the kitchen table. 'I'm going to ask you a weird question, so think hard about the answer before saying anything.'

Sally looked up from her bowl of muesli. 'Sounds . . .' She blinked. 'What's the word?'

'Ominous?'

'That's it.' She sighed and stirred the contents of the bowl one way then the other.

'Did you keep the letters you wrote to Andrew?'

The room seemed to still. Ella couldn't read her mother's face. Eventually, Sally placed her hand on the table and looked directly into Ella's eyes. 'You still need proof I was telling you the truth?'

'No, God, no,' said Ella, shaking her head. 'Sorry, I phrased that badly. It was something Verity said last night about wanting a man who loved her enough to write her letters. It made me think of Andrew writing to you for all those years and not getting any in return.'

Sally's eyes filled with tears. 'I don't like to think about how much that might have hurt him. And they weren't what you might call love letters,' she said. 'They were letters between friends. Friends who weren't just interested in the everyday. I suppose, because we knew each other so well, we could talk about what we really thought and felt, not about each other, but about everything. I was completely truthful with Andrew.'

'It must have been freeing to be able to be so authentic.' Ella wasn't ever completely open, not even with Charlie. She wondered what it would be like to say exactly what she meant and for him to do the same. Did married couples ever truly do that? 'Do you wish now that you'd sent them?'

Sally raised her eyebrows, contemplating the question. 'Yes, if things had turned out differently. I suppose I wouldn't have carried on writing if I didn't wish he could read them. We had a deep connection.' She smiled sadly. 'And I still feel its loss. If he'd read all the things I wanted to say to him over the years, maybe that connection would still be there.' She lowered her gaze. 'But it wasn't right to carry on without your father's knowledge.'

'Let's not get into the rights and wrongs. He was more to blame than anyone, and I haven't exactly covered myself in glory.' Ella poured another tea from the pot on the table and stirred in some milk, all the time wondering how to phrase what she meant. 'Since I got back, I feel like I've been on a steep learning curve. It's

273

felt like I've got to know you properly for the first time in my life, and I suppose I'm hoping I might learn a bit more from your letters. But I completely understand if they're too personal and you'd prefer I didn't.'

She lifted the pot and Sally nudged her mug forwards. She watched the dark liquid flow from the spout until it was three-quarters full. Sally lifted the cup to her lips.

'Mum!'

'What?' The drink hovered near her mouth.

'What about milk?'

Sally looked at the contents of the mug and blinked.

'You have milk in your tea, and even if you didn't, you'd scald your mouth if you drank it now.'

Sally put the mug down and picked up the milk jug, pouring a small amount into her tea, while Ella watched, with a growing feeling of concern.

Something soft brushed against her calf. She looked under the table and saw Hadron. She looked up at her with her piercing green eye, then moved forwards, knocking clumsily against her shins as she weaved between her legs. Ella swallowed. It was the first time the cat had chosen to be near her. She bent down to run her hand over her back, her spine ridged under the silky fur, feeling like she'd passed her hardest test yet.

'You can read the letters,' Sally said. 'I think I'd like us to know each other better, before—' She stood abruptly. 'I'll go and get them now.'

The word 'before' hung in the air when she left.

***

274

Ella scraped the soggy leftover muesli into the food recycling caddy with a churning feeling in her stomach. What she'd asked was an invasion of privacy, but it felt like the means justified the ends. She'd been so wrong about everything, that any insight into her mother's real life, rather than the one Ella had constructed for her, would surely be a good thing?

The doorbell rang. She hurried upstairs and let in Bill the Builder and his mate, promising them a cup of tea in the little library shortly. She heard them say good morning to Sally and she waited in the sitting room for her mother.

Sally appeared in the doorway with a number of notebooks trapped between her cast and her torso. 'I never even tore off the paper,' she said. 'There didn't seem much point since I was never going to send them, so I suppose they make up a journal of sorts.'

Ella stood and took the A4 spiral notebooks from her mother's hands. 'You're sure you're all right with me reading these?'

'Yes,' said Sally. 'But I'd rather not watch you do it. I think I'll pop down to see Hannah, then call in at the library.'

Ella was increasingly uncomfortable with Sally going out on her own. Much of the time, she was completely fine, but would she be safe if she had a lapse of memory when she was out and about? 'Please don't hate me for this.'

'What now?' It was so unusual for Sally to snap, it

seemed to surprise both of them. 'Sorry.'

'It's fine.' Was this the start of the personality change that could come along with dementia? Ella wondered. Was this how it would be from now onwards, her mum slipping away until she wasn't herself at all? 'I'm sorry, Mum, but do you mind if I put an app on both our phones so we can see where the other one is?'

'So, you can check where I am, you mean? In case I get lost.'

She didn't answer.

Sally went to her bag by the side of her chair and took out her phone. 'Here,' she said, then slumped into the seat. 'I'm sorry I'm a grump. I didn't sleep well.'

Ella's mood lifted. If Sally was tired, then maybe she wasn't changing too much. Maybe she was just not on top form. She installed the Find My Friends app on her phone, then on Sally's and connected the two. She showed her how to use it, glancing up often, to see if Sally was taking it in. 'Just remember to keep your phone on when you're out.' She nudged the button on the side to turn off silent mode. 'And answer if I call, okay?'

'Yes, boss.' Sally sighed. 'Have you read the Seamus Heaney poem, *Follower*?'

'No, why?'

'Look it up while I'm out.' Sally rose to her feet and hung her bag over her shoulder. 'I'll look both ways when I cross the road and be back in time for lunch.'

'Mum . . . I don't want—'

276

'I'm joking,' said Sally. 'Sorry, it's going to take a while for both of us to settle into this new . . .' She stopped and scrunched her eyes tight.

'Pattern? Routine?' Ella offered.

Sally sighed. 'Yes. Thank you, love.' She nodded to the notebooks. 'Happy reading.'

When she heard the front door close, Ella picked up her phone and searched for the poem. She came across a YouTube clip of Heaney reciting it, his face close to the camera, mop of greying curls on his head. She pressed play and listened to his Irish accent, describing how his father ploughed the fields, the young Seamus stumbling along behind him, watching, learning, hoping one day to follow in his footsteps.

Then, in the last two lines, the poem shifts to the present and it's Heaney's father who is behind, stumbling in his son's wake. Hadron came over and sat at her feet as Ella's tears dropped onto the screen.

Chapter Thirty-Eight

Ella

Present Day

The date on the top of the first letter was a week after her father's funeral. Even the sight of it took Ella back to the ache of loss in her chest, and the fury that burned inside her. She'd been angrier than she'd ever been in her life and the memory of it was so easy to access because she'd allowed it to sit within her for more than two decades. What a self-righteous fool she'd been. How destructive to hold on to all that negativity. Hopefully, this would be the first step in finally letting go.

Something heavy and warm settled on the top of her feet. She looked down to see Hadron lying over her socks and felt the rhythmic vibration of purring through the cotton. She held her breath, too scared to move in case the spell was broken. The occasion felt momentous, as though she'd finally been deemed worthy by this most discerning of creatures. Hadron looked up at her with her one green eye, then nuzzled Ella's ankle.

Ella let out her breath and started to read.

Dearest Andrew,

The first thing I need to say is that I will never send this letter. It's a peculiar thing to write, since you'll never read it, but I need it here, in black and white, as a reminder for if I get weak and feel like I need to lean on you again. I mustn't and I won't.

You have been my safe place for so long, it will be strange not to rely on you anymore. You've been a sounding board, a stalwart, a cheerleader and, most importantly, a friend. I don't know how I would have got through the difficult years without you to turn to, but now I must. I made a promise, you see, and I believe in promises.

Ella might laugh if she read that. It would be a bitter laugh, I imagine, and it would slice into my heart. She thinks I broke my marriage vows. Did I? I wonder. I suppose, in some way, I did, because I do love you, Andrew. I don't know, if I'd made different choices, whether we could have had a happy life together. You've never made a secret of the fact you wished I hadn't been drawn to the shiny thing that was my husband, but you loved him too, remember? And it wasn't always bad.

I sometimes think it's been cruel of me to carry on communicating with you like this. I hope it hasn't stopped you from finding love. Love, elsewhere, I mean. I hope I've always made it clear you shouldn't wait for me. I never stopped wishing happiness for you. You do, for the people you love the most, don't you? Maybe now my letters will stop arriving, you will forget me. That might be a release. Maybe I should have done it years ago, when I decided I would never leave Neil, despite his betrayal. You know why I couldn't. Timing is everything; they say that, don't they?

If I've been selfish, I'm truly sorry. I suspect I'm about to get my comeuppance for all my wrongdoings. Ella has set off on her trip without a backward glance. I tried not to cry when she left, at least not when she was there, but it feels as though my heart has left with her, ripped out and bleeding, if that's not too dramatic and self-indulgent. I'm not sure she'll ever know quite how much she means to me. I hope, somehow, she doesn't, because I don't want her to know how much this hurts. All of it.

I'm going to leave her to lick her wounds for as long as she needs. I owe her that. I live in hope the bond between us is more frayed than severed. I'm going to carry on building the collection of books for her that I wrote to you about. When I've saved the money, I'm planning to change the box room into a little library, and I'll put a new book in there with an inscription on her birthday, as I have every day since she was born.

I hope, one day, she'll come back and read them all, and know how much I love her. How much I always have.

I'll write again soon, for what it's worth.
Your ever-loving friend,
Sally

Ella wiped tears from her cheeks. This confirmed what she already knew. Sally was truthful. She was innocent.

'You all right, love?'

She jumped at the sound of Bill's voice from the doorway. 'Yes, fine, sorry. I, er, was reading something sad.'

'You want to try A J Pearce's *Dear Mrs Bird*, something uplifting like that,' said Bill. 'It's a proper comfort read.' His gaze dropped to the cat sitting on her feet. 'Nice pair of slippers you've got there. Weird cat, that one.'

She is, thought Ella, *but she's our weird cat*. She grinned at Bill, viewing him through fresh eyes. That book recommendation was probably the last thing she would have expected from the burly man standing in the hallway. She really did need to re-evaluate how she thought of people. The boxes she'd created in her head were only limiting her. 'I'll look that book up, thank you.'

'All right if I make that cuppa?' said Bill.

Ella put the notebook on the ottoman, shuffled her feet from under Hadron and jumped up. 'God, sorry. I said I'd make tea, didn't I?'

'Do you want me to do it?'

She did but didn't feel like it was kind to say so. 'No,

it's fine.' He followed her down to the kitchen. 'How's it going up there?'

'Not bad,' said Bill. 'All the wallpaper's off and the plasterwork's dried out. I had a devil of a job getting that exact print, but I'm not a quitter.' He grinned. 'I should be able to get it slapped on tomorrow.'

'And the bookcase?' She stirred the teabags until the water was almost black.

'Yep, my mate Geoff will have that built by the end of the week.'

Ella put a drop of milk in each cup and handed them over. 'Brilliant. Remember to keep the door closed. I've told Mum it's a mess and I don't want her to see it until it's stripped out. She has no idea what we're planning.'

Bill made his way up the stairs. 'You're a sneaky one, but she's lucky to have you.'

Watching the bottoms of his overalls disappear from view, Ella's thoughts returned to the unsent letters in the notebooks and she hoped, albeit uncertainly, that his words might hold some truth.

Chapter Thirty-Nine

Ella

Present Day

'I found my way home,' shouted Sally from the hallway two hours later.

Listening to the rustling sound of Sally shaking off her coat and hanging it on the banister, Ella put down the notebook she was reading and wiped her face dry. 'I'm in here.'

Sally came through, stopping when she saw Ella's red-rimmed eyes. 'Oh, sweetheart. I wouldn't have let you see those if I'd known you'd find them so distressing.'

'I'm so sorry I put you through all this, Mum,' said Ella, standing and taking her mother in her arms.

'It's not all sad, is it?' said Sally, a question in her voice.

'No, no, not at all.' Ella let Sally go. 'A lot of it is really positive. It's great to read about when Jakub started at the library. I can't believe he's been in your life for ten years and I've only just met him. I'm almost up to present day. I'm sorry I missed sharing all this stuff with you.'

Sally's bottom lip wobbled.

Ella didn't want to upset her. 'I loved reading about you meeting Mina. I had no idea she was a refugee.'

'Yes. They went through a lot when they first came to England from Afghanistan. I'm so proud of what that girl's achieved, running her own business with the baby signing. Her mother was deaf, you know? That's why she knows sign language. Who'd have thought something so good could come out of something so sad? She has the loveliest family,' said Sally. 'Now, what's her husband's name?'

'She did mention him, but I can't remember,' said Ella.

There was a bang upstairs. Sally looked up. 'How's it going up there?'

'Good, yeah,' replied Ella. 'Will be a while 'til they're finished, though.'

'Are you sure I can afford it?' Sally's brow furrowed, making Ella feel like hugging her again.

'Both Charlie and I have been through your finances and it's all in hand. You don't need to worry about any of that stuff anymore.' She didn't say Charlie had agreed they should help pay for the repairs. Sally had tried to hold on to the house because it was Ella's inheritance, so helping with the costs was the least they could do.

Sally sat down and dropped her bag by the side of the chair. 'When's my appointment to get this cast off?'

'Don't worry about that,' said Ella. 'I've got it in the diary.'

'And Glenda should be back soon,' said Sally. 'She'll

help a bit when you've gone back home. I don't want to be a burden to anyone, though.' Tears pooled in her eyes.

'You won't be, Mum. People want to help. And we've got that doctor's appointment tomorrow, haven't we? I promise, I'm not just going to swan back to Australia and leave you and everyone else to get on with it.'

'That makes me a burden to you,' said Sally, fishing a tissue from her cardigan sleeve and wiping her nose.

'No more talk of burdens,' said Ella. She picked up the first notebook. 'I've got a question about the first letter. Can I . . . ?'

'Go on.'

Ella ran her finger along the lines until she found the part she wanted. 'It says here: "*You know why I couldn't. Timing is everything.*" What does that mean? It follows on from you saying you couldn't leave Dad and you seemed to be saying you might have, if something hadn't happened?'

Sally looked at her with a sad smile. 'There was a time, when I learned about your dad's affair – the first one – that I thought our marriage vows meant so little to him I was a fool to keep to my side of the bargain. It was the only time I considered leaving him.'

'And what happened? Why did you decide to stay?'

'You happened, my lovely girl. I found out I was expecting you, and I couldn't deny you your father. It wouldn't have been right.'

A bolt of guilt shot through Ella. 'I'm so sorry you felt you had to make that sacrifice for me.'

'It wasn't a sacrifice,' Sally asserted. 'Whatever your father did, before or afterwards, paled into insignificance in comparison to the joy you brought.'

'But then I left you.' The words caught in Ella's throat.

'And now you've come back.' Sally was smiling at her as though this was enough, but Ella didn't think it possibly could be. She'd denied her mother decades of love. She had one hell of a lot of making up to do.

'Tell me more about Andrew,' she said.

'Are you sure?' Sally rubbed her hand along the chair arm.

'Yes. What does he do, where does he live?' While reading the letters, Ella had gone from thinking this man was the enemy, to understanding he'd been one of the best things in her mother's life.

Sally let out a long breath. 'He always wrote on headed paper,' she said. 'But I don't know if he's still at the same place. I don't know if professor is a job you retire from.'

'He's a professor?' said Ella.

'Yes,' replied Sally. 'At Canterbury Christ Church. Professor of English. There's a reason we always shared our love of books.'

'What's his full name?' asked Ella, her pulse quickening.

'Andrew Walker,' said Sally.

Ella swallowed. 'This is another weird question.' She shifted to the edge of her seat. 'Do you know what his favourite book is?'

286

'Ha,' said Sally, 'that's easy. He bought me a copy years ago.' Her face fell. 'But now it's ruined.'

'What is it, Mum? What's the title of the book?'

'It's *Persuasion*, by Jane Austen.'

Chapter Forty

Ella

Present Day

Sitting in the doctor's treatment room, Ella was taken back to all the times her mum had taken her to this same surgery when she was younger. She'd even gone with her to get the pill when she was seventeen and had her first long-term boyfriend. Verity had been astonished, telling her how lucky she was that she could be so open with her mum. It was like some memories had only recently become available to her again after having been locked away. How had she forgotten how close they were?

Sally had agreed Ella should take the lead and ask the questions. After they took their seats, she outlined her concerns and gave examples of what she'd noted down since her arrival.

The young doctor listened and nodded. 'This is helpful, thank you. Let me just make a note of what you've told me.' She turned to her computer.

The words of Heaney's poem replayed in Ella's head as she glanced nervously to check Sally was okay, then around the room, taking in the bed covered with blue paper, the blood pressure monitor on the desk next to the keyboard that the doctor was tapping on.

The doctor stopped typing and read from her screen. 'I see you've had the cognitive tests that have confirmed dementia, and you're having blood tests to see if there's any abnormalities and you're waiting for an MRI for a closer look at the brain.'

Sally nodded.

Ella reached for her hand and squeezed it. 'Will the appointment letters come to Mum?' she asked, nervously.

'Now we've got your details, and Sally's consent, we can make sure you get a copy of everything by email.'

That was a relief. Having to rely on her mum for updates had been a real concern.

They might need to do more, the doctor continued to explain, like a CT scan and neurological assessments, but they'd decide that when the first lot of results came in.

'Thank you,' said Ella. 'Unfortunately, I have to go back to Australia shortly, so . . .' So what? She wanted to be told something definite: a timeline or, better than that, a cure. She wanted to be told that this was all a bad dream and next time she flew home, she would find her mum riding her bike around Greenwich without a care in the world. 'Can you give me an idea of treatments, and next steps?'

The doctor turned her swivel chair slowly left to right. 'Until we have more information to go on, I'm afraid we can't put a full plan in place. I can see that you being so far away is a concern.' She turned to Sally. 'Do you have people around who can support you?'

Sally nodded. 'Yes. My neighbour, Glenda, and I've got quite a few friends who will look out for me.'

'That's good. We have your details,' the doctor said to Ella. 'We'll keep you both up to date on what's happening.' She smiled. 'And, in my experience, things don't change that quickly.'

Ella wanted her to promise. She wanted her to swear on her life that next time she came to England, Sally's condition would be no worse than it was now.

Instead, she thanked her, checked again that her phone number and email address were on record, and walked quietly back to Circus Street with her mother.

***

The second time Ella approached the university's Creative Arts building, she was carrying a bag filled with Sally's spiral-bound notebooks and the copy of *Persuasion*. She climbed the stairs to the second floor and knocked on the professor's door. She waited. There was no reply. She glanced up and down the corridor, berating herself for not making an appointment. She'd wanted to surprise him, but all she'd done was make a wasted trip.

Ella knocked again and then, when there was still no sign of life inside, she decided to go and find a café and try again later. She was deflated and cross with herself when she started back down the stairs.

'Ella?'

The voice startled her. She saw the figure of the professor silhouetted against the window in the stairwell, but she couldn't make out his features against the bright light outside.

'Is it Sally?' There was panic in his voice. 'Is she all right?'

Ella blinked against the brightness. The figure moved towards her and soon she could make out his face, his expression of concern. 'You knew who I was when I came to see you?' She tried to remember their first meeting to see if there was any hint he was aware she was Sally's daughter.

'Yes. As soon as I saw your name on the email, I knew you had to be Neil and Sally's daughter,' he said. 'But I didn't mention it because it was clear you didn't know who I was. Is Sally all right?'

'Yes,' she said. 'She's fine.' This wasn't the place to tell him the whole story. 'Do you have a few minutes?'

His face relaxed. 'Oh, that's good. That's good. Actually, you've caught me at the perfect moment. I have all the time in the world,' he said. 'I've just delivered my final ever lecture. I was quite proud of it, actually. I centred it on Prospero's final speech at the end of *The Tempest*. Do you know it?'

Ella shook her head.

'It was Shakespeare's last play, and it's thought it was his way of saying goodbye.' He gestured for Ella to follow him up the stairs. 'He asks for a round of applause, saying, "Let your indulgence set me free."' Andrew waved his hands. 'And applaud they did. The whole of the lecture hall stood on their feet and clapped. It was probably the highlight of my career.' They reached his office door and he turned to her. 'Is it vain, to say that?'

'Not at all. I imagine anyone would be delighted to have that kind of response.'

'It was cheating a bit, though, using that epilogue.' He unlocked the door. 'But a dog will have his day.'

'You're retiring, then?'

Andrew leaned back against his huge desk, crossing his arms. 'I am. They wanted to have a party and all that kind of fuss, but I told them I'd prefer to slip away quietly.'

Ella saw this old man through fresh eyes. She'd immediately liked him when she had first met him, but now he was her parents' university friend, the man who had told her mother about her father's affair, the man who had loved Sally for over half a century. 'Why didn't you tell me you knew I was Sally's daughter?'

He shrugged. 'I waited for you to say you knew who I was. Since you didn't, I kept my counsel. I can't tell you how nervous I was.'

Ella could imagine. 'I had no idea. What an incredible coincidence.'

'Especially since I haven't heard from your mother since . . .' He paused and started again. 'I was very sorry to hear about your father. We didn't always see eye to eye, but we were good friends, once.'

'Thank you,' said Ella, a confusing mix of emotions jostling for precedence inside her. There was a time when any mention of her dad would bring the grief rushing up her throat. Now she'd learned he wasn't the idol she'd made him, she didn't know how to respond. 'I'm sorry my mother stopped sending letters.'

Andrew's eyes widened. 'Oh, you know about the letters?' He licked his lips nervously. 'I haven't received one for over twenty years.' He walked to the chair under the window and sat. 'I stopped writing to your mother after about ten years. I had a partner myself by then, and it didn't seem fair on anyone to continue.'

'You have a partner?' Ella's stomach balled. What had she expected? Her mother hadn't been in contact for twenty-one years so she couldn't expect her to remain his number-one priority.

'Had,' said Andrew. 'We parted amicably. We found we were better suited as friends.'

The tightness in Ella's gut released. She sat in the other chair. 'It was my fault Mum stopped writing,' she said. 'I made a mistake.'

He turned to her, looking deep into her eyes.

'I thought you two were having an affair. I accused her of being unfaithful to Dad and, because it all happened at the same time as Dad's heart attack, I sort of . . . well, I thought it might be the shock of finding out that killed him.'

She was expecting anger or resentment, but instead,

Andrew's eyes grew moist, and he reached out a hand for hers. 'That must have been harrowing for you.'

'But I made a mistake,' she said, somehow wanting him to blame her. She didn't deserve his warm hand comforting her.

'Anyone could conflate the events, especially when young and grieving.'

'I'm sorry,' she said. 'I ruined any chance you two had of happiness.'

He squeezed her hand. 'Happiness comes in many forms,' he said. 'I once read that whenever you read a good book, somewhere in the world a door opens to allow in more light.' He smiled sadly. 'I've read a lot of good books, so my world has always been full of light.'

She shook her head. 'You and Mum are two of a kind.'

'I always thought so.'

Ella took the notebooks out of her bag, along with the copy of *Persuasion*, and held them out to Andrew. 'I brought these.'

Andrew took them, eyebrows raised in a question.

'Mum never stopped writing to you,' said Ella. 'She just didn't send them.'

A sound like a suppressed sob escaped from Andrew. 'Does she know you're showing these to me?'

'I asked her if she wished you'd read them, and she said yes. She would have sent them if it wasn't for me. But she doesn't know I'm here. She . . .' The words seemed too heavy to push out. 'She has dementia.'

Andrew's mouth opened, his face full of concern.

'It's early days. Most of the time you wouldn't know anything was wrong. That's why I came on my own, because I don't want to upset her. I didn't know if you'd be angry or resentful because of the way she cut you off. I sort of knew you wouldn't, because you kept writing for so long, but, I don't know . . .'

'You want to protect her. I understand.' He turned to the first page of the notebook, then closed it again. 'I can't read these without her express permission,' he said.

Ella nodded, feeling ashamed of bringing them without her mother's knowledge and incredibly grateful that Andrew was so considerate.

'You're still staying with her?' he said.

'Yes, I'm going back there this—'

'Is she at home now?'

Ella nodded. She'd rung Sally when she'd arrived at the building to check she was all right, and she'd said Nathan had promised to pop in for a cuppa.

'Did you come on the train?'

'Yes.' This was a lot of questions.

'My car's in the car park,' said Andrew, handing the notebooks back to Ella. 'Would you mind awfully if I gave you a lift home?'

Chapter Forty-One

Ella

Present Day

Ella's heart rate quickened when Andrew's classic Mercedes ground to a stop next to the kerb on Circus Street. She watched his face as he looked up at the impressive facade, trying to imagine how he felt. He must have spent a lot of time here when her parents first moved in. She imagined the three of them, much younger than she was now, playing at being grown-ups in the big house, excited for what the future held.

Andrew seemed to have aged in the brief time she'd known him. His face appeared more lined, or perhaps it was the anticipation of seeing Sally again that made him seem more serious and austere. He'd been quiet on the hour's drive, his finger tapping nervously on the Bakelite steering wheel. Ella had been privately amused at how stereotypically eccentric he was, with his big desk, office full of books and quirky old fantail car, just like an English professor from a film.

He jumped and she looked beyond him to see the front door open. She put a steadying hand on his arm, noting how tense his muscles were, but then Nathan appeared on the top step and closed the door behind him.

Nathan gazed admiringly at the car, then noticed Ella in the passenger seat and leapt down to the pavement. 'Nice ride,' he said, walking around the car, nodding his approval.

Ella pulled the chrome handle, then pushed the heavy door open. Nathan held it for her as she stepped out.

'This door's well heavy,' he said, running his hand over the chrome above the window. 'They don't make them like this anymore.'

'That's true. And why would they? No power steering,' said Andrew, joining them on the pavement. 'No air con, unless you count winding down the windows. I don't know why I stick with it.' He smiled indulgently.

'Well, if you want to give it a new home,' said Nathan, 'you know where I am.'

'Andrew, this is Nathan. He lives next door. Nathan, this is an old friend of Mum's.'

'Pleased to meet you.' Andrew shook Nathan's hand.

'And you.' Nathan turned to Ella. 'Your mum's in the garden. She wouldn't let me help with anything. I tried.'

'Ah, thanks, lovely. I appreciate it. All ready for what we talked about?'

'I've just got to write the dedication in the book,' he said. 'I've drafted it, but I'm scared to write it inside in case I spell something wrong and muck it up.'

'Albert Einstein believed that someone who had

never made a mistake was someone who had never tried anything new,' said Andrew.

Ella grinned at Andrew as Nathan left. 'You're the king of wise words, you.'

Andrew held his arms wide, exposing the myriad of wrinkles in the sleeves of his linen jacket. 'You don't stay in my job for decades without learning the odd thing. Do you want to know my favourite quote about making mistakes?' His blue eyes seemed to pierce her.

'Go on.'

'It's from *Anne of Avonlea*.' He kept his eyes on hers. '"We all make mistakes, dear, so just put it behind you. We should regret our mistakes and learn from them, but never carry them forward into the future with us."'

He reached out and squeezed Ella's hand, and she squeezed his back with a huge lump in her throat.

Ella led Andrew down to the kitchen and opened the back door. Blondie's 'Dreaming' was playing, and she saw the old CD player, plugged into an extension lead, sitting on the garden table. Sally sat with her back to them, head tilted, face turned up to the afternoon sun.

'Mum,' said Ella, quietly. 'Mum, I've brought someone to see you.'

Sally turned. Andrew let out a breath. Sally covered her mouth. Her eyes filled with tears, and she stood, stepping forwards as Andrew did the same. He took her in his arms and Ella felt she should look away, but she was mesmerised by the way Andrew held her mother so gently. It was like no time had passed between them.

Sally looked so tiny in his arms. He cupped the back of her head with one hand, the other lay soft across her back.

Hadron appeared from under the table, walked towards the pair, then lay across both their feet, purring. *If I was Queen of the World,* thought Ella, *I'd make that cat Minister for Justice.*

Sally's eyes were closed. A tear made its way down her cheek as she rested her head against Andrew's chest. They stood, perfectly still, as swifts chased each other overhead and Blondie sang out, *'Dreaming . . .'*

Chapter Forty-Two

Ella

Present Day

Walking along Creek Road, Ella felt the familiar nostalgia lifting her chest. She'd had some memorable nights in Up the Creek comedy club when she was younger. She and her friends would purposefully sit near the front, knowing they would be the target of the comedians, loving coming up with heckles and what they thought were witty retorts.

'I remember one time we were here, and this acerbic, older comedian asked Verity what she did for a living. I have no idea why she thought she could mess with him. He was brutal.' She pushed hair from her face where the wind had blown it across her eyes. She looked at Sally and Glenda walking alongside her, a rush of affection for the two of them billowing in her chest. Glenda had only been back a couple of days, but it seemed like she'd never been away. Or perhaps it felt like Ella had never been away because being here now, with those two, was the most natural thing in the world. 'She told him she was a sex therapist.'

'Goodness,' said Glenda. 'Whatever made her say that?'

'She thought it was funny.' Ella laughed at the memory. 'Only, the bloke could obviously see she was too young to be any kind of professional, and he sat on his haunches, asking her about whether she thought all these weird scenarios were normal. She ended up admitting she was a student just to make him stop.'

'Crikey,' said Sally. 'There won't be anything like that in Jakub's set, will there?' She looked up at Ella, who had to look away, holding her hands up and lifting her face to the grey sky as though checking for rain. She didn't like lying to her mum, but she classed pretending they were there to see Bridget Bard-Oh as a white lie, more of a means to an end.

'No. I guarantee you'll enjoy tonight's set,' she said, briefly spying Verity's head peek out of the club's doorway, see them, then dip straight back in. Ella glanced at Sally, but she didn't seem to have noticed. She checked her watch. Exactly eight p.m. All going to plan so far.

Up the Creek had changed since she was last there. There was now an adjacent pub with tables outside. It had a door that led directly into the main room and as they approached, the fabric of the table umbrellas flapped noisily in the wind. The plan was that she, Sally and Glenda would go in through the comedy club entrance, up the steps and into the small bar to make sure Sally didn't get wind of the surprise.

301

'Where are the bouncers?' asked Sally, when they reached the glass doors at the front of the club. 'They usually have to check you off their list.'

Ella glanced at Glenda, who looked like she was about to blurt everything out.

'It's a private show,' said Ella quickly. 'Jakub's trying out new material, so he wanted friendly faces in the audience, not any old randoms, so there's no need for bouncers.'

Sally nodded. 'Very wise. He must feel very . . .'

'Vulnerable?' said Ella. She wondered who would find the right words for Sally when she was thousands of miles away.

'Yes, very vulnerable on that stage with all the lights trained on him.'

They climbed the steps to the wood-lined room with its illuminated Craft Beer sign. Ella led them towards the bar, leaning forwards to view the array of bright bottles lined up on the shelves behind. 'What do you fancy?'

'I got rather keen on fruity gin when I was in France,' said Glenda. 'Do they have a blackberry one?' She turned to Sally. 'You can get all kinds of flavours now, you know. Have you tried any of them before?'

'I haven't, but I'm game,' said Sally. 'I'll have what she's having.' She nodded towards Glenda with a cheeky grin. Ella loved this playful side of her mother. How had she forgotten it existed?

Ella was so nervous, she could hear her pulse in her ears when she handed the drinks to Glenda and Sally.

She took a slurp of her gin and let the taste of sweet blackberry mixed with sharp tonic calm her. Ice cubes clinked together in her glass, and she realised her hand was trembling. She hadn't anticipated she would feel this much trepidation.

'Shall we get a seat?' said Sally. 'It gets busy, and we want to make sure we can sit together. Although, it's surprisingly quiet.' She looked around the bar, then at the doors that led to the performance area. 'I hope Jakub hasn't been too selective. It would be a shame if he didn't get a full house.'

Just then, the door opened a crack and a face appeared, followed by a body dressed in a jewelled halter-neck evening gown split to the thigh.

'Bridget,' said Sally in delight. 'You look incredible.'

Ella stared at Bridget, hardly able to recognise Jakub under all the sparkles and perfectly applied make-up. Everything was exaggerated perfection, from her Brigitte Bardot-style wig, piled high on her head, to the heavy black-winged eye make-up and stacked silver heels.

'Wow,' said Ella. 'Just wow. You are rocking that look!'

Bridget did a twirl. 'Why, thank you, kind lady.'

'Do I call you Bridget this evening?' Ella asked.

'Call me anything you like, darling.' Bridget patted her wig. 'Ladies. Are you ready for the show?'

'We are,' said Glenda, unable to suppress a giggle.

'Then let me escort you to your seats.'

Bridget held out a silk-gloved arm for Sally and led

303

her towards the door.

Ella followed alongside Glenda, her heart pounding, her eyes trained on Sally. Her mum's face was all smiles when they entered the room. The cosy auditorium was swathed in red light, apart from the bright wall behind the small stage, which was illuminated blue with mismatching letters spelling out Up the Creek in a variety of coloured bulbs.

Every seat in the venue was filled, apart from three in the front row. When her eyes adjusted to the boudoir lighting, Ella saw all heads were turned towards them.

Sally stopped when she recognised a few of the stallholders from Greenwich market near the back. 'Hello,' she said. 'How lovely to see you.' Next were a group of mothers she knew from Mina's baby signing group. 'Oh, hello,' she said, saluting and grinning in delight. 'Fancy seeing you here.'

Bridget led her further into the room down a narrow aisle through the centre of the red velvet chairs. Ella watched closely as her mother noticed she knew all the people in one row, then everyone in the next. Her eyes narrowed and Ella could see she had questions.

When Sally saw Andrew sitting next to the only empty chairs in the house, she turned to Ella, her face full of confusion. Andrew came to stand by her side, kissing her cheek. Bridget slipped her arm free and tottered up onto the stage. Sally's eyes flittered from her, to Andrew, then back to Ella. 'What's going on?'

'Take a seat, Sally Harrison,' said Bridget, holding

the microphone in one hand, the other sweeping and gliding like a gloved bird. 'Because we have a little secret to share with you.'

Andrew led Sally by the elbow to the seat next to his. Verity waved from further down the row, where Nathan, Hannah, Mina and Pru were also sitting. Sally's head swivelled from left to right, eyes glistening.

'You thought you were here to see me perform,' said Bridget, pouting and winking a set of eyelashes huge enough to set off a tidal wave, 'but that was a ruse, cooked up by your magnificent daughter, Ella.' She pointed a talon-like fingernail in Ella's direction.

Sally turned to her, open-mouthed, apparently lost for words.

'You might have noticed on the way in here that you recognised one or two familiar faces in the crowd,' boomed Bridget's voice through the PA system. 'And that's because every last person in this room wanted to come here to say thank you for the positive impact you've had on their lives.'

Sally's hand covered her mouth. Tears sparkled in her eyes as she turned in her seat to see all of the faces smiling back at her.

'So, tonight is all about you, Sally. It's about friendship, it's about love and it's about community.' There was whooping from the audience and people started to applaud. Bridget pressed her palm down, shushing the noise. She lowered her voice to a stage whisper. 'Do you know what else it's about?'

Sally shook her head. She took Ella's hand and squeezed.

'It's about books. Lovely, lovely books. When Ella told us her plans to replace your lost library, and asked us to get involved, we came together as a community and decided that replacing your library wasn't enough. We wanted everyone to know why we chose the books we did and what we'd inscribed inside. So, Sally Harrison, tonight I have the great pleasure of hosting the one and only, *Library of Your Life*!'

Chapter Forty-Three

Ella

Present Day

The first person to join Bridget on the stage was Hannah. She took the second microphone and stood centre stage, as if she was always meant to be there.

'My name is Hannah,' she said, to a quick burst of applause. 'And many of you will know me from Greenwich market.' The stallholders at the back whooped. 'Sally has been my friend for decades.' She flicked her long hair over her shoulder. 'Which surprises everyone since neither of us looks a day over thirty-two.'

Bridget lifted her mic. 'Leave the comedy to the professionals. You'll do me out of a job.'

When the laughter died down, Hannah held a book up in front of her. 'The book I've chosen for Sally's library is *We All Want Impossible Things* by Catherine Newman. It's a newish one.' She looked up and pursed her lips, as though holding back tears. 'It's funny and wise and it's comforting, even though the subject matter is terribly sad. Mainly, it's about friendship and the lengths people will go to for an old friend in need.' She focused on Sally. 'You, my friend, are funny and wise and comforting, and it's my greatest pleasure to be involved in this fitting tribute to you, wonderful you.' She blew an expansive kiss towards Sally, then placed the book in a box at the back.

As she stepped from the stage, Ella felt Sally shuddering beside her. She leaned to whisper in her ear. 'Don't lose it yet. This is just the start.'

Sally nodded and wiped her eyes. Her chin was puckered, lips pinched, but Ella could tell she was glowing inside.

Next up was Nathan. He wore a black, slashed top over a neon pink vest, teamed with harem pants and black trainers with a stacked sole. He shielded his eyes from the spotlight and rolled his lips between his teeth. When he started to speak, the microphone was too far away from his mouth, and no one could hear. Bridget stepped forwards and lifted it closer to his face, then gave him a reassuring pat on the back.

'Hi, erm, hello,' Nathan said, falteringly. 'I'm Nathan from next door, and both Sally and Ella have done loads for me, so, erm, I'd like to dedicate this book, *Life of Pi*, to Sally.' He held the book up in a shaky hand and Ella had the urge to climb up and hug him.

'It's about a boy's struggle for survival against the odds.' He looked at Ella. 'The boy does some pretty bad stuff, but, in the end, the reader is left to judge whether it's justified.' He looked out at the audience, squinting. 'I chose this one because I've never felt judged by Sally.

We're nothing alike.' He gestured to his huge afro, then his outfit and smiled shyly when the audience laughed. 'But I've never felt she looks at me differently to anyone else. Acceptance is a rare and beautiful quality.' He fixed his eyes on Sally. 'So thank you, Sally. You're a legend.' He placed his book in the box and left the stage.

To the sound of clapping, Mina walked gingerly to the centre of the performance area. She was dressed elegantly in a white hijab, her strong eyebrows and red lipstick standing out in the light. She was stunning.

She looked at Sally and saluted, then moved her arms, tapping her fingers in her palm and making gestures Ella didn't understand, but knew her mother did. Sally was nodding.

The rest of the room was silent until Mina bent down and picked up the book, showing it to the audience. It was *The Color Purple* by Alice Walker. If Ella wanted to know what Mina had signed, she'd have to read the inscription later, but Sally knew, and that was enough for the whole place to burst into applause.

'I don't know how I'm going to follow that,' said Verity, clomping onto the stage and taking hold of the second microphone. 'It was like when Rose and Giovanni did that silent dance on *Strictly*, wasn't it?' She swallowed, then took a deep breath. 'Mrs Harrison.' She laughed. 'Sorry, but it would still feel disrespectful to call her anything else, because she was my teacher in Year Four. She was the best teacher I ever had. I still remember what it felt like to get a hug from Mrs H.' She pointed at Sally. 'I'm coming in for one of those later.'

Sally nodded, her face shining with pleasure.

Verity held her book up for everyone to see. 'I've chosen *The Secret Garden*, because I think it's the first book I ever read and really enjoyed. And that's down to this lady here.' She extended her hand towards Sally. 'She read along with me, and showed me what it meant; underneath the story, I mean. We talked about friendship and the power of positive thinking and all kinds of stuff I would never have thought about myself.' She grinned. 'I met Ella when I went to seniors, and even though that girl's head was always in a book, we hit it off, and I'm so glad we've had the chance to spend time together again over the last few weeks. These two' – she pointed, her finger, bouncing between Ella and Sally – 'are two of the best and I feel very lucky to have them in my life.'

She did a little bow and added her book to the box.

Ella grabbed her hand as she passed on her way back to her seat. Tears clogged her throat. 'Thank you,' she said. She wanted to say so much more, about how Verity had taught her so much about being brave enough to change your life, but Pru was stepping up to the stage, so she released Verity's hand after one more squeeze and looked at the upright woman standing in the spotlight, tugging at the hem of her jacket.

'I've chosen *To Kill a Mockingbird* by Harper Lee.' Pru cleared her throat. 'Sally and I haven't always seen eye to eye.' She looked down at the stage floor.

Ella's stomach flipped. The evening had been going so

well. Now she could feel the euphoria in the air stilling with every syllable of Pru's monotone voice.

'I thought she was just another privileged, middle-class woman making her presence known and, honestly, I didn't see what all the fuss was about.'

People started to shuffle uncomfortably in their seats.

Pru raised her eyes and tears sparkled in the bright lights. 'But I was wrong.' She smiled briefly. 'And I don't often admit that.'

There was gentle laughter and Ella's shoulders relaxed.

'Sally is privileged, that much is true, but she uses the power that gives her to help others who haven't had the best start in life.' She shrugged and Ella saw an unexpected hint of mischief pass across Pru's face. 'And she is middle class, but there's very little any of us can do to solve that particular problem.'

More laughter seemed to make Pru's spine straighten, her chin lift.

She held up the book. 'This novel is about standing up for what's right in the face of adversity. I chose it because, now I've got over my own prejudice, I can see that's what she does. What she has always done.' She fixed her eyes on Sally. 'I'm sorry I haven't always been the friend you deserved.' Her voice wobbled. She cleared her throat. 'But no matter what lies ahead, please know that I will always be there. Come rain or shine, call on me. I will be there.' There was a fierceness in her gaze that said she meant every word.

'I know many of you have got your own books you want to share with Sally,' said Bridget into the mic, when Pru left the stage, 'and you'll all get your chance, because in a minute, we're going to reconfigure the room so it's groups of chairs and tables. We'll be coming around with drinks, courtesy of the management, and snacks from the lovely people at Cheeseboard.' She paused as the crowd cheered. 'But first, I'm going to have my time in the sun.'

She grinned out at the audience, posing with one leg exposed through the slit in her gown. She patted her wig, batted her eyelashes and looked sidelong from the stage.

'Some of you might not know that it was Sally who came up with my stage name, Bridget Bard-Oh.' She said the *Oh* in a breathy voice and the audience laughed. 'Genius, isn't it? I usually perform comedy poetry, but today I'm going to be a little more serious, because, like all of you here, I have a lot to thank Sally for. I started a poem of my own, but it was a bit shit.' She paused for the audience to stop laughing. 'So, instead, I'll let the original Bard say how I feel about my friend – our friend – who we all agree is beautiful inside and out. This is for you, Sally Harrison.'

She collected a book from the back of the stage and opened it. 'This is Sonnet 104 by the great William Shakespeare. I've known our Sally ten years, not three as in the actual sonnet, so I've amended it slightly.' She winked and started to read.

'To me, fair friend, you never can be old,
For as you were when first your eye I ey'd,
Such seems your beauty still. Ten winters cold,
Have from the forests shook ten summers' pride,
Ten beauteous springs to yellow autumn turn'd.'

Her voice was rich and lyrical. Ella turned to see Sally gazing up at Bridget, a beatific smile on her face. Beyond her, Andrew was mouthing the words of the rest of the sonnet along with Bridget, his face full of rapture.

At the end of the rhyming couplet, Bridget snapped the book closed and grinned out at the audience. 'I hope you've enjoyed our little bookish performances this evening. There's just one more very special woman I'd like to invite to the stage. Can we hear it for Sally's gorgeous daughter, Ella.'

Ella walked up to the stage accompanied by a round of applause and cheering. Her heart thundered and when Bridget handed her the microphone, it almost dropped from her slippery palms. 'Thank you,' she said, her voice unsteady. 'I have a book of my own to give to Mum, but, stupidly, I left it at home, so I'll have to give it to her later.' She grimaced and the audience laughed. 'But I couldn't let tonight pass without saying thank you to all of you for everything you've done for us – for me in the last six weeks, and for Mum for far, far longer.' She grinned, picking out faces in the audience to focus on, each one smiling back at her.

'The last six weeks have been eye-opening for me. In Australia, I live quite an insular life, I've realised. I go

313

to work and come home, and I don't spend much time in my community. Being here, in Greenwich, with you amazing lot, has reminded me what a community can do when it comes together. I'm so proud of Mum for the work she's done over the years as a member of The LCG.' She waited for the cheer to die down. 'The work they do at the library is invaluable, because it isn't just a building, or a hub, it's a living thing where people can meet, work, learn and get support and we're all very fortunate that Mum and her friends fought to keep it open for the benefit of everyone.'

'Since I've been back,' she continued, 'I've been reminded how valuable community is. To my shame, I'd forgotten that. I'd forgotten a lot of things, but I'm delighted to say my incredible mum has put me back on track.' She lowered her voice. 'And do you know how she did it? Through books. She took the messages from all these amazing stories and used them to teach me some of life's most important lessons.'

Ella took a breath, then carried on, 'For years, I didn't want to hear what she was trying to tell me. I closed myself off. I didn't read and I didn't learn those messages. But since I've been back, Mum has reminded me of who I want to be. And, you know what? I want to be like Sally Harrison.'

To the sound of shouts and clapping, Ella stepped forwards and looked directly at Sally. 'I'm so lucky to have you, Mum. I love you and I'm so, so grateful for everything you've done for me.'

314

The room erupted in applause.

'Come on.' Ella gestured for Sally to join her on stage. She stood, took Ella's hand and followed her to the middle of the performance area. Ella picked up two tall flutes from next to the box and handed one to Sally.

Bridget took a third and lifted it into the air, saying, 'To Sally and her library!'

Everyone raised their glasses in unison and chorused, 'To Sally and her library.'

As Sally squinted into the audience, her face was a picture of delight.

Chapter Forty-Four

Ella

Present Day

Ella was exhausted when they finally closed the door behind them that evening. Her mascara was in dark rings under her eyes from all the happy crying, but she didn't care. She was warm and fuzzy and still had all the wonderful things people had said about her amazing mum ringing in her ears.

Sally's face was flushed, her eyes brighter than Ella had ever seen them.

Andrew laid an arm around Sally's shoulder and kissed the top of her head. 'What a night,' he said.

'I still can't take it in,' remarked Sally, a smile in her voice. 'I need a cup of tea after that. I don't know if it's the gin or all those lovely words, but I'm quite giddy.'

'Before you go downstairs,' said Ella, 'I have one more surprise for you.'

Sally's eyes widened. 'More?'

'Follow me.' Ella led the way upstairs to the closed door of the little library. Six short weeks ago, she'd thought this was a junk room. It was only when she discovered the books and the way Sally had continued her tradition that she'd fully appreciated how loved she was. Through rebuilding the library, Ella had learned so much about her mother, but also about herself.

They stood outside the room, Sally looking questioningly from Ella to Andrew. The handle was cold under Ella's fingers. She pressed down and opened the door.

Sally gasped. Her hand flew to her mouth. Ella followed Sally's gaze into the room, taking in the velvet armchair, highlighted by the glow from the copper lamp, the pretty wallpaper, onto the bookcase, the top shelf already full of books.

'I thought you said it was still a mess?' Sally stepped into the room, her face a picture of awe. 'It's exactly as it was. Better, even.'

'White lie, sorry,' blushed Ella.

'It's divine,' said Andrew, following them in. He looked at the bookcase. 'You're going to need more shelves,' he remarked. 'When we collect all the ones you've been given tonight.'

'I can't believe everything that's happened,' said Sally, fresh tears collecting in her eyes. 'A few weeks ago, I was a sad old woman in a ruined house.' She spun slowly, taking in the rejuvenated room and the people in it. 'And now I don't think I've ever been happier.'

'You deserve to be happy.' Andrew tucked his hand into his jacket pocket and drew out the copy of *Persuasion* Ella had handed back to him along with

Sally's letters. 'One more for your collection,' he said, slotting it into the bookcase. 'Now, I'll leave you two alone while I make the tea.'

Ella gave him a grateful smile. When she could no longer hear his footsteps, she turned to Sally. 'I have a book of my own for you.' She went to the bookcase and took out *The Five People You Meet in Heaven*. 'I know this was already in the library, and I don't know what you'd written in the original—'

'It's about forgiveness and redem . . .' Sally shut her eyes tight as she always did when she lost a word.

Ella's heart squeezed. For a brief time that evening they'd all been able to forget Sally's diagnosis and ride a wave of joy and hope. This reminder that Sally was unwell made it all the more important Ella made the most of this precious time with her mum. 'Redemption,' she said. 'Forgiveness and redemption.'

'I wanted so much for you to forgive me,' said Sally, touching Ella's cheek.

'And now I'm hoping for your forgiveness,' said Ella, taking Sally's hand in her own.

'Let's forgive each other,' Sally whispered. 'I love you, my precious girl.'

'I love you too, Mum.'

'Be worthy, love, and love will come,' said Sally, looking deep into Ella's eyes.

They repeated it together: 'Be worthy, love, and love will come.'

Epilogue

Ella

Ten Weeks Later

Ella watched her daughter's face nervously as they drew up outside Sally's house in the hire car.

'Is it called Circus Street because there's a real circus?' asked Willow, her nose pressed to the window.

'Afraid not, although there is a circus on Blackheath, just up the road, once a year.'

'Can we go?' Willow turned to Ella, her nose leaving a smudge on the glass.

'I don't see why not,' said Ella. She'd been trying to say yes to Willow as much as possible recently. She and Charlie had agonised over their decision to move in with Sally in Greenwich. The impact on Willow had been one of their main concerns. They had mooted the idea after they'd decided it was a serious option and had been surprised at her enthusiasm.

'Sasha says she has friends all over Australia because she moves around so much with her dad's work. I could have friends in Australia and England, couldn't I?'

'Yes,' Ella had said, hesitantly. 'But it's not easy to

come back from the UK. It's a long, long way.'

'That's all right,' Willow had replied. 'Harper is still being a meany and Sasha is moving to Perth next term, and if I go to England, I'll be able to see Grandma all the time, won't I?'

Ella had anticipated a change of heart when plans were formalised, but Willow had continued to be excited at the prospect of a new school and time with Sally.

Now she was bouncing in her seat, impatient to start her new life. As soon as Charlie pulled on the handbrake, she unclipped her seat belt and asked if she was allowed out of the car.

'Grandma!' she yelled, when the door to the house opened and Sally stood on the top step, a wide smile on her face. The cast was gone, and she held both arms wide for Willow to run into. Hadron appeared next to Sally and Ella was relieved to see her headbutt Willow's calves. The little girl laughed and bent to stroke her.

'Hello, Sally,' Charlie said, getting out of the car and stretching. Ella joined him and snaked her arms around his waist. He dropped his arms onto her shoulders and gave her a squeeze. They'd been touching each other a lot more since Ella's time in London. They'd stayed up late into the night, talking like they did when they were first a couple, curled together on the sofa, making plans for their future.

They'd been cuddled up close when Charlie had told Ella he wanted to become a geography teacher. 'Since I've got a degree, I'd only have to do a year's course to qualify.'

'That's a brilliant idea,' Ella said. 'Oh my God, you'll be an amazing teacher.' And she knew her kind, patient, funny husband would change lives, just like her mother had.

'And there's a course at Greenwich University. I could apply to start in September . . .'

Ella looked into his eyes and burst into grateful tears.

After that, they agreed Ella would work her resignation period and then they would relocate back to England as soon as possible, ready for Willow to start the new school year. It had all happened so quickly, but, looking up at Willow and Sally, together at last, Ella knew it had been the right decision for all of them. She couldn't deny she'd been relieved when she'd been told the London office would be delighted to hear from her, but for now, her priorities were helping Willow settle in and spending time with her mum.

Andrew had put an offer in on a small terrace around the corner. He'd emailed regularly with updates and to reassure her that Sally was still doing well, but Ella was relieved to see her mother looking fresh-faced and healthy with her own eyes.

'Hello, you two lovelies,' said Sally. 'You must be exhausted. Come inside, I've got the kettle on.'

'Is this the special library?' said Willow ten minutes later, after she'd toured the kitchen and the ground floor, coming to stop at the bookcase in the sitting room. The others followed behind, holding mugs of warm tea in their hands.

'No, that's the next floor up,' said Ella. 'Want to see?'

'Yes.' Willow skipped to the bottom of the stairs and stopped, waiting for her mother to put down her drink and lead the way. Ella took something from her bag, then started up the stairs.

'It's really nice,' said Willow, sitting in the armchair and rubbing the velvet nap on the arms with her finger.

'Thank you,' said Sally. 'It's my favourite room in the house.'

'Please can we get another chair so I can sit in here with you?' asked Willow, making Ella's heart swell.

'Absolutely,' smiled Sally. 'There's nothing I'd like more. Mummy tells me you like to read.'

'I like stories,' said Willow, 'and I'm a good reader, aren't I, Mummy?'

'You are,' said Ella, taking the book from behind her back and presenting it to Willow. 'That's why I bought you this as a little moving-in present.'

Willow read the title. '*Little Women*.'

'It's the first book for your own library,' said Ella. 'I'm going to get you a new novel every year on your birthday.' She turned to Sally and smiled. 'Mum gave that book to me on my eighth birthday, didn't you, Mum?'

'It feels like yesterday,' said Sally, sitting on the arm of the chair. She reached down and opened the cover, her eyes misting when she saw the handwritten inscription. 'What does it say?' she asked Willow.

Willow sat up straighter and read:

Willow,

My lovely girl, I hope you will learn as much from this story as I did, but I also hope you will remember more.

Marmee is one of the wisest characters you will ever find in a book (almost as wise as your grandma, but not quite).

Marmee says, '"When you feel discontented, think over your blessings, and be grateful."'

You are my greatest blessing, and I am so grateful to have you and Daddy and Grandma in my life. As we start this new chapter, I wanted you to know how proud I am of you. You are kind, clever, resilient and funny. My life is so much richer because you are in it.

I know change isn't easy, however resilient you are, and if things get tough, come to me and we will think over our blessings together. I will always be here for you. Always.

I love you.

Mummy

'That's beautiful,' said Sally.

They turned at the sound of a soft skull knocking against woodwork. Hadron shook her head, crossed the room and sat on Sally's feet.

Willow climbed out of the chair and circled her arms around Ella and Charlie. Ella's heart swooped with joy.

'Welcome home,' said Sally, smiling wide, her hands pressed to her heart.

Home, thought Ella. She looked from Sally and Hadron, to Willow, then to Charlie and thought, *Yes, that's exactly where I am. I am home.*

Acknowledgements

My first thanks go to my editor, Elisha Lundin, whose vision and passion for this novel have been invaluable from inception to publication. I couldn't wish for a more generous and wise collaborator and I'm exceptionally lucky to work with you and all the talented, committed team at Avon.

Laura Williams, the very best agent in the business, is next in line for well-earned gratitude. Your honesty, encouragement and support are almost as valuable to me as your humour and friendship.

Librarians extraordinaire, Debra Sullivan and Catherine Percival, and the members of The Friends of West Greenwich Library, thank you so much for your help in the planning stages and for trusting me to write a book partly set in your beautiful library. It was a pleasure to spend time there. The work you do for your community is awe-inspiring.

Next on the gush list is fellow writer, Suzy Oldfield, who is masterful at seeing where my first draft is going wrong and suggesting how to fix it.

Like many people, WhatsApp groups became a support system for me during the pandemic. Thankfully, the habit of the group chat has continued, and that's a boon for this unusually extroverted writer. If you're in any of the following, please know I appreciate and cherish you. You keep me sane: Jeeves and Wooster, Make Mine a Double, Writing Sisters, Claire's Surprise, Thespians on Tour, February Fun, Chislehurst Writing Group, Mark's 50th Malta Mayhem. (We need to rethink those group names, guys.)

To all the amazing book bloggers and the brilliant admins of Facebook book groups, especially The Bookload and The Fiction Cafe Book Club, the work you do to spread the love is deeply appreciated, thank you from the bottom of my heart.

Mum, Bronwen, and dad, Kenneth, thank you for everything, including bringing me up in a house full of books.

John, Eva and Isla, thank you for providing me with so much material… only joking. I love you lot even more than I love stories. And that's saying something.

If you enjoyed reading Sally and Ella's story, I'd really appreciate it if you could leave a brief review on Amazon, and/or any other review platform. Reviews help other readers discover books and help authors to find new readers. It doesn't have to be long, but it can make all the difference. I read and appreciate each and every one. Thank you!